MALEVOLENT

by Jana DeLeon

Three blind mice. Three blind mice.
See how they run. See how they run.
They all ran after the farmer's wife
Who cut off their tails with a carving knife.
Did you ever see such a sight in your life
As three blind mice?

PROLOGUE

Algiers Point, Orleans Parish
June 8, 2015

Emma Frederick bolted upright in bed, her pulse racing. She blinked, unsuccessfully trying to make out anything in the dark room. Storm clouds forming had completely eclipsed the moon, leaving the inside of the house as pitch black as the lawn outside. And a lamp was out of the question. At least for now.

She desperately wanted to dismiss her reaction as the result of a bad dream, but she knew that was a lie. She'd barely fallen asleep when something sent her heart into the stratosphere. She sat perfectly still, holding her breath, praying that her fear was a result of PTSD or an anxiety attack. Seconds ticked slowly by, each one met with absolute silence, and her pulse began to decrease.

Slowly, she let out her breath, feeling some of the tension leave her shoulders and back. It was nothing. Just her overactive imagination or screwed-up mental state. Or both. She wished things would get back to normal. Whatever that looked like.

Crrrrreeeeeaaaaaaakkkkkkk.

1

The sound of the loose step on the interior stairwell sent her body back into overdrive. The night was still. The storm clouds hung over the house, but right now, it was the calm before the storm. No wind at all. Just overwhelming New Orleans humidity. Nothing to cause the old house to make noise on its own.

Someone was coming up the stairs.

She launched into action, silently sliding off the bed and onto the rug. She rose up on her knees and pulled the covers up to make it look as if the bed had not been occupied, then crawled along the carpet runner until she reached the closet. The well-oiled door had been left open a crack, and she pulled it back enough to enter, then crawled inside, closing the door behind her. She pushed her way through the bottoms of several low-hanging dresses and slid the hidden panel on the back wall to the side. She lowered herself a bit more and crawled through the small cutout and into the black space beyond.

Damn it!

She froze for a moment, cursing herself for forgetting her pistol under her pillow. She'd practiced this at least ten times the day before. Why didn't she get it right?

It was too late to go back for the gun now, so she continued along her escape route. The room behind the closet ran the twelve-foot length of the bedroom but was a narrow three feet wide. It had seemed enormous when she was five years old, but twenty years later, it felt as if the walls were closing in on her, slowly sucking the air out of the room. She inched her way to the far end of the pitch-black space and huddled against the wall, waiting.

The master bedroom was the first bedroom the intruder would come to. That's where he would expect to find her. She'd left the bed linens in that room rumpled and the window next to the master bathroom toilet opened a crack. A huge oak tree stood just outside, an enormous branch creating a wooden walkway almost right up to the side of the house. A moderately athletic person would have no trouble getting out that window and into the tree. Emma was more than capable of doing it and hoped her intruder thought so as well.

The *screech* of old hinges echoed through the house and she knew he'd pushed open the door to the master bedroom. She forced herself to breathe normally, in and out, in and out, trying to keep her mind clear and ready to react if her ruse didn't work. Every second that passed, she prayed she'd hear retreating steps on the stairwell, but when the next sound came, she realized he was coming down the hall to the bedroom she'd been sleeping in. Her childhood bedroom.

Her pulse spiked and her head suddenly felt lighter. She closed her eyes and took a deep breath, then slowly let it out, trying to force the dizziness away. The door to the bedroom creaked open and she heard him step inside. She clenched her hands, feeling her nails digging into the soft skin on her palms. One second, two seconds, three. How long was he going to stand there? She heard another footstep and prayed that he was leaving, and then it started.

So low and light that at first, she thought she was

imagining it.

But then the whistling grew stronger.

Three blind mice. Three blind mice.

Both hands flew up and she clenched her mouth, stifling the scream that was straining to get out.

It couldn't be him.

See how they run. See how they run.

She knew it was impossible, but she had to be sure. Had to prove to herself that it was someone else. Before she could change her mind, she removed one hand from her mouth and used it to push herself up from the floor. Inch by inch she rose until she was standing straight up. She couldn't see a thing in the inky black, but she knew where to find the plug she'd carefully placed in the wall the day before. She ran her hand over the wall until she felt the surface variation.

She removed her other hand from her mouth and used both to gently ease the tiny plug from the wall. Leaning forward, she placed her eye right up to the hole and peered into the bedroom. A penlight flashed a beam across the bed, then toward the closet. A dark figure moved along the path of the penlight, only a faint outline of his body visible. She held her breath as he opened the closet door. If he found her hiding place, it was all over.

Sweat formed on her brow and the drops of salty liquid ran into her eyes, making them burn. The closet door closed, and she could have wept with relief. The footsteps continued across the floor and she saw the shadowy figure moving back toward the hallway. She blinked to try to clear her blurry vision, straining to make out something that would tell her who he was.

As he started to leave the bedroom, someone slammed a car door, and he looked back. At that exact moment, the storm clouds parted enough to let a sliver of moonlight into the room, and his face was illuminated.

Her body went completely rigid and her heart pounded so hard she thought her chest would burst. Warm urine ran down her leg and trickled onto the floor around her feet. It couldn't be him. It wasn't possible.

She'd killed him last month.

CHAPTER ONE

New Orleans French Quarter
June 10, 2015

Shaye Archer looked around her empty apartment and felt a ripple of excitement and fear run through her. This was one of those big moments in a young woman's life—when she left home and struck out on her own—but for Shaye, it wasn't just big. It was monumental.

Are you sure you're ready?

Doubt sneaked into her thoughts, as it had since she'd made an offer to purchase the apartment last month. She shook her head and pushed the negative thoughts aside. She'd mulled over this and little else for the past year. She had her bachelor's degree in hand, her private investigator's license issued, her business license, three years of experience, and the financial means to start her own agency. It was time. Every decision she'd made for the last six years had been about getting to this moment.

You can do this.

She smiled. That was more like it.

Now all she needed was her furniture and clothes and

bathroom supplies and a host of other things coming her way on a moving truck, and she'd be in business. Literally.

She cast a critical eye at the front room of the apartment. It was a good-sized room, and its original hardwood floors, brick accent wall, and fireplace gave it a homey feeling. It was supposed to be a living room, but Shaye had other plans for the space. Clients would feel comfortable in this cozy room, and Shaye would feel comfortable having them here, rather than traipsing them through the apartment to the spare bedroom. No, this was definitely the best option for her office. All she had to do was find the right furniture for the space and she was good to go.

A horn sounded out front and she jumped, then immediately grew frustrated with herself for being so touchy.

You're in the French Quarter. There's going to be a lot of noise.

Much more than she was used to when tucked away in the back bedroom of her adoptive mother's huge historical home in the Garden District. The only sounds that drifted into her bedroom there were made by the lawn crew who arrived every Wednesday morning to work their magic on the beautifully landscaped yard. The noise level in the heart of New Orleans would be both higher and different. In a couple of weeks, she'd be adjusted to the nuances of her new home and everything would be back to normal. She just needed to be patient. Not her strong point.

She headed to the front door and swung it open as the moving truck eased up to the curb. Her initial plan had been to throw her clothes in a duffel bag and a couple of boxes and haul it all over in her SUV, but her mother, Corrine, had insisted Shaye take her bedroom furniture and the couch and tables from her sitting room. Shaye couldn't find a good argument against that plan. She'd chosen all the furniture herself, and it was good quality. It would last her a long time, and taking it with her allowed her to eliminate one more thing from her long list of things to do.

Hence the need for the moving truck.

Two young, athletic men jumped out of the cab and rolled up the back door of the truck.

"This is a great location," one of them said, and smiled.

"Thanks," she replied, but didn't return the smile. He'd been trying to flirt with her since they arrived at her mother's house to load, but Shaye didn't want to give him any indication that she would consider him an option. Men were at the top of her list of things *not* to do. Not now. Maybe not ever. The idea of sharing her daily life and thoughts, especially her past, with someone other than Corrine caused a rise of panic in her that hadn't diminished yet. She wasn't sure it ever would.

One step at a time.

Shaye could hear Eleonore's words echoing in her mind, and as much as they annoyed her, she also knew her psychiatrist's sentiment was right. She sighed. It was beyond frustrating when things you didn't like were also your reality.

"Where do you want the living room furniture?" one

of the movers asked.

She directed him inside and showed him the dining area off the kitchen that would serve as living and dining. If it weren't for Corrine's forcing her to a table most evenings, Shaye would have eaten every meal curled up on the couch in front of a television, and now that she didn't have anyone else to consider, that's exactly what she planned to do.

The men made quick work of the furniture, expressed their thanks at the generous tip she gave them, then headed off. Shaye pulled her long, dark brown hair back into a ponytail and looked around the kitchen/dining areas trying to figure out the best arrangement for the two end tables. Only one fit next to the couch. The other would stick out into the walkway, so she moved it over to a corner. She could put a lamp on it and call it done...claim the minimalist look. Whatever kept her from dusting too often.

"Hello?" A woman's voice sounded from the front of the apartment.

Shaye frowned and stepped through the doorway from the kitchen into her future office. A young woman with auburn hair and pale skin stood in the doorway, clutching the door handle and looking nervously around.

"Can I help you?" Shaye asked, figuring the woman was lost.

"Are you Shaye Archer?"

Shaye hesitated a second before answering. "Yes." She wasn't expecting company, and she'd never seen this woman before.

"My name is Emma Frederick. I, uh…I think I have a problem that needs a detective. Your website gave this as your office address…"

Shaye's puzzlement switched to amazement. When she'd launched her website two days before, she hadn't anticipated clients before she'd even gotten them a chair to sit on. But then, she hadn't anticipated clients showing up at her front door without an appointment, either. Apparently, there were a lot of things she hadn't expected when setting up her business.

"You're in the right place," Shaye said. "I'm just moving in today and some of the furniture hasn't arrived yet."

Emma's expression shifted to disappointment. "Oh, well, I can come back. Can I make an appointment?"

Shaye started to say yes and schedule something for next week when everything would be in better shape, but then she took a closer look at Emma. Her hand on the doorknob shook, and with her other hand, she pulled at the bottom of her blouse. Two threads stuck out and the hem in one spot sagged a tiny bit. Her skin, while pale naturally, wasn't only naturally pale right now. It was beyond that, almost blanched.

Emma Frederick was scared.

"No, please," Shaye said. "Come in. There's a couch in the living room, and I have my laptop to make notes."

Emma hesitated a second, then stepped inside, closing and locking the door behind her. She followed Shaye into the living area and took a seat at the end of the couch where Shaye indicated.

"I would offer you a drink," Shaye said as she grabbed her laptop from the kitchen counter, "but I don't even have a cup unpacked yet."

"That's okay," Emma said. "I'm too nervous to drink anything. I guess you noticed."

Shaye pulled the end table she'd just stuck in the corner over to the middle of the room across from Emma and sat on it. "Right now, you're in the safe zone," she said, repeating the words Eleonore had said to her so many times. "Tell me about your problem."

"I think I'm being stalked."

"You think?"

"Yes. No. I mean, I'm sure I'm being stalked."

Emma's responses grew more hesitant, and Shaye knew she was reconsidering being here at all. Shaye's heart went out to the woman. Her confusion and fear were things Shaye understood all too well.

"Do you have any idea who's stalking you?" Shaye asked.

Emma nodded. "It looked like my husband."

Okay, Shaye thought. At least they were moving into normal territory. Spousal stalking was far more common than people might think, and often deadly. "I assume you're separated?"

"Not exactly."

Shaye's back tightened. If Emma had felt she had no other option left other than running away, and her husband had found her, the situation could be even more dire than

Shaye had originally thought. "Are you hiding from him, and you think he's found you?"

"I...no." Emma took a deep breath and blew it out. "You see, I killed my husband last month."

Shaye blinked. Surely she'd heard incorrectly. "I'm sorry. I don't understand."

"That makes two of us."

"Maybe you should start at the beginning."

Emma nodded. "I met my husband, David Grange, a little over a year ago at a party in the French Quarter. I had just moved back to the area from Dallas. I got a scholarship to nursing school there and stayed for a couple years for a great job that I got after graduation, but the city never fit, if you know what I mean. So I packed up my car and headed back home to NOLA. David was an army sergeant stationed at Fort Polk and was in New Orleans for the weekend. He was charming and handsome, and we had a whirlwind courtship. We married just six weeks after we met."

"Grange? You didn't change your last name?"

"No. Given my professional licenses and contacts, it was easier to keep my maiden name."

Shaye typed some notes on her laptop as Emma talked, trying to fathom marrying someone she'd known for only six weeks. Imagining herself married was a big enough stretch, but the six weeks thing had her completely stumped.

"The first six months were great," Emma said. "David worked four days on base and then could be here for three.

We lived in an apartment here in the French Quarter. I'm an RN at New Orleans General in critical care, so I scheduled my shifts to match his. It didn't always work out, but we spent as much time together as possible. We never fought. Never even argued, not about anything important." She paused for several seconds and appeared to be gathering her thoughts. "Then he was deployed to Iraq. When he returned, he was different. Nothing that you could specifically point to at first, but I could feel it the moment he arrived."

Emma gave Shaye a sad smile. "I suppose it sounds melodramatic, but I don't know how else to describe it."

"I understand what you're saying," Shaye said. Shaye had a finely honed ability to zoom in on any difference in someone she knew. She only had to glance at Corrine when she walked in from work to know if her daily dose of stress had been from her caseload as a social worker or the bureaucracy she continually railed against, but Shaye doubted anyone else noticed the same subtleties that she did.

"While he was deployed," Emma continued, "some things changed here. My aunt passed away, and I inherited her home in Algiers Point. My parents died in a car accident when I was five, and my aunt raised me. She was my parents' only living relative and she never married, so she was the whole extent of my family."

"I'm sorry. That must be hard."

"Thank you. I spoke with David, of course, and we both agreed that selling the house was foolish. More people were moving to Algiers and restoring the old homes. Property values were starting to rise and were only going to get higher. Besides, I had no intention of leaving Louisiana again, and Algiers is a short ferry ride from the French Quarter. After Iraq, David's time in was over and he would be home for good."

"So when David returned, you'd already moved to the house in Algiers Point?"

Emma nodded. "After our tiny apartment in the French Quarter, I thought he'd be happy with the space we now had. It's a beautiful old house and my aunt was meticulous about maintaining it, but he was totally disinterested. It was as if he'd walked into a hotel room rather than his own home. Before he deployed, he used to always talk about finding a place with a garage so that he could work on old cars. It was a huge interest of his, but when I showed him the oversize garage, he barely nodded, then went back inside and sat in front of the television the rest of the day."

"PTSD?"

"Probably. Given my profession, I've seen it before, but every time I made an attempt to get him to talk, either to me or to a professional, he shut me down." She took a deep breath and blew it out. "Then he got mean. It was subtle at first—insults that he claimed were just joking—but it progressed to direct and abusive. When he hit me, I knew I had to get away from him. If you could have seen the look on his face...the absolute rage. I knew, that given time, he would kill me."

"Did you go to the police?"

"Yes. I did everything by the book. I've worked enough emergency room shifts to know the drill. Everything was documented, then I got a restraining order, and the judge ordered him off the property. Since it was inherited, he had no claims to it."

"I'm going to take a guess that he didn't feel the same way."

"You guessed right. The police hauled him away in handcuffs, but he was out the next day."

"Did he come after you?"

"Not like you'd think. He was smart about it. He knew the exact distance he had to remain from the property. Every morning, on my way to work, he was standing on the same street corner, just far enough away from the house to keep him from being arrested, watching me as I drove by." She crossed her arms and shivered. "The worst part was the smile."

"He was enjoying torturing you."

"Yes, and there was nothing I could do about it."

"What about David's family or friends? Couldn't they help?"

"He told me he didn't have any family living. Every time I asked him about his childhood, he clammed up and refused to talk. I got the impression it wasn't very good. He always said I was his family and his future, and that's all that mattered. As for friends, he didn't really have any. Not close, anyway. He'd been in the military for eight years, but the guys he knew there were either still serving or had gotten out and scattered to their home states. Sometimes he went for a beer after work with coworkers, but there wasn't anyone close to him. Except me, and now I wonder if I was ever as close as I thought."

"Given a probable bad childhood and the strain of combat, you might have been the only person he let in."

"Maybe so, but looking back, I don't feel like I got very far. I realize I didn't know him for very long before we married, but I swear, I didn't see any signs of the complete turnaround he did. I'm trained to notice these things, and I'm far too practical to have stuck my head in the sand because I was in love." She blew out a breath. "I'm sure you know the facts about stalkers."

Shaye nodded. "If they want to get to you, they eventually will. A piece of paper is little defense against obsession. You have to be prepared to protect yourself."

"And I was. I knew how to shoot a pistol, so I dragged my aunt's out of her closet and made sure it was in working order. I loaded it and kept it on me, even at the hospital. I knew it was illegal, but I figured I'd rather take my chances with the police than walking across a dark parking garage without protection."

"I don't blame you."

"I thought I was being safe, but as it turns out, the gun didn't protect me at all."

Emma stopped talking and her jaw flexed. Shaye knew it was hard—telling someone the worst thing that had ever happened to you. Reliving every moment. Every moment that felt like a year.

"How did it happen?" Shaye asked, hoping the prompt would push Emma past the mental block she'd constructed to protect herself.

Emma stared at the wall behind Shaye. "I was cooking. It was my day off and it was sunny with a cool breeze. The kitchen window was open and I remember a lawn mower running somewhere nearby. I didn't hear David come in, but I'll never forget that moment when I knew he was there. I had just finished washing a cucumber in the sink and was about to slice it when the whistling started."

"Whistling?"

Emma swallowed hard and nodded. "'Three Blind Mice.' When he came back from Iraq, he'd whistle it every time...every time he changed into the monster."

Shaye frowned as she made a note. Professionalism required her to be objective and focused on the facts, but she couldn't deny that was creepy as hell. "I can't imagine..." She started her reply but stopped when she realized she was being disingenuous. Shaye might not be able to imagine exactly how Emma felt, but she had a damned good idea.

"It was the most terrifying moment of my life," Emma said. "Even more horrifying than when I killed him." She looked directly at Shaye. "When I have nightmares, I don't see his death. I only see that sink, the water still running, the knife in the bottom—stainless steel gleaming against white porcelain. I feel my pulse racing, the blood draining from my face, my hands shaking, my heart pounding in my chest that's constricted so tight I can't take in even the smallest of breath. And then I hear the whistling. I wake up screaming, soaked with sweat, sometimes violently ill."

Shaye felt her back tighten and her pulse tick up a notch as Emma talked. She knew all about those kind of dreams—the kind where you lived everything as if it were happening over and over again. The kind that made you wish, in the darkest moments, that you'd just drift on to the never-ending dreamless kind of sleep.

Emma shifted on the couch and shook her head. "I'm sorry. That's not the kind of information you need."

"I'm here to listen to anything you want to tell me," Shaye said.

Emma shot her a grateful look. "I couldn't move. Not at first, but then he grabbed my shoulder. His fingers dug into my skin and I'm sure it hurt, but I don't remember anything except the rage that coursed through me. Anger and fear and a million other emotions that all arrived at the same conclusion—he was there to kill me."

Shaye nodded, no doubt in her mind that Emma was right.

"I felt the cold, hard butt of the pistol as he pressed it to my temple," she said. "I actually saw it, just like everyone says, my life flashing before me. I always thought it was a cliché, but it was real, my dad teaching me how to ride a bicycle, the mermaid cake my mom made for my fifth birthday. It was all there, for one suspended second, and then it was gone."

She leaned forward on the couch and looked Shaye directly in the eyes. "I was going to die."

"So you had nothing to lose."

Emma nodded. "David was an expert martial artist. While he was away, I started studying kung fu. I never told him because I wanted it to be a surprise. With only six months of lessons, I'm not very good…"

"But you caught him by surprise." Shaye's respect for Emma ticked up another notch. Most people would have frozen, died right there in front of the sink, too frightened to even raise a hand.

"I lifted the knife from the sink, praying as my fingers curled around the handle. As soon as I had it in my grip, I ducked and whirled around, knocking the pistol out of his hand with my arm, and sliced his throat with the knife."

Emma's voice broke on the last words and she sniffed. "I knew what I was doing…with the knife."

"Because you're a nurse."

"Yes. I severed the carotid on the right side of his neck. His eyes were so big, his entire expression one of disbelief. He flung his hands over his throat. The blood squirted out from between his fingers. I…I knew it would be a lot. I've seen that artery nicked and it was bad, but I didn't expect…"

"No amount of education could prepare you for something like that."

"But I'm a nurse. I know…"

"You know what the body is supposed to do, but you couldn't know how you would react if you were the one who caused it. Your training is to treat injuries, not cause them."

Emma's eyes widened and Shaye silently cursed. "I'm sorry," Shaye said. "I didn't mean to upset you."

"No. You didn't upset me. Quite the contrary. I've been struggling to understand my reaction, my emotions, and I never thought about it that way. Thank you." She shook her head. "It didn't take long for him to lose consciousness. Probably only two or three minutes, but it seemed like forever. I was afraid to move, even for the phone, but when he finally passed out, I grabbed my cell phone and called 911."

"How did the police handle it?"

"David was dead when they arrived. The clean cut coupled with the heightened emotional state maximized blood loss. The policemen who responded were thorough. One of them had taken my statement when I'd filed on David for the abuse. He was so kind. The other was less so—older and rather abrupt, but I didn't care. I just wanted it all over."

"Was there an investigation?"

"Yes, but it was short. Given the evidence, the prosecutor declined to press charges and I was free to get on with my life. As well as one can after, you know."

"Give it time," Shaye said, slightly aggravated at herself for repeating her psychiatrist's words again. It was even more irritating when the woman was right.

"I know. I kept telling myself that, and for a couple of days, things started to ease a bit, enough to get a glimpse of normal. But then..."

"Tell me about the stalking."

"At first, I didn't think anything of it—an item out of place in my house, a noise outside in the middle of the night, a door open that I thought I'd closed. Noises happen, and given my mental state, it was completely reasonable to assume I'd moved or opened something and forgotten. But then I started feeling like I was being watched. I never saw anyone, but I could feel someone out there, hiding in the shadows."

"What about your friends? Did they notice anything odd?"

"I don't really have any close friends. I met David right after returning to New Orleans, and we spent all our available time together before he left for Iraq. My high school friends had all married and moved away. I went to the movies a couple of times with coworkers, but then my aunt died and all my free time was wrapped up in going through the house and getting it ready for David to come home."

"Did you make a police report?"

"And tell them what? That I could feel someone watching me? I had no proof, and the only person who wanted to harm me was dead. They wouldn't have taken me seriously. Hell, I wasn't completely convinced myself. Not until two nights ago."

"What happened?"

Emma told Shaye about the break-in. About hiding in the secret room behind the closet. About the whistling and seeing her husband in the glimmer of moonlight.

Shaye didn't take a single note while Emma spoke. She

didn't even try. Every inch of her was right there with Emma in that secret room, peering through that tiny hole…seeing an impossible nightmare right there in front of her. When she finally finished, Emma collapsed in tears. Shaye jumped up and grabbed a paper towel from the roll on the counter and handed it to her.

Emma wiped her eyes and nose and sniffed for a minute more. Shaye sat back on the end table, feeling helpless and completely out of her element. She'd spent the past three years working for a local agency, earning her hours to get her license, but she'd never worked on anything with an emotional component, and certainly not a deadly one.

"I'm sorry," Emma said once she regained a semblance of control. "I thought I could handle repeating it."

"Please don't apologize. What you described is horrifying. I'd be more concerned if you weren't upset."

Emma gave her a small smile. "Do you think I'm crazy?"

"No." Shaye's response was immediate, and more importantly, the truth. "I think you're traumatized, and rightly so, but I see no evidence of crazy. What about an alarm system? You didn't mention one."

"My aunt installed one right after Hurricane Katrina. Things got rough in the neighborhood for a while, and a senior living alone was an easy target. So it's old, but it was working fine until two nights ago."

"The night the man was in your house?"

Emma nodded. "I tried to set it before I went to bed

and it was dead. We'd had a big storm that afternoon and lightning fried my satellite, so I figured it took out the alarm as well. At least, that's what I tried to convince myself, but if I really believed it was all nothing, I wouldn't have planned an escape route in my old bedroom. I wouldn't have staged the master bedroom to look like I was sleeping there and had left through a window. Deep down, I knew something wasn't right."

"Did you go to the police after you saw the man?"

"Yes. First thing the next morning."

"I take it they didn't believe you."

"An officer took my statement, and two detectives came to my house to check out the doors and windows. But with no sign of forced entry and no hard evidence, there was nothing they could do."

"I have to ask, are you certain your husband died?"

Emma nodded. "He bled out. I know he did. And I saw the body before he was cremated. He was dead. I'd bet my RN license on it. But…"

"How could he be stalking you now?"

"Exactly."

Despite the fact that Emma's story was impossible, Shaye had already come up with a possible scenario. It was a matter of proving it. "I have an idea. I believe that you are being stalked, and that the man stalking you can't be your husband. You saw him in the moonlight, and given the heightened state of emotion, you could have been mistaken. Maybe the man was similar enough in appearance for you to mistake him for your husband."

"But the whistling."

"He might not have had living relatives or close friends, but your husband didn't live in a vacuum. If he turned on you, wouldn't it make sense that others might have gotten the same treatment?"

Emma frowned. "Yes, that's possible, sure, but why come after me? I don't have much in liquid assets and have never had trouble with other people beyond the normal job kind."

"That is what I'm going to find out."

Emma blew out a breath. "So you'll take the case?"

"Yes. But you're going to have to discuss your husband at length. I'll need to know everything about him in order to find out who else could have known details about him and about you."

"Apparently, what I know about my husband is a whole lot of nothing, but I will do anything to stop this. Anything at all." She glanced at her watch. "My shift starts in thirty minutes, though."

"That's okay. I'll want to start checking into your husband's background...coworkers, military buddies, anyone who might be able to shed some light on things."

"Great. I'll email you all his personal information. Will that work?"

"That's fine. I'll do some poking around and then call to schedule another meeting. Are you still staying in the home?"

"No. I booked a hotel close to the hospital. I'm afraid to go back home, but I can't afford to live like a vacationer forever." She sighed. "I've always loved that house, but now, I can't imagine spending another night in it. I started thinking about selling right after I…right after David…"

Emma pulled a checkbook from her purse. "You'll need a retainer. How much?"

"My rate is seventy-five an hour plus expenses. A thousand is fine for the retainer."

"Is that enough time?"

"I won't know until I get started, but let's not worry about that now."

Emma wrote a check and passed it to Shaye, then dug a business card from her purse and handed Shaye that as well. A number was handwritten on the back of it. "That's my cell phone number. I can't answer during shift—hospital rules—but I check it on breaks. If it's critical, call the hospital and they'll page me."

Emma rose from the couch and pulled her purse over her shoulder. Shaye followed her to the front door. As Emma stepped outside, Shaye put a hand on her shoulder. "Ms. Frederick, can I ask you a question?"

"Please, we've got to be close to the same age. Call me Emma, and of course you can ask a question."

"Why me? You could have hired someone with far more experience."

Emma smiled. "A nurse I work with recommended you. She said you would believe me even when no one else would."

Shaye frowned. "Who is the nurse that recommended me?"

"Clara Mandeville." Emma turned and hurried off down the sidewalk. She jumped into a black Nissan Altima parked a couple buildings down and pulled out into the afternoon traffic. Shaye watched as the car faded into the distance.

Clara Mandeville.

The name sent Shaye careering back nine years.

Back to the first day for which she had any memory.

Chapter Two

Corrine Archer poked her head inside Eleonore Blanchet's office and gave her friend a pleading look. "Please tell me you don't have a client coming anytime soon."

Eleonore raised one perfectly arched eyebrow up and gestured to the chair in front of her ornately carved antique desk. "I cleared my afternoon."

Corrine plopped into the cushy leather chair. "Am I that transparent?"

Eleonore smiled. "I've known you for twenty-six years. I've written prescriptions for people I've known less than an hour."

"That's comforting." But not untrue. Eleonore had been working her way through medical school when she'd taken the position of tutor and nanny to a twelve-year-old Corrine, who'd just lost her mother. The two had bonded so well that the friendship continued after Eleonore finished medical school. Eleonore was the one person in the world, besides her father and Shaye, who Corrine completely trusted.

Eleonore turned to open the credenza behind her and

pulled out a snifter and an individual serving of scotch. She poured it in the glass and pushed it across the desk along with a package of shortbread cookies.

Corrine sighed and lifted the glass for a sip. "It's really unnerving...having someone know you so well."

"Especially when you're not sleeping with them."

"If my dry spell continues, I might consider it."

Eleonore snorted. "You're not having a dry spell. It's a voluntary drought. Things are probably starting to wither."

"I am not withering. Jesus, Eleonore."

"Uh-huh. When was the last time you had a date?"

Corrine frowned, searching her mind for something that could be passed off as date-like. "Last month. The art festival," she said, feeling slightly triumphant that she'd come up with something to pass muster.

"The art festival that you helped sponsor? Where your 'date' was one of the artists? The very gay artist?"

Damn it. Was there anything that happened in New Orleans that Eleonore didn't know about? "We had dinner and he held my hand," Corrine argued.

"The word 'date' implies the potential for romance. You weren't sporting the right equipment, honey."

"Fine. Then I have no idea when my last date was. Does sometime after puberty narrow it down?"

Eleonore shook her head. "You and I both know that if you wanted male company, there is no shortage of men who'd take you up on an offer."

"Of course. But would they be interested in Corrine Archer, social worker and general worrywart, or *that*

Corrine Archer, daughter of a state senator and sole heir to Archer Manufacturing?"

Eleonore gave her a sympathetic look. "I know it's hard to trust anyone. Hell, I'm not saying if I were in your situation that I could do any better. But I don't even have to be a psychiatrist to know that it would be a good thing if you made your world just a little bigger."

"What do you want me to do—join one of those meat market dating sites?"

"God no. Unless you want to, of course, and then I'd say go for it. I was thinking more along the lines of friends with boobs."

"You cannot be serious."

"Surprisingly enough, you can enjoy an afternoon wasting time with the same sex as well as the opposite sex. Granted, the opportunities for fun are slightly different. And given that my idea of weekend frivolity is not taking off my pajamas until midafternoon, you need to branch out."

"And you think finding female friends is somehow easier than finding a date?"

"It's not?"

"Hell, it's harder. The only women I run across are either socialites with an IQ lower than their bra size or women whose children I'm taking away because they're horrible people. Netflix is a better option than either of those."

"Because there are only two kinds of people in all of New Orleans."

"You know I hate it when you're sarcastic."

"No. You hate it when I'm right. I'm almost always sarcastic." Eleonore leaned back in her chair and gave Corrine a pointed look. "Want to talk about the elephant in the room?"

Corrine took in a deep breath and blew it out. "She's not ready."

"We won't know that for sure until she tries."

"You're her psychiatrist, and more importantly, you're my friend. Why won't you tell her to wait?"

"Because as her psychiatrist, it's not my job to tell her what to do. It's my job to find out what she wants to do and help her emotionally facilitate that. I'm afraid that trumps being your friend."

"You're a sucky friend." Corrine flopped back in her chair and glared at Eleonore. "God, I hate it when you get all logical and professional."

"Everyone does. You can't make her stay."

"I know, but I thought maybe if you talked to her…"

"What the hell do you think I've been doing for the past nine years?" Eleonore sighed. "Look, the truth is, I've talked over every possibility for issues with her. The bottom line is that she's determined to go it on her own."

"What if she can't do it?"

"Then she can move back in with you until she's ready to try again."

Corrine's back tightened as she thought of the one million things that could go wrong. "And if she relapses? What if being on her own is so hard it sets her progress back?"

"That's possible, but what if she proves you wrong? Shaye is the most brilliant client I've ever worked with, and she's had three years working at a detective agency. It's not like she walked out of your house, threw open a door, and yelled that she was for hire. She's got a bachelor's degree in psychology and criminology, and she's fantastic at reading people and the general energy in a room. If anyone can do this, it's Shaye."

Corrine took a big sip of the scotch, taking some time to absorb everything Eleonore said. It wasn't anything she didn't already know, but it helped to be reminded. "She woke up screaming this morning. That hasn't happened in months."

"It's probably the stress of the move coming out in her subconscious."

"Do you think...when she dreams...is it about what happened to her?"

"Only Shaye can answer that."

Corrine tapped her finger against the side of the glass, her concern for Shaye warring with her professional ethics and the thought of putting Eleonore and *her* professional ethics on the spot. Before she could change her mind, she pushed forward. "I know you can't talk about the things Shaye has told you. She's told me very little—I think because she wants to protect me—but what she revealed is bad. Really bad."

Eleonore nodded. "Really bad doesn't come close. Twenty years I've been doing this, and I've never seen the level of abuse Shaye suffered. Never heard nightmares so vivid and so terrible. Don't ever want to hear them again, either."

Corrine's respect for her friend shot up even more. "How do you handle it? Listening to all that horror?"

"Yoga usually, but this time…after fifteen years of sobriety, I had to start attending AA meetings again."

"Oh no!" Corrine sat up straight in her chair.

"Don't worry," Eleonore said. "I had one lapse. I'm not drinking again."

Corrine felt tears form in her eyes and she sniffed, trying to hold them in. Eleonore wouldn't want or appreciate her sympathy. She took her sobriety as a personal show of strength, and Corrine knew just how disappointing the lapse was to her friend.

"I know I can't make her stay," Corrine said, "but I don't know how to stop worrying. She's been through so much, and we don't even know…" Corrine choked, trying to hold back a sob.

Eleonore nodded. "We don't even know who did it to her."

"He could be living across the street, walking down the sidewalk behind her, selling her coffee in the morning."

"Yes. And he could have been doing all those things while she was living with you."

"It's not the same. I know my neighbors. I know the guy selling me coffee—I used to tutor him in math."

Eleonore frowned. "I'm not telling you there's nothing at all to worry about. I would be worried if I were you. Hell,

I'm worried and I'm not you. But it's been nine years, Corrine. No one has come after her. We have no reason to suspect he ever will, and that's assuming he's still alive or not in prison. She has no memory, therefore she poses no threat."

Corrine bit her lower lip. "What if the night terrors aren't just her mind's horrific way of working things out? What if she's remembering?"

"If we don't know that for sure, how could he?"

"You're right. I just have to keep reminding myself of that. God, I feel like such a mother."

"You are her mother, and you have plenty of good reasons to be concerned."

"So what do I do?"

"You worry because that's who you are, and you try not to let it drive you crazy."

Corrine shook her head. "I don't have that far to go."

"None of us do."

He stared across the hotel parking lot as Emma pulled her Nissan Altima in a spot near the elevators. She glanced around as she climbed out of the car, her jerky movements and hurried walk giving away her unease. He smiled. She was just like everyone else in the world—predictable.

When he'd seen her put a suitcase into the trunk of her car, he'd already known she was headed for a local hotel, trying to hide. But her practical side had her staying close to the hospital where she worked instead of jetting out of town. It had taken him little time to locate her car that morning and even less time to convince the pea-brained girl working at the front desk to give out her room number. But then Mama had always said women were stupid.

Emma had been in the house the night he'd entered. He was sure of it, and more than a little surprised that she'd managed to slip away. The bathroom window and the tree were a surprising leap for Emma, and one he never would have expected her to make. It almost made him smile just thinking about it. Emma thought she'd won, but she'd actually done him a favor. He'd jumped the gun, going into the house so soon. If he'd found her sleeping, he wouldn't have been able to keep himself from strangling her until the last dying breath crossed her lips.

And it would have been premature.

He lifted his hand and formed a gun with his fingers, sighting her in. It would be so easy to kill her now. Maybe even the easiest kill he'd ever made. But what would be the fun in that? Even the amount of fear she exhibited now had his blood coursing stronger through his veins. His heart rate was elevated with excitement. He imagined what it would feel like when she was truly terrified.

And she would be.

At 11:00 p.m., Emma pushed open the door to the break room and filled the largest cup she could find with

coffee. She dumped in three packets of sugar for good measure and carried it to the corner table, still stirring as she sat down across from Clara Mandeville.

"You planning on staying awake for the next week or so?" Clara asked.

"Just until this shift is over." Emma took a sip of coffee and cringed at the bitterness. She opened another packet of sugar and started the stirring all over again, wishing a Starbucks latte gave her the same energy regular coffee did.

"You pulling a double?" Clara asked.

"Yeah. Heather called off again."

The sixty-two-year-old Creole woman gave her a disapproving look as only Clara could manage. "That's three times already this month. Marcy needs to fire her."

"Please. As long as Heather is supporting Marcy's worthless son, she'll never be fired. That would put him right back on the couch at Marcy's house."

Clara sighed. "I know you're right, but I don't have to like it. You've had enough on your plate the past couple weeks. She should have asked someone else to fill in."

Emma felt the warmth from Clara's words as if she'd wrapped her in a blanket. If Emma's aunt was Emma's surrogate mother, then Clara was her surrogate aunt. The older woman had taken Emma under her wing when she'd started at the hospital a year ago and had been a blessing in so many ways. With almost thirty years at the hospital, Clara's knowledge and experience was as vast as any middle-aged doctor and better than many. But it wasn't just the medical part of the job at which Clara excelled. She had an ability with people that Emma had always envied. No matter the situation, Clara knew just the right words to say.

Having trouble with a difficult patient? Call Clara. She'd set them at ease and have them smiling before she left the room. Ready to kill an egotistical doctor? Call Clara. She'd have him apologizing and calling her ma'am in a matter of minutes. Feel like you're drowning in hospital red tape? Call Clara. In a matter of minutes, she'd have everyone doing his job.

In short, Clara was magic.

"I'd like to say Marcy's a stone bitch," Emma said, "but the truth is she asked for a volunteer and I offered."

"Why in the world would you do that? I don't think the church is looking to make more saints anytime soon."

Emma smiled. "If the church tried to make me a saint, lightning would probably strike the place."

"Then why are you pushing yourself like this? Marcy may be conveniently ignoring the dark circles under your eyes and that skin of yours that's whiter than any white woman is supposed to be, but you can't deny it to me or yourself. You're exhausted. You need to rest."

"How am I supposed to do that when I know someone is after me? Every night, I climb into bed with good intentions, but as soon as I close my eyes, I imagine him there, standing right above me. Then my eyes flash open and I sit upright, holding my pistol and every light on. What's the point?"

"I thought you were staying at a hotel?"

"I am, but it hasn't been the sleep aid I thought it would be. I just can't relax. When my body gets so tired that my mind can't keep me awake any longer, I finally doze off, only to bolt upright ten or fifteen minutes later, my heart jumping out of my chest like I'm having a heart attack."

Clara shook her head. "That is horrible, but you can't continue like this. If you don't get some rest soon, I'm going to be pulling a double and you'll be at the top of my patient list."

"I know. Believe me, it's not my choice."

"And you think working a double is going to make it better?"

"No, but I think being in a brightly lit building, surrounded by lots of people, will keep me from having that heart attack I'm afraid of."

"Did you even think about my suggestion?"

"Yes! I went to see her today."

"And?"

Emma's thoughts flew back to her exchange with the young PI, and that same feeling of hope that she'd had when she finished talking to Shaye coursed through her again. "She believed me. Just like you said she would."

Aside from Shaye and the New Orleans detectives she'd spoken to, Clara was the only other person Emma had told about the man in her house. And like Shaye, Clara had never once indicated that she thought Emma was firing on less than eight cylinders. The older nurse had simply done what she always did—offered a solution.

"What did you think of her?" Clara asked.

"Intelligent and tough but empathetic. She asked all the right questions and showed the appropriate amount of concern, even though I could tell she wanted to shout at me to get the hell out of Dodge."

"Well, why don't you?"

"That would only change geography. It wouldn't stop me from being afraid that he'd follow me. Besides, being somewhere else would put me at a disadvantage. I know this city. I have people here that I can trust. Somewhere else, I'd be completely alone."

"Exactly what I'm saying. If you did things right, even the stalker wouldn't be able to find you."

"For how long? I inherited a bit of money and I have some savings, but I'm not rich. Eventually, I'd have to take a job, and since I'm not up on the criminal element and such, that means ponying up identification. Then I'd be looking over my shoulder every second of every day. That's not living."

Clara frowned. "You may be right on that one, but you can't keep going like you have been, either. You're starting to look like one of those *Twilight* vampires."

"At least I'm in the right city for it—vampire lore and all."

"Bunch of hooey if you ask me. So are you going to hire her?"

"I already did. I didn't have time to tell her everything, but I emailed her some information on David on my break. She wants to start by looking into his background."

"Something you should have done before you married him."

"Yeah, well, hindsight's twenty-twenty. Anyway, I left her a retainer and she's going to start right away."

"Good. I think you made a wise decision in hiring her."

"I have to admit, I was a bit taken aback when I first saw her. She looks far younger than she must be, but then we've both seen the advantages of great genetics."

"We have, but she is young. Twenty-four, give or take a year."

Emma stared. "Twenty-four? Okay, now you've got my curiosity in overdrive. How do you know her?"

Clara looked over Emma's shoulder and stared at the wall for several seconds. "I was working the emergency room nine years ago on the night the police brought her in. One of the old guard, Detective Beaumont, had found her wandering in the middle of the street, weaving like a drunk. She was clothed but only barely, the material hanging on her like rags. She was dirty and smelled of human excrement. Her hair was matted in big knots all over. She had long cuts in her hands and on her wrists, and was covered in blood that turned out to be her own."

"Had she been in an accident?"

"The police couldn't find a car anywhere nearby, and she wasn't talking, so we didn't know. The rookie cop decided she was drunk or a junkie, but Detective Beaumont said something wasn't right about the whole thing and insisted on staying while the staff checked her out."

"I take it Detective Beaumont was right?"

"And then some. Tests for narcotics and alcohol were negative. She was staggering because of blood loss. Once we got her onto a gurney, she all but collapsed, eyes wide open and vitals strong, but she was nonresponsive."

"Shock?"

"I'm sure. Dr. Thompson was working the ER that night, so we were lucky."

Emma nodded. Dr. Thompson was one of the hospital's oldest doctors and took his time with patients. He was the nursing staff's favorite.

"He sent her straight off for X-rays and that's when all hell broke loose," Clara said. "That poor girl...it was unlike anything I'd ever seen before and something I hope to never see again." Clara looked directly at Emma, her big brown eyes misting up. "So many broken bones, some of them old injuries and some more recent, and none had ever been set right. My guess is, she'd never even seen a doctor."

Emma's stomach rolled. "Oh my God."

"Then Dr. Thompson started his physical exam." A single tear rolled down Clara's cheek and she swiped it away. "That girl had been violated in every way possible. There were cuts all over her body and a brand in the middle of her back in the shape of a pentagram. I had to leave the room for a few minutes. It's the only time I've ever gotten sick on the job, but I'm not ashamed of it. An hour after he finished the exam, I found Dr. Thompson in his office crying."

Emma's chest constricted and she struggled to keep

her own tears at bay. What Clara described was unfathomable, that someone could abuse a child to the point that even veteran medical staff struggled to handle it. What kind of monster could do that?

"We cleaned her up as best as possible and treated the wounds on her hands and wrists. She didn't stir, not even for a minute. Not until the next night when she woke up screaming. Me and one of the new nurses ran in and tried to calm her down, but it took some convincing before she stopped looking ready to bolt."

"Did she tell you who did that to her?"

Clara shook her head. "She didn't remember. Didn't remember a single thing before waking up in the hospital. It was as if her mind had simply erased it all."

"Self-preservation?"

"That's what I think. What happened to her was so horrible her mind made it all go away. She didn't even know her name. Had to pick one out for herself." Clara sniffed. "Based on her bones, Dr. Thompson estimated Shaye's age at fifteen or thereabouts. He couldn't be certain of the year, but he was certain she was a minor. We were about to call social services when Miss Archer showed up. Detective Beaumont had served on a charity board with her and had given her a call. I all but yelled hallelujah when she took a personal interest in the case."

"Charity board? Wait, Archer? As in Archer Manufacturing and State Senator Archer?"

"His daughter."

Emma frowned, completely confused. "I don't get it.

What was a New Orleans socialite supposed to do? Pay her hospital bill?"

"Corrine Archer may be one of the wealthiest women in New Orleans, but she's the salt of the earth. And the best damned social worker we have in this city."

"Corrine the social worker is *that* Corrine?" Emma gasped. "Pierce Archer's daughter? I never realized..."

"Which is a testament to the caliber of woman she is. Corrine could be sitting in a ten-thousand-dollar leather chair in a boardroom or soaking up rays in the Bahamas full time, but she chose to help children. And against her father's wishes, I might add."

"I'm absolutely blown away. I had lunch with her one day at a hot dog vendor outside of the hospital." Emma shook her head, some of her faith in humanity instantly restored. If a woman of means like Corrine Archer chose to spend her time in the trenches helping children, then there might be hope for the future.

"Corrine doesn't usually throw her weight around. She wants to be seen and treated as any other social worker, but in this case, I was hoping she'd pull out her last name and get things done."

"Why?"

"Because it was clear that Shaye had been through a horror the rest of us couldn't even begin to imagine. Putting her in a group home or with foster parents wouldn't have done a bit of good. The girl needed serious medical and psychological treatment, and Corrine could afford the best of everything."

"You're saying she took custody of Shaye herself?"

"Yes, ma'am. Corrine had her father pull some strings, and Shaye was placed in Corrine's custody. Corrine got her entrenched in her home, cleaned up, and spending time daily with Eleonore Blanchet."

"I've always heard she's the best."

"You've heard right. Eleonore brought that girl from the brink of madness back to reality—her new reality." Clara shook her head. "Shaye had several surgeries to correct broken bones that hadn't been set property. It took Eleonore a year before she could get Shaye to leave Corrine's house, except for doctors' visits."

"But that was only nine years ago. She seems so normal. How in the world could someone come from what you described to the woman I met today?"

"Money to hire the best of the best, time, and a spirit that couldn't be broken. Shaye could read and knew math up to multiplication and division, so they assumed she'd received at least an elementary education. Corrine hired the best tutors she could find and they worked with her every day in Corrine's home. Shaye grabbed right on to those books and surprised everyone with her intelligence. In three years' time, she took the GED and started college. When she turned eighteen, the state released her and Corrine adopted her. Shaye worked for a local detective agency while she was going to college and as best I know, has never looked back."

Emma shook her head. "That is the most incredible, awful, wonderful story I've ever heard. Did they catch the person who abused Shaye?"

"No. With Shaye's memory gone, the police didn't have much to go on."

"I guess a child abuser isn't likely to file a missing persons report on their victim."

"Got that right. The police circulated her picture through all the national databases, sent it to schools and churches, and even did those commercials, but they didn't get any hits."

The reality of Shaye's situation crashed into Emma like a freight train. "If Shaye has no memory of her abuser, then she has to assume that anyone she comes in contact with could be her attacker. My God. Every day is some form of nightmare."

"I would imagine so, although she seems to have found a way to balance it out and try to live a normal life."

"That's why you thought she'd believe me...because of her own extraordinary story."

"I think it's no coincidence that Shaye became a private investigator. She doesn't have answers for herself, and my guess is she doesn't want anyone else to live in the shadow of darkness like she does."

Emma took another drink of her now-lukewarm coffee, trying to fathom what a normal day was like for Shaye. For all intents and purposes, Shaye was born at age fifteen, with a lifetime of baggage and no claim ticket to tell her where it had come from. The fact that she was sane, much less accomplished, was a testament to Shaye's strength and Corrine's determination.

For the first time in weeks, Emma's bleak outlook cleared just a little. If Shaye could go through all that and come out the other side not only sane, but educated, and eager to help others, then Emma had a chance of regaining her own life and sanity.

CHAPTER THREE

The room was dark and damp. The old bricks that made up the walls were crumbling in some places and growing moss in others. She didn't know the length of the room in feet, but she knew it was exactly thirty steps long and twenty steps wide. When it rained, water crept in where the brick met the concrete floor. If it rained hard, the entire floor was drenched. She stood as long as she could, but if it rained for too long, her weakened body couldn't keep her upright and she eventually had to sit down. The water soaked into her clothes and made the room freezing in the winter and sticky hot in the summer.

She couldn't remember how long she'd been in the room. Several summers and winters had passed. Maybe five. Maybe more. When you sat in the dark every day, it was hard to know how much time passed. But as bad as the room was, it was worse when he came to get her. He'd stick her with a needle and she would go to sleep, but not completely. She could remember what happened, how he bathed her and dressed her, then took her to the red room with all the candles. There were other people in the red room. People who hurt her, along with the man.

But she didn't want to think about that.

Thinking about the red room made her want to die.

She'd tried to kill herself once. Had slit her wrists with a piece of broken brick. The man had been so angry when he found her. He'd wrapped her wrists to stop the bleeding. Every day, he'd returned to the room to make sure the cuts didn't get infected, and every day, he'd made her pay for her attempt to escape her prison. Made her pay so badly, she'd never tried again.

Thunder boomed outside and she slid to the center of the room, curling her arms around her legs. Her right foot throbbed from the minimal movement. Maybe it was broken, but as long as it couldn't get infected, the man didn't care. Her teeth began to chatter, and she hoped the storm was short. She wouldn't be able to stand on her foot, not for more than a minute.

As the water began to creep into the room, she squeezed her arms tighter around her legs and prayed. God hadn't heard her yet, but he was the only thing she had left.

Shaye bolted upright in bed as thunder shook her bedroom walls. She squinted a bit as the bedroom light hit her eyes, then zeroed in on the baseboards, looking for water. The old hardwood floors were as dry as a bone. She flopped back onto her pillow and blew out a breath. Lately, every time it rained, she had the same dream. So far, most of the summer thunderstorms had rolled through the city during the day, but a few had broken the night stillness with booming thunder and pounding rain.

She closed her eyes, wondering if she'd be able to get back to sleep, but with every roll of thunder, her heartbeat ticked up a notch. She flung back the covers and walked down the hall and into the kitchen. It was a short walk and an easy one. No light switches to fumble around for in the dark. The only time Shaye was in the dark was when the power went out, and even then, she had a lantern and a whole nightstand drawer full of flashlights, located right above the drawer filled with batteries.

No complete darkness. No candles. Not ever.

She grabbed a bottled water from the refrigerator and flopped down on the couch. The television was mounted on the wall in front of her, but the cable guy wasn't due until tomorrow, so right now, it was just a big black monitor, providing no distraction whatsoever. At least the Internet guy had made a call that afternoon. Television she could do without for a night or two, but having no Internet was akin to having no hot water. It just wasn't a livable sort of thing.

She rubbed the bottle of water across her forehead. The air-conditioning in the apartment was good, but the humidity from the storms made the air inside stale and muggy. Her laptop sat on the end table where she'd left it before she went to bed, so she flipped it open and fired up a movie on Netflix. At least it provided a little bit of noise to drown out the storm.

Staring at the dark television in front of her, she tried to force her mind from the dream but she couldn't. Was it real? She had no doubt the girl in the dream was her, but what she didn't know was if the dream was true. Had that really happened to her? Was that the reason she was terrified of the dark and hated even the sight of a candle? Or did she fear those things for other reasons and the dream was a made-up story that her mind had created? Its way of expelling her demons?

Would she ever know?

She blew out a breath. Eleonore told her that her mind had blocked the past in order to protect her from a mental break. Given the extent of her physical injuries, Shaye had no doubt that was true, but Eleonore also thought that one day, when she was strong enough, she might start to remember. The problem was, right now, everything Shaye saw was only in her dreams. Nothing flashed through her mind or caught her attention when she was awake. Only when she was sleeping did the darkness creep in.

The dream felt real. She could feel the terror the girl felt, the horribly painful throbbing of her foot, the awful desperation when she began to pray.

Shaye's foot had been broken. It was one of the many things she'd had surgery to fix after she'd gone to live with Corrine. Two long scars across her wrists indicated a suicide attempt, and one made by a child who had seen it in the movies but didn't know that you should cut long ways if you were serious about dying. But again, were those things that she knew to be true manifesting themselves in her dream, or was the dream giving her a glimpse of her past?

As much as the dreams terrified her, she hoped they were real. Because if she never remembered, then the people who'd done this to her would get away with it.

Emma hurried across the hospital parking lot, one of the hospital security guards in tow. Jeremy Walker was a nice man and more importantly, a big man and a retired cop. When her shift had ended, she'd sought him out specifically and asked if he would walk her to her car. It was a little after 2:00 a.m., and most of the city had shut down for the night. But it was midweek. Come the weekend, at 2:00 a.m., some parties would just be getting started.

"How you doing tonight, Miss Frederick?" Jeremy asked as they walked.

"I'm doing all right," Emma said. "Thanks for asking."

"I'm glad to hear it. You've had a rough time of it lately, and I'm sorry for that."

"Things will get better, right? Isn't that what you always tell the victims—that time heals everything?"

"I reckon that's what we say."

Emma looked up at him. "You don't think it's true?"

Jeremy frowned, his dark eyes troubled. "I don't guess I do. I don't think there's enough time to repair some things. Some things just become part of a person, like their skin color. It doesn't have to define them, but it's always with them."

"That's an interesting way to look at it, and I agree with you. I don't doubt that at some point I'll be as happy as I was before, but I don't think I'll ever be the same, if that makes sense."

"Yes, ma'am, it does. Most people go through life with a false sense of security...until something happens. Then you start to take a closer look at the way you do everything and the risks involved."

"Like walking to my car alone at night in a dark parking lot?" Emma smiled.

"Two weeks ago, you'd have been waving and hurrying out that door without so much as a backward glance."

Emma stopped in front of her car. "Well, I appreciate you walking me out here."

"Any time. And I mean that. You don't go traipsing around here like you're some superhero. They gave me a badge and a gun for a reason."

Emma placed her hand on his arm and gave it a squeeze. "You're the best, Jeremy."

He smiled. "I'm going to tell my wife you said so. Sometimes she needs a reminder. Now, go on and get out of here."

He took a couple steps back from her car but stood and waited as she pressed the button to unlock her car door. Clearly, Jeremy didn't consider the job done until he saw taillights. She pulled on the door handle, but the car was still locked. She pressed the button again, waiting to hear the *click* that indicated the lock has disengaged, but it never made a sound. She pulled on the handle again, just to be sure, but it didn't budge.

"Is something wrong?" Jeremy asked.

"The keyless entry isn't working. Something else to take care of, I guess." She pulled her car keys out of her purse, disengaged the slave key, and manually opened the car door. "I can't remember the last time I used a key to do this."

Jeremy nodded as he pulled her door open. "Technology has taken over the world. Not that I'm complaining, mind you. I'm not one of those old people always bitching about progress. Last night I talked to my granddaughter in Tokyo on the computer. Nope, you won't hear me complaining at all."

"That's great," Emma said, trying not to think about all the times she'd Skyped with David. All the emotions she felt seeing her husband so far away and in a war zone. Back then, she couldn't wait to see him again. Now she was afraid she'd never stop seeing him.

Jeremy shut her door and stepped back from the car. She tried to start the car, but it didn't make a sound. She tried again. Nothing. She opened the door and stepped out. "It won't start."

"Probably your battery," Jeremy said, "which would explain the remote not working. Pop your hood and I'll take a look."

She reached back into the car and released the hood latch. Jeremy lifted the hood and shone his flashlight onto the battery cables.

"One of your cables is loose," he said. "I don't suppose you have any pliers?"

"I'm afraid not."

"No worries. I can get it fixed up well enough to get you home. You got pliers there?"

"If I don't, I can get them."

Jeremy pulled a package of gum from his pocket and popped a piece in his mouth. He offered Emma one but she declined, then watched in confusion as he carefully folded the foil wrapper. Her confusion cleared when he stuffed the wrapper in between the terminal and the wire cap to hold it in place.

"It will conduct power because it's metal," she said. "Ingenious."

"Done it more times than you can guess. Probably still carry gum because of it. Don't chew it much anymore because of my dentures. Go ahead and try her again."

Emma hopped into the car and gave it another try. The engine roared to life and she grinned at Jeremy as he closed the hood. "Lifesaver," she said.

Jeremy smiled. "All this flattery is going to ruin me."

"I've never had that happen before," Emma said. "Is it common?"

"I wouldn't say it's common, but it happens. When was the last time you had the car in for service?"

"Last month. They did an oil change and the usual once-over."

Jeremy nodded. "Most likely, it got knocked loose. Or someone removed the terminal and didn't tighten it well when he put it back on. Make sure you get that tightened before you drive it anywhere else."

"Absolutely! Thanks again, for everything."

"You have a nice night, Miss Frederick. What's left of it."

Emma shut the car door and backed out of the space. She could see Jeremy in her rearview mirror, still standing where she'd left him, watching her drive away. As soon as she rounded the corner, the smile she'd forced for the old security guard vanished and her anxiety shot up another notch.

Maybe Jeremy was right and the terminal was loosened during her last service, but she didn't really believe that. The service had been over a month ago. What were the chances that it just happened to pick now to pop off? Emma had never been a big believer in coincidence.

It was him.

Clutching the steering wheel, she fought back the anxiety that threatened to take over. She had to remain calm. Scared people made mistakes, and she wasn't about to become the ditzy heroine who ran back *into* the spooky house.

Still, when she got to the hotel, she would valet her car. Damn the twenty dollars a day plus tip.

She refused to be scared. But she was going to be careful.

CHAPTER FOUR

Shaye hesitated in front of the door to the police station. The morning work crowd hustled down the sidewalks, hurrying to make the nine o'clock shift. Artists, toting their wares, made their way toward Jackson Square, hoping to make some money off the tourists. Everything was so normal, except for the part where she was standing in front of the police station.

Shaye hadn't been in this building for nine years, and if she was being honest, she didn't really want to go inside now. But that same honesty forced her to admit that she'd accepted long ago that if she hung her hat out as a private investigator, the odds of her needing to pay the occasional visit to the New Orleans police was going to be high. Before she could find a reason to put it off until after lunch, Shaye pushed the door open and stepped inside.

A bench sat against the wall on the left side. A reception desk stretched across the right side, separating the tiny lobby from a sea of desks occupied by police officers. A lot of New Orleans may be just going to work, but the police station was already jumping. Three drunken young men sat at one desk, their fraternity letters emblazoned on their shirts. One of them caught sight of her and nudged the others, causing them to break out into "You've Lost That Loving Feeling." Clearly they'd seen *Top Gun* one too many times.

Two women, either prostitutes or exotic dancers, sat at another desk, their expressions shifting between anger and boredom. At some desks, people talked in raised voices, maybe a decibel below screaming, while others leaned across the desk, whispering and looking embarrassed.

Shaye scanned the faces for the policeman she'd come to see, but she couldn't locate him.

An older man with silver hair, what was left of it, studied her over the reception desk. "Can I help you?"

"Uh, yes," Shaye said. "I'd like to speak to Detective Beaumont."

"A lot of people would, but he retired last year."

"Oh." Shaye was a bit taken aback at first, then she chided herself. Detective Beaumont had sported a full head of gray nine years ago. It shouldn't be a surprise that he'd retired. Unfortunately, that left her with no one to talk to...no one she trusted, anyway.

"Would you like to talk to someone else?" the sergeant asked.

"I guess so. I'm looking for someone who can talk to me about David Grange's murder."

The man's eyes narrowed. "You with the paper? Because we don't just hand out information to reporters."

"No. I'm a private investigator. I was hired by the deceased's wife."

The sergeant raised one eyebrow, his expression clearly shouting "bullshit."

Shaye reached for her purse and fumbled with her wallet, trying to pull out her ID. Finally, she managed to get the identification out and presented it to him. The sergeant leaned over to look at the card, then looked back up at Shaye.

"You're a little young, aren't you?" he asked.

"I'm twenty-four. Some might consider that young, but I'm legit."

The man shook his head. "Pretty girl like you...why would you want to be a PI? Chasing down cheating husbands and insurance fakers? It's a thankless job."

"I'm not looking for thanks. I'm looking for the truth."

He snorted. "Girl, you got a lot to learn, and I'm betting it's going to be a bumpy ride. But what the hell do I know? Thirty-two years at this job and I still get up and drive to work every day. I'll get you someone to talk to."

He turned around in his chair and yelled, "Vincent! Someone here needs to talk to you."

A heavyset man with short silver hair and glasses looked over at Shaye and frowned. "Send her back!"

The sergeant turned back around. "That's Detective Vincent. He was the senior officer on the Grange murder. I'm sure he can help you." But his tone when he delivered the last statement didn't instill confidence.

Shaye took a deep breath and walked past the reception desk and into the sea of police officers and criminals, preparing herself for the complete waste of time that talking to Detective Vincent was probably going to be.

As she approached his desk, he grabbed a stack of folders in one of the metal chairs and shoved them into the only bare corner of his desk. He motioned for her to take the seat and plopped back into his chair, glancing at his watch and then his computer screen.

"I'm Detective Vincent," he said. "What can I do for you?"

"My name is Shaye Archer. I'm a private investigator, and I was recently hired by Emma Frederick to look into some things concerning her late husband, David Grange."

The detective's eyes widened slightly when she threw out the private investigator part, but he managed to force the bored look back into place. "I don't know what it is you or the Frederick woman needs to know. The man's dead and she killed him. From where I sit, it seemed like a good idea. Not sure what more there is to investigate."

"Ms. Frederick thinks she's being stalked."

Vincent sighed and slumped back in his chair. "This again?"

"Are you the officer she spoke to a couple of days ago?"

"I'm afraid so. Look, I listened to everything she had to say, drove to her house, and me and my partner checked every square inch of the place. There was no forced entry, and Ms. Frederick told me she'd changed the locks after the other incident. I can't make something out of nothing."

Shaye's back tightened and she struggled to maintain her cool. "Ms. Frederick saw someone in her house. How can that be nothing?"

Vincent shook his head. "Emma Frederick is a nice woman who went through something horrible. Regular people aren't prepared to be attacked, much less kill their attacker, especially when they're married to him. I'd be more worried if she *didn't* have some trauma after what she's been through."

"You think she imagined it." No wonder Emma had been so worried that Shaye wouldn't believe her. Someone was stalking the woman, and the cop who should be trying to figure out who it was didn't even think there was anything to investigate.

"Of course she imagined it. What other possible explanation is there?"

"I don't know. I suppose someone could have been in her house but you failed to find the point of ingress."

"Got yourself a live one, Vincent," said a young policeman at the desk next to Vincent's. He looked at another cop standing next to him and grinned.

Vincent shot them a bored look. "I didn't *fail* to find anything because there wasn't anything to find."

"Maybe. But I'm being paid to make sure."

"So make sure. It's not my dime."

His dismissive tone was the last straw for Shaye. Since when had the burden of proof shifted to the victim? "And if I find something you missed?"

Vincent's jaw flexed. "Look, you seem like a nice girl. You should be down in the Quarter, partying with your girlfriends and looking for a husband to get you that piece of the good life."

Even though she knew he'd said it to get to her, Shaye bristled. "The day I need a man is the day I check myself into a convent."

Vincent smirked. "But yet you're here needing something. And I'm a man."

Shaye smiled. "I'll acquiesce to the first comment. I'm not convinced of the second."

"Ooooh." The other cops sounded off in tandem as Shaye rose from the chair.

"Thank you so much for your time, Detective Vincent. Since that's all you gave me." She slung her purse over her shoulder and headed for the exit.

"You go girl," one of the prostitutes said as Shaye passed. "Don't take no shit from a man or you'll end up like me."

Shaye gave her a nod and picked up her pace, letting the door to the station slam shut behind her. To hell with the cops. Hoping for some help from Detective Beaumont had been a reach to begin with. She had no reason to expect a cop who didn't even know her to offer up information. Before she'd even said a word to Detective Vincent, she'd expected him to scoff at her profession and the case, but she hadn't expected the level of derision he'd shown toward her client. Clearly, Vincent had problems with women, and even more of a problem with someone finding out he'd been wrong.

Shaye had every intention of making that potential problem a reality.

As the precinct door slammed shut behind Shaye Archer, Detective Jackson Lamotte sat at his desk nearby watching as two rookie cops starting razing Vincent. It wasn't smart of them. Vincent had rank and could make their jobs miserable, a fact he knew all too well since he'd been partnered with Vincent a year ago. But he couldn't blame them for their delight. Vincent was a sexist asshole and a lazy cop to boot. Sure, he'd taken down his share of bad guys back in the day, but now he seemed content with cruising straight into retirement on past performance.

Jackson had known exactly how things would go the moment Shaye sat down at Vincent's desk. At least, he'd known how things would go from Vincent's end. With her cool demeanor and quick comebacks, Shaye had surprised him. For someone so young, she wasn't easily intimidated.

He looked out the window and watched as she crossed the street and went into a café. Vincent's irritated voice sounded behind him as he argued with the rookies. Jackson glanced back and decided the argument would probably take a while, and then Vincent would need a break to recover from his hard morning. Vincent always needed a break, and lately, every morning was hard. Basically, unless dispatch forced Vincent off his desk, Jackson wouldn't be needed or missed. Maybe when the man retired, Jackson would get to do actual full-time work again. Shuffling paper at his desk was getting old.

He rose from his chair and grabbed his cell phone and wallet out of his desk drawer. No one even looked his direction as he wove in between the desks and made his way out of the precinct.

It was too late for the work crowd and too early for the tourists, so he easily spotted Shaye at a table in the back corner, sipping on a latte. Only one other table was occupied—two old men arguing over gas prices and the best place to get a haircut. They barely nodded as he made his way past them. Shaye, however, was another story. Her gaze locked onto him as soon as he stepped in the café, and never wavered as he walked directly toward her. Her eyes widened for an instant as he stopped at her table, but she recovered quickly.

"Can I help you with something?" she asked.

"No. But I think I can help you."

She gave him a disgusted look. "Take a hike, perv."

Jackson let out a single laugh. "Shit. No, that's not it." He pulled out his ID and held it out for her to see. "I'm a detective."

"That's too bad."

"There's days I feel the same way. I heard your exchange with Vincent. Do you mind if I sit down?"

She studied him for a moment, then pointed to the chair. "Suit yourself."

As Jackson pulled the chair out and sat, a waitress sauntered over and smiled at him. "Your usual, Detective?"

"That would be great," he said. "Thanks, Christi."

"First-name basis?" Shaye asked.

"Café...police station. Seems a natural progression."

"I suppose so."

Christi returned with a large mug of black coffee and sat it in front of him. He added a packet of the fake stuff and stirred. "About Vincent, I would apologize for his behavior, but I don't figure you'd care, and he's not my responsibility."

Shaye raised one eyebrow. "Honest and direct. That's something I don't get often."

"Yeah, well, I'm lazy and lying requires too much effort."

Shaye's lower lip trembled and he could tell she wanted to smile, but he hadn't completely breached her defenses.

"I'm glad you stopped across the street," he continued. "I probably wouldn't have followed you more than a block. Maybe less."

The smile finally crept through. "So why are you expending so much of your valuable energy pursuing me into coffee shops?"

"Emma Frederick hired you?"

"Yes."

"Can you tell me why exactly?"

Normally, Shaye would never give out information about a case, but Detective Lamotte wasn't just anyone, and given that he'd heard her conversation with Vincent, he already knew most of it. The case part, anyway.

"She's being stalked."

"How can you be sure?"

"Because she said so. Look, Detective Lamotte—"

"Call me Jackson."

"Okay, Jackson, I don't know when the police department's policy changed from helping victims to mocking them, but I don't like it. Emma Frederick is a nice woman who is scared to death, and you guys are telling her she's imagining things."

He understood her anger, but he didn't think she was right. Not completely. "In my job, I'm not allowed the luxury of what I believe to be the case. Only what I can prove."

"Which is a great concept if I were gathering evidence for a murder trial, but my goal is to *prevent* her from being murdered. Consider my services a preemptive strike."

"The implication being that the police arrive at the party after it's already over."

She held her hands up and tilted her head to the side. "You said it."

And unfortunately, there was a huge element of truth in the statement. Cops rarely actively prevented crime. They investigated it. Past tense. But if someone had the means to hire a private investigator, they could go on the offensive. "I'll be the first to agree that having someone check into things gives Ms. Frederick an advantage most don't have. But I also know more about the situation than you do. You see, Detective Vincent is my partner."

"And you're sitting here with me. Are you trying to piss him off?"

"Not directly, but if that's a side effect of our conversation, I'm okay with it."

She smirked. "We can both agree on that. Have you been partners long?"

"A year, but it feels like a ten-year journey through hell."

"I can imagine. Did you work David Grange's murder?"

Jackson nodded. "And I checked out Ms. Frederick's house after she came in and claimed someone had been inside the night before."

Shaye shifted in her chair, and Jackson could tell she was dying to let a million questions fly, but she was still playing it cool. He had to give her credit. She was doing a credible job of it.

"Is it like Vincent said?" she finally asked.

"Yeah. Not that he knows firsthand, mind you. He pretty much stood around in the living room and nodded. I did all the heavy lifting."

"And there's no way someone broke in?"

"There's always a chance. Locks aren't perfect. With the right tools, an expert could be inside in a second. But…"

"Nothing was stolen, so that lets out professional thieves, and locksmiths don't usually let themselves in strangers' houses simply to terrorize them."

"Pretty much. None of the windows had been messed with, and I couldn't see signs of tampering on the door locks, either. A pro wouldn't leave signs, but most break-ins aren't conducted by pros. No footprints in the backyard, and we'd had heavy rain earlier that evening. The backyard is covered with shade trees, so grass is at a premium. There's no way to get to the back door without leaving footprints across the lawn."

"So he entered through the front door."

"*If* he entered, that's the only option that I can see, but it's not a great one. The front porch is visible by at least eight houses on the block, and Emma herself said she always leaves the porch light on."

Shaye sighed. "You don't believe her either."

"I believe Emma thinks someone was in her house that night. I believe she thinks she's being stalked, and she may be right."

"But?"

"But if someone is stalking her, there's no way it's her husband. David Grange is dead. I saw the body myself, and trust me, no one comes back from a severed carotid. Not after he's bled for as long as he did. I understand you believing that Emma is being stalked. She's your client and it's your job to take her at her word unless you have good reason not to. But given the evidence, you can't possibly believe her stalker is David Grange."

"I never said I did. I made the necessary phone calls yesterday. Everyone seems quite clear on the fact that David was dead before the paramedics arrived. And no one doubts that the corpse they handled was indeed David Grange. Honestly, I don't think Emma believes David is her stalker either, but I do believe someone is following her. He's just being very clever about it, because as long as Emma has no proof, she has no protection. But too many odd things have happened to her, and I'm not a big fan of coincidence."

Jackson tapped one finger on the table. Sometimes he hated how the rules and the law tied his hands when he couldn't find enough proof to back up his theories. The reality was, Emma Frederick had gotten to him. And if he was being honest, he believed someone was watching her. Despite the fact that she was clearly frightened, he found her logical and more importantly, sane. Maybe not every strange incident that had happened to her in the last couple of months could be attributed to PTSD or coincidence. Like Shaye, he wasn't a big fan of it either.

"Can you tell me anything about David Grange?" Shaye asked.

"He was abusive. Ms. Frederick got a restraining order. He violated it and attacked her, and she killed him. One of her neighbors corroborated him striking her."

"Really? She didn't tell me that."

"She might not know. The officers who worked the abuse complaint questioned them. A retired gentleman who lives next door was trimming his rosebushes and could see them arguing through Emma's kitchen window. He saw David hit her."

"Trimming his rosebushes, huh?"

"Ha. More likely, he was out pretending to trim the bushes so he could be nosy, but either way, it was a good thing for Ms. Frederick. Between the eyewitness report and her hospital records, we had no question of credibility, and because of that, it was easy to forgo any charges against her for David's death. The DA took one look at the file and said 'Thank her for her service to society and cut her loose.'"

"So you didn't investigate any further? You didn't check out David any further?"

"Why would we?"

She sighed. "You wouldn't. Your case was closed."

Jackson frowned. "Why do you want to know more about David? You've already agreed that he can't be the stalker."

"Yes, but someone who knew certain traits about David is, and no one was stalking Emma before she killed her husband."

"Okay. I'll give you the personal traits item. And I agree the timing is suspect, *if* we assume that the stalking is a recent occurrence. But it could be that someone was stalking Ms. Frederick before she killed David and she simply wasn't paying close attention then because she was focused on her marital problems."

"That's fair enough," Shaye said, but he could tell she didn't like conceding the point. "But if we assume someone was stalking Emma before David returned from Iraq, then the question is why? She doesn't strike me as the sort of woman who goes around making enemies."

"Agreed. I don't think Ms. Frederick is intentionally seeking out trouble, but by virtue of her job, she could have gotten a rise out of someone unstable…say someone who lost a loved one under her care and is looking for someone to blame."

Shaye frowned.

"You're wondering if someone would really take things that far over something so innocuous," he said.

"No, not at all. I have a limited amount of faith in humans as a species, and have little problem imagining someone that petty and insane."

Jackson marveled at the way she easily processed a diabolical mind. "You are a wealth of comfort, Ms. Archer."

"People can see their friends, mother, priest for comfort. That's not part of my job description. But in my next meeting with Emma, I'll ask about her patients."

"Even though you're still leaning toward the David connection theory?"

"Yes. Again, it's the timing and the personal information, and that whole coincidence thing."

If he was being honest, Jackson agreed with her. Assuming Emma Frederick had a stalker, it was more likely someone connected to her dead husband rather than a patient. But the thought of this young, inexperienced woman tangling with the kind of person who'd go on a revenge kick over a piece of shit like David Grange had him feeling more than a little uneasy.

"How old are you, if you don't mind my asking? Jackson asked.

"Why do you want to know?"

"Fair enough. Because you look too young to hold a private investigator's license. And that's a compliment, not an insult."

"I'm twenty-four and an overachiever."

"Good for you. Who did you intern with?"

"Breaux Investigations."

Jackson knew the agency by reputation. They operated a clean business, mostly handling insurance fraud and disability cases. He'd never heard of them delving into the felony end of things.

"What?" Shaye asked. "You have that look."

"What look?"

"The one where there's something you want to say to me, but you're figuring I'll tell you to mind your business."

"Or something less polite given your love of truthful and direct. Tell you what, instead of the big brother speech, I'll just split the difference and say 'Please be careful with your investigation.'"

"Of course, but why the advice?"

"If someone is stalking Emma Frederick and you get in the middle of it, you'll just be an obstacle in the way of what he wants."

Her expression darkened a bit, but he could tell it was a conclusion she'd already come to herself. She might be young, but she wasn't as naive as he expected.

He rose, placed some money on the table for Christi, then pulled a business card out of his wallet and handed it to Shaye. "That's my cell number. If you run into trouble or get a hold of evidence that I can work with, give me a call."

She took the card and nodded. "Thank you."

"No problem." He crossed the café and opened the door. As he stepped outside, he glanced back and saw her tucking his card into her purse. Maybe she'd be all right. A stalker versus a young, pretty, and inexperienced PI didn't seem like a fair match, but there was something about Shaye Archer that made him think she was a lot tougher than she appeared.

He hoped his impression was correct. Because if the stalker turned out to be real, she was putting herself right in the line of sight of someone mentally unhinged.

CHAPTER FIVE

Emma pulled on her top and grabbed her purse. Housekeeping carts lined the hotel hallway, and she said hello to the ladies as she passed. She'd been so wound up when she got to the hotel early that morning that it had taken her hours to fall asleep. Even though she'd partaken in the minibar and tuned the television to infomercials. It was now 10:00 a.m. and she'd finally given up the thought of getting any real rest.

The only good thing about today was it was her day off. First, she was going to grab some breakfast in the hotel restaurant, then she was going to see to her car. She got into the elevator and pulled out her cell phone, then dialed the car dealership.

"Hi," she said when the service adviser answered. "This is Emma Frederick. I had a problem with my car battery last night. Can I bring that in today and have someone check it out?"

"I'm sorry, Ms. Frederick," the service adviser said, "but we're already overbooked. June in New Orleans. Everyone's got AC problems. I could probably fit you in next Monday."

Emma stepped out of the elevator. "No, that's okay. I'll just find a service shop to take a look. It's probably nothing."

"Well, if they find it's anything but the battery, give me a call back. Your car's still under warranty."

"Thanks." She hung up the phone and walked into the restaurant. "Can I get a toasted bagel with cream cheese to go?" she asked the hostess.

"Certainly," the girl said. "I'll have one of the servers get that right out for you."

"Great." She walked over to the nearest table and sat down. Given the late hour, only a couple of tables were occupied. Everyone else had headed off to their business meetings or out into the Quarter for tourist pursuits. She pulled up Safari on her phone and tried to think of the name of the garage her aunt had used to service her car. It was in Bywater and it was someone's name, but that's as much as she could recall.

She did a search for "car repair" and "Bywater" and the garage name popped right up on top of the list. Andy's Auto Repair. That was it. She pressed the button to call and by the time the server brought her bagel out, she'd talked to a nice man named Jimmy who said he'd be happy to take a look at her car any time that day. She paid for the bagel and headed out to the valet.

Given the time of day, the drive from the hotel to Bywater only took ten minutes. Jimmy was tall and skinny and probably all of twenty years old. She explained the situation with the battery, and he took her keys and assured her he'd check it out and would have it back to her in thirty to forty-five minutes. Then he pointed down the street to a café and said they had the best coffee and doughnuts in Bywater.

She thanked him and set off down the street. The bagel had filled her up just fine, but a latte and doughnuts sounded like a much better option than spending the next thirty minutes hanging around the waiting area of the garage.

Halfway down the block, the skin on the back of her neck started to prickle. She stopped short and spun around, scanning the street. There were probably fifteen people in her view—a couple of vendors changing signs outside their shops, two mothers pushing strollers down the sidewalk, three young boys with bicycles talking at the corner, a crowd of older men hovered over the engine bay of an old Mustang, and some random couples and individuals making their way to wherever they were going.

No one looked out of place. No one was looking at her.

But she could feel eyes on her.

She turned around and continued down the street, chiding herself for being so jumpy. Now was not the time to get paranoid. It was broad daylight, and she was in the middle of a street with a bunch of other people. He wouldn't be foolish enough to approach her here. Not when there were witnesses.

At the end of the street, she checked for traffic and was just about to cross when she heard someone yelling behind her.

"Ma'am! You dropped this."

She turned around and saw a boy of probably fifteen or so approaching on a skateboard. His long blond hair was dirty and pulled back into a ponytail. The rest of him didn't look much cleaner than his hair.

He stopped in front of her and stepped off the skateboard. "You dropped this." He held up a light blue scarf with white stars.

Panic raced through her body and she felt her knees buckle. She took two steps backward and leaned against the wall of the nearest building. "Where did you get that?"

The boy stared at her as if she'd lost her mind. "It's just a scarf."

"Where did you get it?"

"Some dude down the street. He said he saw you drop it and asked me to bring it to you. Are you going to take it or what?"

He took a step closer to her and presented the scarf again.

Even though it made her stomach roll, she took the scarf from the boy. Her hand felt as if the silk were burning it. "What did the man look like?"

The boy shrugged. "Like a white dude."

"Please. It's important."

The boy stared at her for a bit and she thought he was going to tell her to take a hike, but something in her tone must have convinced him to talk. "He was good-sized. Not skinny or nothing. Had really short black hair. Military cut, you know?"

With every word the boy spoke, Emma's breathing became more and more shallow. "How old was he?"

The boy shrugged. "About your age, I guess."

"Did you see which way he went?"

"That way." He pointed behind them.

"Have you ever seen him before?"

"Nah, but folks come from all over to have their cars fixed at Andy's. I ain't ever seen you before, either. I need to get going. I got work to do."

"Yes, of course. Thank you."

"No problem." He gave her a nod, then put one foot on the skateboard and rolled off down the street.

Emma pushed herself off the wall and headed back to Andy's, forcing herself to walk rather than run. That scarf had been a Christmas gift from David.

One of the items that she'd boxed up last week and thrown away.

By the time she reached Andy's, she was drenched with sweat and her pulse was racing. She pulled open the door to the shop and stepped into the tiny waiting area. A small refrigerator full of bottled water stood in the corner. She hurried over to grab one of the bottles, but her hands shook so badly that it slipped from her grasp twice before she got it out of the refrigerator and onto the end table located next to the fridge.

She managed to get the top off and chugged back a big gulp. The cold water burned as it ran down her dry throat. She plopped down on an old wooden chair with a red-and-white plaid cushion, then put the cap back on the bottle and rubbed the cold plastic across her forehead. Her heart pounded in her temples, causing her head to ache. She drew in a deep breath and slowly blew it out, trying to calm herself, but it wasn't very effective.

Someone had gone through her garbage and taken the scarf. What the hell kind of person did that? Crazy. She answered her own question, and the answer didn't do anything to calm her nerves. It only made things worse.

She sat the water on the table and pressed her hands to her temples, silently willing the pounding in her head to cease. The description of the man that the boy gave her fit David. But David was dead. She knew he was dead. The paramedics and the coroner knew he was dead.

But he was still attacking her, even from the grave.

Who was doing this? David had casual buddies, but no particular friends that she was aware of. No outraged person had contacted her after his death. In fact, no one had contacted her at all except the oil company he'd been working for, and all they wanted was to know where to send his final paycheck. Granted, the fact that she'd been the one to cause his demise probably prevented people from wanting to acknowledge his death at all, but surely if someone were angry enough to stalk her, they would have made themselves known before now.

She drew in a deep breath and huffed it out, feeling slightly dizzy. She leaned forward and propped her elbows on her knees, still clutching her head. She closed her eyes and silently willed the pounding headache to subside and her racing pulse to slow the hell down.

"Miss Frederick?"

Her head flew up and her eyes crossed as a wave of dizziness washed over her. She blinked several times and finally Jimmy came into focus.

"Are you all right?" he asked.

"It's just a headache," she said.

"I've got some aspirin if you need it."

The amount of concern in his expression made her wonder just how bad she currently looked. Probably pretty awful. She struggled to get up from the chair and into a standing position, hoping that if she appeared more collected she might actually become more collected.

"No thanks," she said. "I've got some in my purse. I was just resting for a minute to see if it would go away."

Jimmy nodded. "Sometimes I get those bad ones…migraines they call them. I have to sit in a dark room with my eyes closed for a couple hours before they'll go away."

"You should try breathing pure oxygen from one of your tanks the next time it happens," she said, automatically slipping back into nurse mode.

"Really? I ain't never heard that, but I'll sure give it a try. Thanks."

Emma forced a small smile. "Have you looked at my car?"

"Yes, ma'am. I got your battery problem all fixed up. Good thinking using the chewing gum. I ain't seen that one in a while."

"I can't take credit for that. The security guard at the hospital knew that trick."

"It's an old one, but it works. Anyway, you're all nice and tight now, and I didn't see any other problems with the car. Being that it's only two years old and a Nissan, there's usually not a lot that's going to go wrong."

"Could the battery cable have come loose by itself?"

"They don't really do that, ma'am. When was the last time you had it worked on that they would have disconnected the battery?"

"About a month ago at the dealership. Could it have been loose then and finally came off last night?"

Jimmy frowned. "The chances of it happening that way are low. I mean really low. If it had been a day or two ago that they worked on the car, I'd say sure. But a month is a long time. You would have had problems a while back if the dealership had left it loose."

Emma tried to absorb everything Jimmy was saying, but her pounding head was making connecting the dots hard. "So it probably wasn't a mistake by the dealership, and it couldn't haven't come loose on its own accord." She stared at him. "Are you saying someone did it intentionally?"

Jimmy shifted a bit, looking more than a little uncomfortable. "Given what you've told me about the last repair, that seems the most likely explanation."

"He wanted me stranded in that parking lot." Emma felt the blood drain from her face and she sank onto the chair again. "Oh my God."

A million scenarios flashed through her mind, each one worse than the next. If Jeremy hadn't been with her, would he have attacked her then? Or was he simply playing more games with her, like with the scarf?

"It's none of my business," Jimmy said, "but I have to say I don't like the way this is headed. If someone's bothering you, I think you should talk to the police."

Suddenly, the walls of the tiny room felt as if they were closing in on her. She jumped up from the chair, desperate to get away from there. "What do I owe you?"

"No charge."

"I have to pay you something for your time."

Jimmy touched her arm. "You can pay me back by being careful and getting help."

Her eyes stung with unshed tears. Everything—David's death, the break-in, the scarf, the car, and now the concern of a stranger, had her completely undone. "I will," she said. "And thank you. Thank you so much."

"You let me know if you need anything." He handed her the keys. "It's parked up front."

Emma took the keys and rushed out of the building. She jumped into the car and pulled away, the tires screeching as she rounded the corner. She turned the air on full blast and directed it toward her face. The overwhelming desire to run coursed through her, but the one thing that eluded her was where to run to. The only answer she could come up with was "somewhere safe."

But she didn't know where that was.

Shaye was looking up information on David's employer when a call came in from Emma. If she hadn't seen her client's name in the display, she wouldn't have known who it was. Emma's voice, which had been low and smooth, even when she'd been obviously upset, was high-pitched and frantic.

Shaye gripped her phone. "Slow down so that I can understand you."

"He disconnected my battery," Emma said, slowing her pitch and pacing enough for Shaye to understand. "If the security guard hadn't walked me to my car last night, I would have been a sitting duck. But that's not the worst of it. Today when I took the car to be repaired, some kid on a skateboard gave me a scarf that some other guy told him I'd dropped."

Shaye frowned, certain that between the car battery and the scarf, she'd missed something important, but she had no idea what. Although she could understand Emma now as far as speech went, she was making no sense. "I don't understand the scarf part."

"I know. Sorry. I had to stop talking for a minute so that I could breathe."

Shaye heard Emma intake and blow out several breaths, and her concern ticked up another notch. If Emma had been frightened before, she was terrified now.

"I didn't drop the scarf," Emma said. "It was one David gave me last Christmas. I threw it out with a bunch of other stuff last week. I didn't want anything in the house that reminded me of him, so I started going through everything and put it all in a trash bag and threw it out. I know I did. And that scarf was in there. I'm certain it was in there."

Shaye felt her back tighten. Emma was rambling, but Shaye couldn't blame her. She didn't understand all the particulars, but what she understood so far was that someone had gone through Emma's trash and recovered the scarf, then had a kid deliver it to her. The things she'd feared most about this case were all coming to fruition. Someone was hell-bent on terrifying Emma, and even worse, he'd had no trouble finding her.

Which meant he was following her or had a tracking device on her car.

"I understand how scary this is," Shaye said, "but I need you to do your best to stay calm, and I need to see your house. Can you do that? Can you meet me at your house?"

"Yes. No! He's got to be following me, right? I took my car to a mechanic my aunt used. I've never been there before today. If I go to the house, he'll follow me there. He'll see you. And when he finds out you're a private investigator, he might come after you, too. I can't have that on my conscience."

"Take a breath. I agree wholeheartedly that I don't want him to find out what I do, but surely there's some way of going there that he wouldn't find suspicious. What about a Realtor? You said you were looking into selling."

"I already have a Realtor. She lives in the neighborhood. If he's been watching, he's already seen her at my house measuring."

"Okay," Shaye said, trying to think of another reasonable cover. She glanced around her mostly empty apartment and smiled. "What about an interior decorator? You said the house was old. Doing some updates before you list it would improve value, right?"

"Yes. That's what the Realtor said, but if he's watching, how would he know you're a decorator?"

"Don't worry about that. I have an idea. What time is your shift?"

"I'm off today."

"Great. Then can you meet me there in an hour?"

For several seconds, there was only silence, and Shaye wondered if Emma was going to flat out refuse.

"You're sure you want to do this?" Emma finally asked.

"Positive. And please don't worry. It's going to be fine."

"Okay. I'll meet you there in an hour."

"Great." Shaye jumped up from the couch and grabbed her purse. "Don't go in the house until I get there."

"I'm not about to. And Shaye?"

"Yeah."

"Thanks for not quitting on me."

"Never."

CHAPTER SIX

Shaye slipped the cell phone into her purse and hurried outside to her car. Corrine had recently redone several rooms in her house. The big books with fabric swatches and floor samples were in the coat closet. She hoped. With any luck, Corrine would be at work and unavailable to ask a million questions or launch into trying to convince Shaye to move back home.

Unfortunately, luck was not with her that day. Corrine's car was parked in front of the house, which meant she'd probably run home for some paperwork or other items she'd taken home to work on and forgotten that morning. Shaye parked behind her and headed into the house and opened the coat closet. She was relieved to see the sample books still sitting on the shelf.

As she pulled the books down, Corrine came out of the hallway from the kitchen.

"Shaye," she said. "I didn't expect to see you."

Shaye grinned at her adoptive mother. "Are you complaining about it?"

"Of course not." Corrine walked over and gave her a hug. "I just figured you'd be busy unpacking or decorating.

Well, maybe not decorating." She looked down at the books in Shaye's hands and one hand flew up to her chest. "Be still my heart. You *are* decorating."

"Sorry to disappoint you, but I'm working a case."

Corrine's eyes widened. "A case? So soon?"

"The client showed up yesterday while I was moving in."

"Please tell me it's Nancy Drew and the Case of the Matching Drapes."

Shaye laughed. Corrine's worry sometimes made Shaye feel as if she was being smothered, but she knew Corrine's heart was in the right place. And given the amount of horrible things Corrine saw and heard every day, Shaye gave her more leeway than she would have on the overprotective vibe.

"I'm afraid not," Shaye said. "I need to meet with the client and neither of us want anyone who might see that meeting to know what I do. She has an old house, so…" Shaye held up the books.

"You're pretending to be a decorator." Corrine bit her lower lip. "I don't know whether to be happy that you won't be flashing your PI status around or worried that you and a client think you need to hide it."

Shaye leaned over and kissed her forehead. "Don't worry about either. It's a meeting with a client in her house in broad daylight. Everything will be fine."

"But you'll call me when the meeting is over, right?"

"I'll call. I have to dash."

"Okay. Love you."

"Love you too." Shaye hurried out to her car and tossed the books on the passenger's seat. She waved at Corrine, who was standing in the doorway, a worried look on her face. Shaye shook her head as she pulled away. Most younger people were annoyed when their parents got into overprotective zone, but then technically, Corrine had never gotten out of it. Not where Shaye was concerned.

And Shaye would be the first to admit that sometimes it was a little frustrating, but she couldn't get irritated with Corrine. The woman had quite literally saved her life. The best medical care, the best tutors, the best mental health care. Without all those things, Shaye had no doubt that she could not have become a productive adult. Corrine had taken her in as a teenager, one with no past, and given her the future she couldn't have gotten from the state. The fact that Corrine was only twenty-nine when she took Shaye in made the woman even more impressive. She'd been only five years older than Shaye was now, and Shaye couldn't imagine taking on the responsibility of caring for a perfectly healthy child, much less one with the issues she'd had.

Shaye's past might be a forgotten trip through hell, but she'd won the lottery in Corrine.

She merged onto the highway and drove over the bridge to Algiers. The historic community was a mixed bag, depending on the street you drove down. Some homes looked as if they needed to be bulldozed. Other blocks held some beautifully renovated homes and others in the process of being improved.

Emma's aunt's house was one of the nicer homes on

the block. Emma claimed her aunt had taken good care of it, and it showed. The siding on the outside was painted light gray and showed no signs of buckling or peeling. Turquoise shutters and trim provided an upbeat feel to the home, and huge rose azalea bushes made it homey. It was a shame that such a pretty place was the location of such horrible things.

Shaye parked at the curb and grabbed a small duffel bag from the backseat, then climbed out of the car. Duffel over her shoulder, she walked around to the passenger's side to collect the sample books. As she closed the car door, Emma pulled up and parked behind her.

Shaye took a good look at Emma as she climbed out of her car and hurried toward Shaye. The circles under her eyes were darker than the day before, or maybe her skin was paler, if that were even possible. Her movements were twitchy and she glanced around as if she thought something was going to attack her any moment.

"Let me help you with those," Emma said and took some of the sample books. She looked down at them and then back at Shaye. "Sample books," she said, her voice low. "That's perfect."

"I told you to trust me."

A tiny bit of panic left Emma's eyes and she nodded. "Then let's go inside and take a look at these samples," she said in her regular voice and glanced over Shaye's shoulders.

Shaye heard footsteps behind her and turned to see a tall, heavyset woman, probably in her thirties, walking with a cane. Her long brown hair was pulled back into a ponytail and her makeup was a little too dark for the middle of the day.

"Patty." Shaye watched as Emma forced a smile and waved her hand between the two of them. "This is Patty. She lives in the neighborhood and is my Realtor. This is Carla. She's one of the decorators I'm going to talk to about updating a few things in the house before I get it on the market."

Patty stuck her left hand out to Shaye. "My right side doesn't cooperate as well," she said as Shaye shook her hand. "I'm glad you're thinking about doing some updating. I wouldn't put too much money into it, though. The house is going to bring a great price simply because of the condition it's in, but a little updating to the kitchen and the master bathroom wouldn't hurt."

Emma nodded. "I'm going to talk to a couple of people, then if you have time, I'd like to get with you and see what you recommend."

"Of course. Just let me know when you're ready. Me and the house aren't going anywhere. It was nice to meet you, Carla."

"You, too," Shaye said and followed Emma up the sidewalk and onto the front porch.

"MS," Emma said. "It's heartbreaking. She can't be much older than I am, but she can't walk without a cane. Yet every day she gets a mile in. Most able-bodied people don't bother to walk at all, and she's out struggling for every step."

"That's tough," Shaye said as she watched Patty slow down to cross over a section of broken sidewalk.

Emma pushed the door open and they stepped inside. "Do you want something to drink?" Emma asked.

"That would be great."

Emma waved Shaye toward the back of the house. "The kitchen is this way. I have no idea what I've got in the refrigerator, so we may have to settle for water."

"That's fine." Shaye followed Emma down the hallway to the kitchen and took in the small room while Emma dug around in the fridge.

"Do you keep a set of spare keys for your car somewhere?" Shaye asked.

"Yes. In the drawer next to the sink. Why?"

Shaye pulled open the drawer and pushed the stuff inside around, looking for a car key. "Because he couldn't open the hood of your car without one. There's no key in the drawer."

Emma whirled around. "He must have taken it when he broke in."

"Probably so."

The window over the sink was closed but the curtains were open, and Shaye could see the nosy neighbor as he stepped outside and peered toward Emma's window. Shaye lifted her hand to wave at him and he hurried off to the other side of the lawn.

"That's Mr. Abshire," Emma said. "He doesn't miss much."

Shaye turned around and took the can of diet soda that

Emma offered her. "Was he standing in his front window waiting for you to pull up?"

"Probably. If he wasn't so old, and was remotely sneaky, I'd think *he* was the stalker."

Shaye smiled at the thought of the man she'd just seen—who had to be eighty years old if he was a day—sneaking into Emma's house. "He'd never make it up those narrow stairs. And if he did, going back down them would get him."

Emma nodded. "True. Aunt Margaret moved to the bedroom off the kitchen the last couple years she was living. It's tiny, but the stairs got to be too much for her. I was terrified that she'd fall and no one would be around to help her."

"I suppose Mr. Abshire wasn't as nosy when it was only your aunt here to spy on."

Emma smiled. "Oh, Mr. Abshire would have totally hooked up with Aunt Margaret if she'd given him the time of day."

Shaye was glad to see Emma smile. She'd been worried that being in the house would make Emma even more panicked than she was when she'd arrived, but she seemed to be relaxing some with their casual conversation. Unfortunately, Shaye needed to get down to business.

"Is it all right if I look around?" Shaye asked.

"Of course."

Shaye opened her duffel bag and pulled out a small tool set that she tucked into her back jeans pocket, then grabbed her cell phone from her purse and left both bags on the kitchen table. "I'm ready for my grand tour."

Emma guided Shaye through the downstairs rooms. Shaye took pictures as they went, not because she spotted anything of relevance but because you never knew when something might become relevant. Her goal was to keep Emma from returning to the house until the stalker was apprehended. The windows were all intact and showed no signs of tampering, just as Jackson Lamotte had said. Not that Shaye had doubted him, but she wouldn't be doing her job if she didn't check herself.

They headed upstairs and into the master bedroom with its connected bath. Emma showed Shaye the bathroom window she'd left open and the tree branch outside that could have been used for her escape.

"Is the alarm box in the master bedroom closet?" Shaye asked.

"Yes." Emma opened a door and Shaye entered the small walk-in and opened the panel on the security system box.

"I looked at it that night," Emma said, "and it all looked fine to me, but I'll be the first to admit I have no idea what I'm looking at. The cop who searched the house looked too, but he didn't mention anything being wrong."

Shaye pulled the tools out of her back pocket and went to work on the electrical outlet that held the power adapter. "He wasn't looking as closely as me." She worked the electrical plug out from the wall and held it up for Emma to see. "It's not wired."

Emma's eyes widened. "But isn't there a battery for

when the power goes out?"

Shaye nodded and lifted the battery out of the security panel box. She pulled the right battery terminal off and looked at it, but it appeared okay. When she pulled the left one, it snapped off completely, leaving small bits of a clear plastic substance in her hand.

"What is it?" Emma asked.

"Superglue. He broke the terminal and glued it on to make it look like it was still connected."

The bit of color that had returned to Emma's face, left. "But how did he get inside the house to begin with? I changed the locks."

"If someone has the right tools and knowledge, they can pick a lock. What did David do in the military?"

"He was infantry, but he trained to repair their trucks and other equipment."

Shaye nodded and made a mental note.

"Why would that matter?" Emma asked. "I mean, we've agreed that it can't be David…"

Shaye placed the battery back in the panel and closed it. "No. But it's probably someone who knew him."

"Someone who might have the same skill set. I see."

"Have any of David's coworkers or military buddies shown up?"

"I was just thinking about that last night, but the answer is no. I've only met a handful of people that David knew, so it wasn't like I was close with any of them. I assumed it was because of the way he died. I mean, what do you say to the widow who killed her husband?"

"Probably not 'can I have your number'?"

Emma stared at her for a moment, then broke into laughter. She laughed so hard she stumbled backward into the bedroom and sat on the edge of the bed, tears streaming down her face. Shaye stepped out of the closet and closed the door behind her, happy that Emma enjoyed her joke. Eleonore had used the same ploy so many times in therapy when things got difficult for Shaye to handle. This was the first time Shaye had tried it herself.

Emma finally regained control and wiped her eyes with her fingers. "Oh my God. I needed that so badly. I can't even remember the last time I laughed. I mean really laughed."

"Have you thought about talking to someone…I mean, about all of this?"

"Yes. And I will." Emma looked up at her and smiled. "You're a good person, Shaye. I know my discernment hasn't been all that great recently, but I'm sure I'm right about you."

Shaye felt a blush creep up her neck. No matter how much Eleonore had worked with her, Shaye still found compliments uncomfortable. On one hand, it pleased her to know she was appreciated, but deep down, there was some dark part of her that whispered that she didn't deserve them.

"I'm glad you laughed," Shaye said. "I would have had to return the retainer if you hadn't."

Emma smiled, then sobered. "Do you think it means something that none of David's coworkers or old military buddies contacted me?"

"No. I was more interested in if someone had. Staying away seems normal under the circumstances."

"And if someone had gotten in touch?"

"If it was a simple 'sorry and let me know if I can do anything,' then I still don't see any cause for alarm. But this guy is playing with you, and sitting down with you for coffee would be another ego boost for him."

"Oh. That's a horrible thought. I'm glad they all stayed away."

"Me too, but if anyone shows up, you let me know."

Emma nodded and rose from the bed. "Let's go look at my old bedroom."

They headed down the hall and into the bedroom that Emma had occupied as a child. Emma opened the closet door and pushed the clothes aside to show Shaye the panel at the back. Shaye got on her hands and knees, slid the panel back, and peered inside.

The room was narrow and dark, and Shaye imagined Emma huddled in the far corner, hearing the whistling on the other side of the thin plaster wall, her pulse racing. If hiding in this room had been the only thing that could save Shaye from an attacker, she probably would have died. Even now, her breathing was somewhat shallow.

She backed out of the closet and looked over at Emma, who was fingering the edge of a lamp. "Is it supposed to be for winter storage?" Shaye asked.

"I don't really know. I found it when I came to live with Aunt Margaret. She'd only recently moved in and didn't even know about it." Emma gave her a sad smile. "I was only five when my parents died and I came to live here. I thought it was the coolest thing ever. How many kids had a secret room in their closet?"

"Narnia."

"Exactly. Except no cold and no witch. I used to crawl inside and stay there for hours, reading books with a flashlight. Even though Aunt Margaret never had children, somehow she knew to leave me alone when I was there. That somehow I felt safe, and inside the closet, I could work things out."

"You're lucky you had your Aunt Margaret." Something Shaye knew firsthand.

"Extremely lucky." Emma looked back at the closet and frowned. "But now it doesn't feel safe. I mean, it saved my life, but I didn't feel safe in there. I was scared to death. I can't even imagine crawling back in there."

Shaye knew exactly how Emma felt and didn't blame her one bit. "Let's see the rest of it and get out of here."

"I thought you'd never ask."

They finished with the upstairs, then Shaye checked out the backyard and immediately saw what Jackson had meant when he said an intruder would have left prints if entering through the back of the house. The giant oak trees created shade over a good two-thirds of the backyard, leaving much of the ground bare. There was no way to approach the house from the back without creating evidence of passage.

As Shaye exited the house, she caught sight of

something sitting on the steps leading up to the front porch. She walked over and saw it was a card in a bright pink envelope. She picked it up and checked both sides, but didn't see anything to indicate who the card was for. Behind her, Emma closed and locked the front door and Shaye turned around.

"I found this on the steps," Shaye said.

Emma turned and looked at Shaye's outstretched hand. Her eyes widened and her hand flew up over her mouth. "It can't be," she whispered. "Open it."

Shaye opened the envelope and pulled out a birthday card. Before she even opened it, she already knew who it was from.

Happy Birthday, my darling. David

"He was here," Emma said. "I told you he's following me. There's no other way he could have found me at the repair shop."

Shaye frowned and stuffed the card back in the envelope. "Can I keep this?"

"Yes, please. I don't ever want to see it again. I don't want to see any of that stuff again."

Shaye slipped the card in her duffel bag. There was really little purpose in keeping it, except that she didn't want Emma to have to deal with it. The likelihood of finding a print for the stalker was low. He had been clever so far, so Shaye couldn't imagine him slipping and leaving a print on the card. And the card would have been handled by any number of store employees and however many people pulled it off the shelf to look at it, then put it back.

"Stay calm," Shaye said. She looked up and down the street, but didn't see anyone holding an "I'm a stalker" sign. Still, leaving the card on the porch steps when they were inside was brazen.

Unless he'd had someone else do his dirty work again.

"Too bad Mr. Abshire is busy in the backyard. He might have seen who delivered the card."

"Oh! That's right. The stalker could have sent someone else, like he did with the skater kid."

"Did the skater kid give his name?"

"No."

"Can you describe him?"

"Maybe fifteen or so. Long dirty blond hair in a ponytail, and I mean dirty blond both in color and in condition. He looked like he needed a good scrubbing. His eyes were light green and he had a tattoo on the back of his hand—an eyeball. It didn't look like professional work, and to be honest, it was a little creepy."

"What color was it?"

"Black. Why, do you know him?"

"No, but I think I'd like to meet him."

"You think he knows more than he was telling?"

"Maybe. If he's a street kid, probably. They don't miss much, but they're not exactly big on volunteering information, either."

"So what do we do now?"

"We get back into our cars and head back to New Orleans."

"But we were going to talk. If he's following me…"

"That's why we're going to meet at Landry's. There's a parking lot next door and plenty of people around. He won't make a move in public. That's not his play."

"Are you sure? I don't want you taking any chances. If you think he could come after you…"

"If he's been watching, then he saw the sample books. He has no reason to think I'm anything but what I'm putting myself out to be."

"I guess," Emma said, but Shaye could tell she wasn't convinced.

"After lunch, you're going to change hotels."

"He'll find me again," Emma said, sounding totally defeated.

"Maybe, but it will probably buy you a few days. You told me you picked a hotel close to your job. When he realized you were no longer staying in your home, those are probably the first places he checked."

A flush ran up Emma's neck and cheeks. "I'm so stupid! I'm sure you're right."

"You're not stupid. You just don't think like a criminal. That's a good thing."

"Seems like it would be an advantage right now."

"Don't worry. I've got that part covered. Let's go get something to eat."

Emma nodded and headed to her car. Shaye tossed the sample books and her duffel bag into her car and hopped inside. As Emma pulled away, Shaye started her car and headed down the street.

He was getting bolder.

That gave Shaye more opportunity to expose him, but made it that much more dangerous for Emma.

He lowered his binoculars as the cars rounded the corner and disappeared from view. The attic window was tiny but provided a perfect view of Emma's house. He could even see inside the open windows. It had been so kind of Mrs. Pearson, the homeowner, to go see her new grandchild in Arizona, and so unfortunate that she'd returned home before his work was finished. In a day or two, her family would grow concerned and the police would pay a visit, but there would be nothing to indicate he was there, except Mrs. Pearson, and she wasn't going to talk.

Emma wouldn't return to the house. Not to live. Not even to stay overnight.

She had done everything she could to keep him out—set the alarm, rekeyed the locks—but there was no lock he couldn't pick. He'd learned that skill long ago, when it was the only way to buy his freedom. And the alarm was a joke. Most home alarm systems were. Even commercial systems were lacking, which was good. After all, a man had to make a living, and working a regular job wouldn't allow enough time for his hobbies.

He smiled. Every man needed a hobby.

He wondered about the woman who'd met Emma at the house. Mama would say she was just another whore, but he couldn't manage his life with such a simplistic viewpoint. Even a whore could put a kink in his fun, and that just wouldn't do. The fabric sample books implied interior decorator, but her casual jeans and tennis shoes didn't convey that at all. Even stranger, the "decorator" had kept the card he'd left on the steps. Why would she do that?

He supposed she could have seen Emma's panic and offered to get rid of it for her, but he'd fully expected Emma to run to the police with what she thought was hard evidence. It wouldn't be, of course. A card owned by Emma and found on her property was hardly a smoking gun. The cops still wouldn't have anything to go on, and the last time he checked, they didn't offer bodyguard services, anyway.

He frowned, thinking about the decorator again.

Something told him she needed a closer look. He had big plans for Emma, and no one was going to get in his way.

CHAPTER SEVEN

Shaye pulled up to the curb just down the street from Andy's Auto Repair and parked. The street was the usual mix of old buildings, some residential, some retail, some commercial. Shaye had never been interested in travel—too much change too fast. Too many unknowns, but she wondered how many cities offered the same sort of eclectic blend within a one-block radius, especially in areas with no high-rise buildings.

She walked down the sidewalk toward the café that Emma had been walking to when the skater had accosted her. A couple of teens were standing on the corner, so she headed toward them. They stopped talking as she approached and gave her a once-over.

"Hi, guys," she said. "I'm looking for a skater who lives in the area. Dirty blond hair in a ponytail. Maybe fifteen."

One of the teens narrowed his eyes at her. "You a cop?"

"Do I look like a cop?"

"No, but that don't mean nothing. Why you looking for this skater dude?"

Shaye pulled out her license and showed it to the boys. "I think he saw the man who's stalking the lady who hired me."

"No shit!" The second teen shook his head. "That's fucked up. If some dude was stalking my moms, I'd cut him."

"Is that what you're going to do?" the first teen asked. "You gonna cut him?"

"Unless he presents a threat, that would be illegal," Shaye said.

"But he's stalking some lady, right?" the second teen said. "So if you find the dude, then he might try to attack you. Could you cut him then?"

"I'd probably just shoot him," Shaye said, assuming the blunt truth would work best with these two.

The two boys looked at each other and nodded.

"Badass," the first one said.

"I think I've seen the dude you're looking for," the second one said. "He hasn't been around too long. I seen him before at the docks. That's where the skaters do their thing."

"Thanks," Shaye said. "I appreciate it."

"No problem," the first one said.

"I hope you get him," the second teen said. "The stalker, I mean."

"So do I," Shaye said, then headed back to her car. The docks were only a couple of blocks away. With any luck, the skater would be doing "his thing."

It took only a couple of minutes to drive to the dock,

and Shaye's spirits lifted a bit when she saw several skaters using the concrete forms as their own personal obstacle course. She parked and headed for the docks, easily spotting the long blond ponytail as she walked. When she got close to the docks, she stood and watched until the boy looked her way, then she motioned to him.

He stopped skating and stared at her for several seconds, but didn't move. Probably deciding whether to approach her or flee. She must not have looked threatening, because he finally picked up his board and shuffled over to her.

"Who are you?" he asked, stopping about ten feet away.

"Shaye Archer." She pulled out her license and showed him. "I'm a private investigator. I'm hoping you can help me."

The boy held up his hand. "Look, I ain't know nothing."

She smiled. "You don't know what I'm going to ask."

"Yeah, well, I don't want no trouble is all. I don't like the cops."

"At the moment, I'm not crazy about them myself. Look, there's a lady I'm trying to help because the police won't. You brought her a scarf this morning."

He gave her a wary look. "Yeah, I remember. She acted like I held out a snake or something. She's not saying I stole it, is she?"

"Nothing like that. The man who gave you the scarf has been following her."

His eyes widened. "He's a creeper? Oh man. I wouldn't have done it if I'd known that. No wonder she was scared. Shit, I feel bad now." He looked genuinely upset.

"It's not your fault. You were just being nice."

He shrugged.

Shaye pulled out her cell phone and opened an image she'd loaded of David Grange. "I wanted to know if this is the man you saw."

She turned the phone around to show the boy. He squinted at first, then finally moved closer. Shaye knew David wasn't the man the boy saw, but wanted to give him a starting point for a description. When he frowned and continued to look at the photo, she started to wonder.

Finally, he shook his head. "It wasn't him, but the dude looked a lot like him." He pointed to the phone. "This guy has a square jaw. The other guy didn't."

"But he looked like this—a lot or a little?"

"Enough to be related. I mean, dude had on sunglasses, but yeah, I can see where people might think they were the same guy. Unless they was looking really close."

Related.

David had told Emma that he had no living relatives, but then he probably hadn't told her he'd abuse her either. What if everything he'd told her was a lie? A brother would be a good choice to seek revenge for Emma's killing David. In fact, it was the most logical speculation she'd come across so far.

"What's your name?" Shaye asked.

The boy hesitated for a moment. "Everyone calls me Hustle."

"You live around here?"

"You're standing on my front porch."

Shaye glanced around, but all that stretched for a hundred yards was dock and parking lot. "You live on the streets? How old are you?"

"Old enough." His jaw set in a hard line.

Shaye held in a smile. She'd used the same line on Jackson Lamotte, and had probably been as irritated by the question as Hustle was now.

"Look, I'm asking because I know a social worker. If you're underage, she can help."

He took a step back and pulled up his shirt to expose three long scars running across his belly. "Last time someone 'helped' me, they stuck me in a house with the guy who did this."

Shaye's stomach rolled. "Your foster parent did that?"

He dropped his shirt and looked away.

Shaye knew this kid—not personally, of course, but knew him from so many of the stories that Corrine had told her about the cases she worked. It wouldn't do any good to detain him. If they put him in a group home or new foster home, he'd only be there as long as it took to get away. If Corrine hadn't taken her in, and Shaye had experienced more trauma in a group or foster home, Shaye had no doubt she would have done the same thing. There were plenty of great foster parents and lots of good people working in group homes, but in every crowd, there were the ones that weren't so great. Weren't so nice.

"Where are your parents?" she asked.

"Never knew my pops. My mom got killed last year by her ex-boyfriend. Said he was gonna get her for breaking it off with him, and he did. The coward did that shit while I was in school, wasting my time in history class when I could have protected her."

Shaye's heart ached for this boy. She knew better than anyone what it felt like to be physically beaten down, to be afraid of everyone you came in contact with. But she'd had Corrine. This boy had been dealt the horrible blow of his mother's murder, then an abusive foster father. She wanted to do something to help him, but she knew he wouldn't allow it. Couldn't, because he couldn't afford to trust her, either.

She pulled out her wallet and emptied it of the eighty dollars in cash inside. She handed it to Hustle. "Take this. Get something decent to eat."

He looked at the money and frowned. "Why you giving me money?"

"Because when I was fifteen I had no one, but a social worker took me in, gave me everything I needed to get healthy and get an education. She even adopted me. I was lucky. And I'd like to call her to help you, but I know you won't accept it. So the least I can offer you is money for food."

"You was on the street?"

She nodded.

He studied her for a couple seconds more, then took the cash and stuffed it in his pocket. She pulled out a business card and handed it to him. "This is my cell number. If you change your mind, call me. Anytime."

He took at the card and nodded. "Thanks," he said, then dropped the skateboard and took off.

Shaye stood there until he disappeared around the end of the dock, wishing she could have done more and praying that one day he would be ready for help. Finally, she turned around and headed back to her car. Hustle had given her something to think about.

It was high time to dig into David Grange's past.

Emma pulled her makeup bag out of her suitcase and placed it on the vanity. It had taken her an hour to get to the new hotel. It was only five miles away from the first hotel, but she'd driven up the highway and around every borough of the French Quarter making sure she wasn't being followed. When she was finally convinced no one had tailed her, she'd pulled into the parking garage and registered for a single night. If she didn't feel okay tomorrow morning, she'd find another place. Maybe it was crazy, but Emma didn't care. She was done ignoring that nagging feeling that something wasn't right. She hadn't felt safe at the other hotel, and she'd had good reason not to. New Orleans had plenty of hotels and she was traveling light. If she had to move every day, she'd do it.

But for how long?

The question was one that kept creeping into her thoughts and it never failed to frustrate her, mainly because she didn't have an answer. How long would it take to identify her stalker, and once he was identified, how long would it take Shaye to convince the police of the danger, and even if they believed her straight off, how long would it take to apprehend him? A day? A week? And even if they apprehended him quickly, could they do more than issue a restraining order?

She flopped back on the bed and blew out a breath. Too many unknowns. Maybe Clara had been right. Maybe she should just leave. Pack a larger bag, get in her car, drive as far as a tank of gas would take her, then fill up and do it again. If Patty could sell the house quickly as she claimed, Emma should have enough money to survive for quite a while without working. Years, if she was careful, but eventually, she'd have to take another job. Would he still be looking for her? Or maybe the key was to take a job with a doctor's office and not a hospital, or maybe even private care. The demand for in-home care was growing every day. She could effectively fall off the employment grid if she was patient and waited for the right opportunity.

It was all so much to think about. And when she went down that path, the sheer number of things that would have to be done overwhelmed her. She rose from the bed and checked the dead bolt again. The first thing she was going to do was take a long hot shower, with the bathroom door open, the shower curtain cracked so that she had a good view of the door, and her pistol sitting on the toilet. Then she was going to order a hamburger, wine, and cheesecake from room service and do her damnedest to forget how frightened she was.

Shaye frowned when she heard the knock on her front door. She glanced at her watch. Eight p.m. Too late for the cable guy, who'd never shown, and too polite for a robber. Since she could count the number of people who knew where she lived on one hand, she bet herself a large pizza that it was Corrine.

She put her laptop on the end table and hopped off the couch. When she pulled open the door, she found herself staring at the smiling and hopeful faces of Corrine and Eleonore. "Double trouble," she said.

"We come bearing housewarming gifts," Corrine said and held up two bottles of wine.

Shaye felt herself weaken just a bit. It was her favorite wine from Corrine's special stock.

"Uh-hmmm." Eleonore held up a cheesecake.

"You guys don't fight fair," Shaye said and waved them inside.

"We're a parent and a psychiatrist," Eleonore said. "The fact that you even assume we'd fight fair tells me I have more work to do with you."

Shaye grinned. "Break open that cheesecake before I grab it from you and kick you out."

Eleonore put the cheesecake on the counter and opened the empty drawers one at a time.

"I've been too busy to unpack," Shaye said, "or to shop. There's some plastic utensils on the stove that I had leftover from Chinese food, and some paper plates in the cabinet behind you."

Corrine sighed and opened one of the bottles of wine. "It hurts my heart to hear you say you're too busy to shop. You're a woman, and an Archer. Surely there's something you need to buy."

"I just ordered office furniture," Shaye said as she grabbed a package of plastic cups from the pantry and slid them in front of Corrine. "I might even get a rug. That should make you happy. That's purely for decoration."

Corrine gave the plastic cups a look of dismay. "What color is the rug?"

"I don't know. I haven't picked it out yet."

"You're just trying to mollify me with a theoretical rug."

"Yes. Is it working?"

Corrine handed Shaye a cup of wine and smiled. "Maybe a little."

Shaye took a sip of the wine and sighed. "This stuff is wonderful." She sat the cup down and pulled open the refrigerator. "Eleonore, I have bottled water and Diet Dr. Pepper. What's your preference?"

Eleonore dumped a huge slice of cheesecake onto a paper plate and slid it over to Corrine. "I'm going to go wild and have the Dr. Pepper." She cut two more pieces and they all stepped around the counter and back into the living room. Eleonore and Corrine sat on the couch while Shaye perched on the edge of the end table that had never made it back to the corner.

"So," Eleonore said, "Corrine tells me you already have a client."

Shaye took a big bite of the heavenly cheesecake and nodded. "A nurse. Really nice woman."

"Cheating husband, I suppose," Corrine said and sighed. "You're probably going to get a lot of that."

"Not this time. Her husband's dead."

"Well, I guess killing him is one way to ensure he doesn't cheat," Eleonore joked.

"Actually," Shaye said, "she *did* kill him, but not for cheating."

"Oh!" Corrine sat up straight. "You didn't tell me it was a murder case."

"It's not," Shaye said. "The guy was abusive and had a record. She had an order of protection, he broke in the house to attack her, and it didn't work out the way he intended."

"Good for her," Corrine said.

"Sounds like she deserves a piece of this cheesecake," Eleonore said. "Don't tell me the DA is pressing charges."

"No," Shaye said. "He didn't pursue it."

"Smart move," Eleonore said. "The last thing you want during the next election is to be the prosecutor who picks on abused women."

Corrine frowned. "Wait a minute. Is your client Emma

Frederick?"

Shaye looked at her mother, a bit surprised. "Yes. Do you know her?"

"Not well, but I've spoken to her at the hospital over some of my charges and liked her. I heard a little about what happened to her. She's so nice. I can't believe she has more problems after everything she's been through. So what's the case, or can't you say?"

"There's no confidentiality laws for PIs, if that's what you mean. Decorum dictates that I don't go around blabbing, but since you're here and asking, maybe you can give me your professional opinions."

The two women looked at each other and frowned. Shaye already knew what they were thinking—if she wanted the professional opinions of a social worker and a shrink, this case was a doozy.

"My client is being stalked, but he's very clever. So clever that the police didn't believe her."

"But you do?" Eleonore asked.

"Yes." Shaye told them about the first incidents that Emma had. "But he's escalating." She went on to tell them about today's events with the scarf and birthday card.

"Oh my God," Corrine said when she finished. "That's why you took those sample books from the house today. You were afraid he might be watching."

Shaye nodded. "She's selling the house, so interior decorator was a logical cover. I don't want him to know Emma has help."

"Damn straight you don't want him to know,"

Eleonore said. "I don't think I have to tell you how bad this situation is. I assume you've gone to the police with this new evidence?"

Shaye squirmed a bit. "Not yet."

"What the heck are you waiting for?" Corrine asked, practically hopping in her seat.

"The lead detective kinda pissed me off," Shaye said. "He basically implied that Emma was weak, and it was all in her head."

Eleonore shook her head. "The woman killed her husband—a man with far more strength and skill than she had—and she's the weak one? When was this detective born, the 1700s?"

"Actually, he's probably only a little older than you," Shaye said.

Eleonore looked over at Corrine. "And you ask me why *I* don't date. Look at the pool I've got to choose from."

Corrine rolled her eyes. "Because every fiftysomething in New Orleans is that guy. Your dating excuses are as bad as mine."

Eleonore turned back to face Shaye, not bothering to acknowledge Corrine's statements. "Surely there's someone else you could talk to? The New Orleans Police Department has got to employ at least one person with a brain."

"There was one guy," Shaye said. "The rude detective's partner. He's younger, like me, and didn't seem to like the old detective any more than I did."

"So he doesn't think your client is frail and imagining things?" Corrine asked.

"He said he found her credible, but without evidence, his hands are tied."

"But you have evidence now," Corrine said. "The scarf and the card."

"Yes," Shaye agreed, "but what can he do? We have no idea who the stalker is, and the police aren't in the business of playing bodyguard in case someone is in danger. They don't have the resources, and unfortunately, a nurse who lacks political or economical connections isn't going to get anything beyond the norm."

"She's right," Eleonore said. "I don't like it and I still think it should be reported, but right now, this is still a case of harassment by an unknown party. The stalker hasn't made a physical threat."

"So the police should only concern themselves with investigating crime rather than preventing it?" Corrine argued. "You know the threat is coming."

"That's exactly what I said to the younger detective," Shaye said.

Eleonore shook her head. "He's getting off on terrifying her—the scarf, the card—purely psychological stuff."

"And when he gets bored with that?" Corrine asked.

"He'll kill her."

CHAPTER EIGHT

Shaye tossed and turned in her bed, unable to relax. Every time she started to doze off, Eleonore's words echoed through her mind on stereo. Before she'd even asked for her opinion, Shaye already knew that Eleonore would say the stalker's ultimate plan was to kill Emma. He was a cat with a mouse, playing with her until the fun was gone. But hearing Eleonore say it made it more real. More immediate.

Her foot began to ache and she flung the covers off and sat up, drawing her leg up so she could rub her foot. She'd had two surgeries to try to fix the damage, and they'd succeeded in allowing her to walk without a limp, but the pain was never completely gone. It remained there, lurking just beneath the surface, ready to spring up at a moment's notice to remind her that she wasn't the same as other people and never would be.

Rain must be coming. It always ached more when it rained.

The massage didn't seem to be working, so she climbed out of bed and headed into the kitchen for aspirin. She'd learned the hard way that the longer she waited to take something, the worse it got, and it took twice as long for the pain to subside.

The bottle of aspirin was still on the kitchen counter where Corrine had left it. Between the stalker talk and the wine, her mother's head had probably been on the edge of explosion. At least, that was the way she described it. Shaye dumped a couple of aspirin into her palm and tossed them back with a big gulp of water. Time to grab her laptop and head back to bed.

Then she heard a scraping noise outside.

She froze, trying to identify the source and location of the sound, but all she heard was the low rumble of distant thunder. She went back to her bedroom and grabbed her pistol, then systematically checked every window in the apartment. The streetlights were dim, and with the impending storm, no moonlight was available to improve visibility.

The street appeared quiet. No sign of movement, not even an automobile.

Then she heard the noise again.

This time she was certain it came from the courtyard between her apartment and the building next to hers. She grabbed a spotlight from her bedroom closet and placed her ear against the side door that led into the courtyard. It was quiet now, but that didn't mean someone wasn't out there. The storm hadn't moved in yet, so the air was still— no wind to blow things around and create the noise. And the only items contained in the courtyard were the trash cans for the building occupants and a tiny wrought iron table and two chairs that sat under a tree in front of the back wall of the courtyard.

She sat the floodlight on the floor next to the door, disarmed the alarm, and inched back the dead bolt. She turned the doorknob slowly, then pushed the door open a tiny bit and slid her foot against it to keep it from closing again. She switched her pistol to her right hand and reached down to pick up the spotlight with her left, then she counted to three and threw the door open.

She jumped out, clicked on the spotlight, and directed it down the breezeway toward the brick wall. The breezeway was empty, but twenty feet away, one of the trash cans moved. She trained her pistol on the cans. "I've got a weapon. Come out of there."

The can rattled again and its shadow cast across the breezeway morphed as if something behind it had moved. Her finger tightened on the trigger and she felt her chest constrict. Her pulse beat in her throat and her temples, pounding like a jackhammer. She inched forward.

"Come out or I'll shoot."

One of the cans swayed and a black-and-white cat jumped on top of it and let out a loud meow. She jumped back, and the breath she didn't know she'd been holding came out in a whoosh.

"Damn it, cat. Are you trying to get shot?"

The cat sat and started cleaning its paw. Shaye shot it a disgusted look and hurried back inside. She locked the door, slid the dead bolt into place and leaned back against it, willing her pulse to slow. All that aggravation and stress over an alley cat.

If you were still living with Corrine, you'd probably be asleep.

She pushed herself away from the door and headed into the kitchen. To hell with sleep. If her mind worked better at night, then so be it. She'd work at night and catch a nap in the daytime. What was the use of being your own boss if you couldn't make the rules?

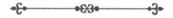

From the rooftop across the street, he watched as she slammed the door to her apartment shut. He lowered the night-vision goggles and frowned. He'd been right. She was no interior decorator. He'd thought he recognized her when he saw her at the house. It had taken him several hours to locate the old copy of *New Orleans Magazine* that had the picture he remembered. The girl in the photo was younger than the woman he'd seen with Emma, but he was certain it was the same person.

Shaye Archer.

Once he had a name, it took no time to find out everything he needed to know about Shaye's life, her family, and most importantly, her new business venture. He'd almost tired of clicking on links when he came across her website. He'd smirked when he read the home page. Private investigator. What in the world were poor little rich debutantes going to think up next to waste everyone's time? The thought of that inexperienced, frail-looking girl getting the better of him was laughable.

But she *was* messing up his game.

He wanted Emma alone and frightened. Allies and others who would bolster her confidence and keep her from falling apart would interfere with his fun. No way was he allowing a stupid twit like Shaye Archer to detract from his pleasure. Something would have to be done, but first, he had to make sure he knew where to find her when he was ready to strike.

When he saw the address on the website, he figured she was using the apartment for both her living quarters and her office, but he needed to be sure.

It had been a simple matter to put fish behind the trash cans in the breezeway, then drop fishy liquid from the freezer bag along the sidewalk to where he'd spotted the cat. Then he'd climbed atop the building across the street and waited. He'd wondered, at first, if he'd miscalculated, because lights were on in the apartment. She might be working late, but that wouldn't indicate she was living there. But when she'd burst outside barefoot and wearing gym shorts and a tank, he knew she'd been in bed.

With every light in the apartment on.

Apparently, Miss Archer was afraid of the dark.

CHAPTER NINE

Jackson slipped his cell phone into his pocket and looked across the desk at Vincent. So far, he'd spent the morning at the very dangerous job of completing paperwork and fetching Vincent coffee. He could almost feel himself aging in place. "We got anything up right now?" he asked.

"Paperwork from that drug bust last week," Vincent said. "Since you had the better view of everything that went down, I figure you need to do the write-up."

Translation: Because I'm lazy, I waited out back while you busted in and did all the hard work. Because I'm super lazy, I think you should do all the paperwork as well.

"Yeah," Jackson said. "I started it already. Got about thirty minutes or so on it to finish. If that's all, I'm going to take off for an hour or so. I got to talk with my landlord about some maintenance problems."

Vincent barely glanced at him. "Sure. Take whatever you need. If we get a call, I'll let you know."

Jackson struggled to keep the disgusted look off his face. They weren't likely to get a call unless no one else was available or Vincent downed a case of energy drinks and a bucketful of courage. The man apparently intended to spend the rest of his career cruising into retirement, and if he had his way, Jackson would be sitting in the passenger's seat, snoozing along.

At 10:00 a.m., the drive across the French Quarter was a fairly easy one. He located a parking spot half a block away from the café he was looking for and headed up the street. It was a tiny place, maybe fifteen tables total, and had a surprising amount of natural light from front and side windows. At a table in the back corner, Shaye was easy to spot. There were only two other patrons, an elderly couple sitting near the front. Otherwise, the place was empty.

Shaye was watching as he came in, and he gave her a nod and headed for her table. As he slid into the chair across from her, he noticed the huge coffee cup with a single packet of artificial sweetener in front of him.

"Black, right?" Shaye asked.

He poured the sweetener into the cup and stirred. "Good memory."

"It's not a difficult order."

"No, but most people wouldn't have noticed."

"I'm not most people."

"Touché." He knew Shaye wasn't most people. He wouldn't have admitted it to anyone, but only a few minutes of exposure to the young PI had fascinated him. Had him wondering what made someone like Shaye Archer tick. When he'd gotten back to the police station, he'd pulled out his personal cell phone and searched the Internet for information on her. He'd expected to find a Facebook page full of pictures with college girlfriends and family. He'd been shocked when the first five pages were full of news articles about Shaye and her missing past.

He'd spent two hours reading through the stories and finally risked searching police records, even though he knew if Vincent caught him, he'd crawl all the way up his ass to Alaska. If Vincent never heard the name Shaye Archer again, it would probably be too soon. Jackson doubted his so-called superior officer had made the connection between Shaye and the girl Detective Beaumont had pulled off the street years ago, even though he was working at the precinct at that time. But then these days, Vincent didn't seem to notice much besides the clock hitting five.

If the news articles had been disturbing, the police reports had been downright horrifying. Even now, sitting across from her, he marveled that she could sit there so normal, so sane.

So beautiful.

He took a drink of his coffee. Where the hell had that come from?

"You said you wanted to talk," he said, forcing all thoughts of anything but business out of his mind.

Shaye nodded. "A couple of things have happened. Emma isn't interested in being mocked again, but you said to call if I got something."

"Definitely. What's going on?"

Shaye told him about Emma's car trouble and the returned scarf.

"Do you think the skater could identify the man?" he asked.

Shaye opened her phone and showed Jackson a picture of David Grange. "I tracked him down and showed him this photo. Obviously, the man who had the scarf wasn't David, but the skater said it looked enough like him that they could be related."

Jackson blew out a breath. "Which supports Emma's insane claim that she saw her husband in her house. With only moonlight, looking through that tiny hole in the wall, and terrified, I can see why that's the first thing she thought."

"That's not all. Yesterday, I met her at the house to have a look around." Shaye pulled a card out of her purse and slid it across the table. "He left this on her front steps while we were inside. It's a birthday card—one that she'd thrown away."

Jackson stared. "In broad daylight?"

"Yeah."

Jackson pulled out the card and saw the inscription "Happy Birthday, my darling. David."

He slipped the card back into the envelope and looked at Shaye. Her expression reflected everything he was thinking—this was bad. Whoever was after Emma Frederick was crafty and cruel, and seemed to have no fear of discovery. The more unpredictable, the more dangerous.

"I assume Ms. Frederick is staying somewhere else?" he asked.

"She's been staying in a hotel since the night he broke

into her house. Given that he found her at the shop in Bywater, I had her change hotels yesterday. She probably burned a tank of gas driving around before checking in, just to make sure no one was following her." Shaye tapped her fingers on the table. "He's not going to stop. Not until she's dead."

"I know."

"Is there anything you can do about it?"

He knew the question was coming. Had known it since he'd heard about the car battery and the scarf. "Not officially. Not until there's some sort of threat."

He didn't blame Shaye for the disgusted look she gave him. At the moment, he felt the same way.

Shaye shook her head. "You and I both know that everything I just told you *is* a threat. Hell, he's coming right out and telling Emma he can get to her any time he wants to."

"The law doesn't see it that way, and even if we could convince other people that everything Emma says is the gospel, we have no idea who this person is. We can't arrest a shadow." He blew out a breath. "How much do you know about David Grange?"

"Very little. I tried the usual Internet searches, but it returned sixteen thousand matches. I went through a couple hundred pages before giving up. The images were the same."

He nodded. "We checked for a criminal record when Emma filed her report on the assault and it came up clean. I imagine a person like Grange would keep a low profile. I wouldn't expect to find him posting selfies on Twitter or anything."

"I didn't really have an expectation that I'd find anything, but I had to try."

Jackson ran one hand through his hair and blew out a breath. "Look, there's nothing I can do in a professional capacity...not on the record, anyway. But let me see if I can run down anything on David Grange—brothers, cousins."

"That's my plan for the day. I've got a meeting with his former boss in an hour, but if you can find out something, I won't turn down the help."

"It's a long shot, but I'll give it a whirl. I might not be able to get to it until this evening, though. If Vincent catches me helping you, he'll have me demoted."

"For helping a woman being stalked?"

"For helping someone without hard evidence, especially the woman who cut him off at the knees and got him razzed by rookies for an hour."

She gave him a rueful look. "At least that's something. So he's really that big of a douche bag?"

"And then some. He's been looking for a way to take me down a peg ever since they assigned me to him. So far, he's managed to submarine my career through inactivity. If I gave him a reason to cause me more grief, he would take it in a heartbeat."

"Why don't you complain to his superior?"

"I'm the new guy. Maybe when I've been there a couple years, and if my nose is clean, someone will listen. But right now, the old guys see me as a new face that probably won't last long. A lot of guys do a turn in New Orleans, then move on to the suburbs for less stress and a higher paycheck."

Shaye frowned. "I owe you an apology."

"How do you figure?"

"I've been judging you unfairly. My mother is a social worker, so I hear all about the politics of government work. I wasn't extrapolating that same set of nonsense to police work. It was shortsighted of me."

"The politics are the most frustrating part of my job."

"My mother's as well, and that's saying a lot in both cases given what you do. Anyway, I appreciate any information you can provide, but I don't want you to risk your job or your reputation in doing it."

"There's way more at stake than my job."

Shaye's expression darkened. "Yeah."

"Remember when I told you to be careful? I'm telling you again. I'd bet anything he saw you at Ms. Frederick's house. If he thinks you're in the way…"

"I had a cover…interior decorator, complete with sample books. But I'm being careful. I'm always careful."

He nodded, but her assertion didn't do anything to lessen the nagging dread that was starting to consume him. Given her past, Shaye Archer was probably one of the most careful women in New Orleans. But she still wasn't any match for a psychopath.

Especially an unknown one.

CHAPTER TEN

Emma rushed across the hospital parking lot to the entrance. She'd parked in the visitor area, and if anyone had a problem with it, they could kiss her ass. If someone insisted she park in the garage with the other employees, she'd give them her two minutes' notice. She'd been struggling with the decision all morning at the hotel. She'd had room service for breakfast and lunch, too scared to leave her room, all the time dreading going to work because the hospital was the easiest place to find her.

When she entered the hospital, she headed straight for the security office and was relieved to see Jeremy watching the monitors. He looked up as she entered and smiled. "Afternoon, Ms. Frederick. You get your car looked at?"

"Yes. I wanted to thank you again for getting it running. I took it to the mechanic yesterday."

"They get you back to a hundred percent?"

"Yes, but that's what I wanted to talk to you about. The mechanic said there was practically no chance the terminal came off accidentally."

Jeremy frowned. "He thinks it was deliberate? But who would do that?"

"I've been having some trouble since David…anyway, I think someone's following me, trying to scare me."

Jeremy straightened in his seat, clearly concerned. "If someone's bothering you, then you need to go to the police."

"I have, and there's nothing they can do. There's been no threat, and I have no idea who it is. But I'm not interested in becoming a victim in order for them to have a clue."

"Of course not!"

"Anyway, all of this is to say that I parked in the visitor's section in front of the building, so please don't have me towed."

Jeremy nodded. "And don't you go walking out to that car without me."

"I won't. Thank you."

"Be careful, Ms. Frederick."

Emma nodded and headed out of the security office. She was so preoccupied that when she rounded the corner into the hallway, she almost ran right into a bouquet of flowers.

"Oh," she said as she drew up short, then took a step back. "I'm so sorry."

"That's okay," a voice said, and the flowers lowered.

A man's face emerged and his eyes widened. "Emma?"

She slowed her racing mind long enough to focus on the man with the flowers. "Stephen. It's been a long time."

She'd dated Stephen for three years of high school. He was the only child of one of New Orleans's "good" families and had a bright future ahead of him following in his father's footsteps as a lawyer. He was good-looking, popular, and intelligent, but he'd been more invested in their relationship than Emma. When she got word of her college scholarship in Dallas, Stephen had begged her to stay, even said he'd marry her, which probably would have sent his highbrow parents over the edge. But aside from knowing she wasn't remotely ready to be a wife, Emma also wasn't convinced that Stephen was "the one."

The breakup had been heart-wrenching. She hadn't wanted to hurt him and had been surprised with how badly he'd taken her rejection of the marriage proposal, but over the summer, his feelings cooled and they were on decent terms when she left for school. He even helped her pack her car. They'd stayed in touch by email for six months or so, then as most college students do, they got involved in their campus lives, and communication got less frequent until it finally stopped altogether.

"When did you move back?" he asked.

"About a year ago."

"You look great," he said with a huge smile. "But then, you always did."

"Thanks. So do you." And he did. He'd put on some bulk since high school, and his long wavy locks were darker and military short, but he still had the chiseled face and wide grin.

"Do you work here?" he asked. "Wow. That's a stupid question given that you're wearing a badge."

"I'm a critical care nurse."

"Wow. That's a tough area."

"It is, but it's also very rewarding. I considered working for a specialist—weekday office hours and a regular schedule were tempting—but ultimately, I felt trauma was my calling."

"I bet you're great at it. You were always the calm in the middle of a storm." His smile vanished and he shuffled in place. "I heard about…you know. I'm really sorry, Emma. I can't imagine how horrible all that has been for you."

"Thank you. It's been…something. I don't know that I can even describe it."

"If there's anything I can do, please let me know. I know we haven't been in touch for a while, but I'm always there for you. We should get together for lunch or dinner and catch up—whatever works for your schedule."

"That would be great."

He put the flowers down and pulled a card out from his wallet and handed it to her. "Business hours you can reach me at the firm. My cell number's on the bottom."

Emma took the card and slipped it into her pocket. "Thank you. I'll give you a call as soon as I catch a break."

"It was good seeing you again," he said, and gave her arm a squeeze.

"You too. I have to run or I'll be late for my shift."

She gave him a wave and hurried down the hall to clock in.

It had been nice seeing Stephen again—a smiling face from her past. She'd been gone for so long that most of her old friends had moved. A couple still remained, but they were knee-deep in baby diapers, a completely different place in life than Emma. Maybe when all of this was over, she'd take Stephen up on that offer for a meal and conversation. Right now, she wasn't about to take the chance of bringing someone else into her circle. She was already worried about Shaye. She didn't need another person on her conscience.

Shaye walked down the hallway of Wellman Oil and Gas and knocked on the door at the end of the hall. The nameplate on the door read "Richard LeDoux—Operations Manager."

"Come in," a deep voice yelled from inside.

Shaye opened the door and stepped inside. The man behind the desk waved at her as he yelled at someone on the phone. He was a big guy—muscles clearly visible beneath his polo shirt with the oil company logo on it—and younger than Shaye had expected. She'd figured that the man yelling behind the door would be midfifties. To have this position so young, Mr. LeDoux was either born into the right family or had serious skills. Since his last name wasn't Wellman, she was going with the latter.

"That's not negotiable," he said and slammed the phone down. He looked up at Shaye and waved her to the chair across the desk from him. "Please sit. I'm sorry for the language. No, that's not true. I'm not really sorry as the jackass deserved every word I said, but I apologize that you had to hear it."

"That's all right. I've had a word or two for jackasses in my day."

He smiled. "Kindred spirits then. What can I do for you, Ms. Archer? Greta said you needed some information on a former employee? You don't look like a cop or one of those hard-ons from an insurance company."

"I'm neither." She pulled out a business card and passed it to him.

His eyebrows went up. "PI? You look like you should still be in college. You must be one of those annoying overachievers."

"I suppose you would know."

He stared for a moment, then laughed. "Yeah, I guess I would. So what can I do you for, Shaye Archer, Private Investigator?"

"I wanted to know what you could tell me about David Grange."

"Well, he used to work here and now he's dead."

"I know the highlights. I'm working for his wife."

Richard frowned. "I didn't think the state was pressing charges, given the circumstances and all. That's what they said on the news, anyway."

"There are no charges against my client for David's death. She hired me because she's being stalked, and the stalker is leaving her mementos related to David."

"Seriously? Man, that is screwed up." He shook his head. "I don't know what I can tell you aside from his job description and pay range. There were several levels of management between us, so aside from a brief conversation the day he interviewed, I never really talked to him."

"Would you be willing to check his personnel file and see if he listed any next of kin other than Emma?"

"Sure. If you think it will help."

"I honestly don't know, but I'm checking everything I can. Would it be all right if I spoke to the employees who worked with him?"

Richard reached for his keyboard and started typing. "You'll want to talk to Charlie Evans. The assistants work in pairs, so if anyone knows something about David, it will probably be Charlie." He stopped typing and looked at the screen. "And it looks like you're in luck. Charlie's crew just got back from offshore."

He grabbed his phone. "Hey, send Charlie Evans to the conference room. There's someone who needs to speak to him." He hung up and rose from his chair. "I hope it's okay if I set you up in the conference room. I would stick around but I have a meeting with the owners in ten minutes."

"That's no problem at all."

Richard opened his office door and she followed him back up the hall to the first room on the right. He flipped on the light and waved her inside. "I'll have Greta check that personnel file for you. If you need to talk to anyone else, let her know and she'll run them down if they're here, give you contact information for them if they're not."

"Thank you. I really appreciate all your help."

He grinned and winked at her, then hurried back down the hallway. Shaye poured herself a cup of water from the cooler in the corner. If Charlie Evans was as helpful as Richard, and actually knew something relevant, today might start looking up.

A couple of minutes later, a scruffy blond-haired man walked into the conference room and gave her a wary glance. Shaye put him late twenties to early thirties, and he had a look about him that said he was no stranger to trouble.

"The boss says you wanted to see me," he said.

"Yes. My name is Shaye Archer." She stuck out her hand. Charlie gave it a single shake and released it almost immediately. "Why don't you have a seat?" she said.

Charlie pulled out one of the chairs and dropped into it, his arms crossed. Shaye shut the door to the conference room and sat on the same side of the table as him but a little ways down. Enough space to keep him from being crowded, but no table in between to make him feel like he was on trial. Eleonore had taught her well.

"I'm a private investigator working for David Grange's wife," Shaye said.

Charlie's eyes widened. "This is about David?"

She nodded and his shoulders relaxed a little. Apparently, Charlie thought his own butt was in a sling. Now that he knew the summons wasn't about him, he wasn't as anxious. "Ms. Grange has had some trouble lately. Someone is harassing her, and they seem to know a lot about David and their marriage."

"She don't know who it is?"

"No. But he's gone so far as to break into her house, so she's rightfully scared."

"Why don't the police do something?"

"They don't have any evidence to work with."

Charlie snorted. "And Emma ain't got the clout to make them jump. Cops suck."

"The rules suck."

He shrugged. "Amounts to the same thing for the people who need help, doesn't it?"

"Yeah, I guess it does. Can you tell me anything about David—specifically about family, friends, his past?"

"Ron got him the interview. Said they were cousins. He didn't talk about no other family, except Emma, of course."

"Was he friends with any of the other employees?"

"Not really." He shifted in his chair, clearly uncomfortable. "Look, I know you ain't supposed to speak ill of the dead and all, but the truth is I didn't like David much. He was weird—nice one minute, then he'd completely lose his shit the next. It's hard to be around people when you don't know what's going to set them off."

"What do you mean?"

"Well, like this one time when we was offshore, some of us were playing poker. Willie was talking smack about his own mom, saying as how she was a crazy bitch who'd ran his dad off and probably caused his heart attack. David gets all antsy and tells Willie to shut up—that he didn't know anything and maybe his dad was just another piece of shit that abandoned his family because it was convenient."

"Willie's talk made David mad."

"More like furious. I know it probably sounded bad, but in Willie's defense, I've known his family my whole life and his mother is definitely a crazy bitch. I'm surprised his dad stuck around as long as he did."

"What did David do?" she asked.

"Willie told him to shut up since he didn't know nothing about nothing. David's face turns dark red and before we knew it, he flips the table over and launches across it, grabbing Willie by the throat. It took four of us to pry him off of Willie. If we hadn't been there…"

"You think David would have killed Willie?"

"I know it. If you coulda seen the look on his face. I ain't never seen anyone look that way. Don't ever want to again."

"Did you report what happened to management?" she asked, even though she was pretty sure she already knew the answer.

"No. Willie didn't want to be on the hook for someone losing his job. A couple of us tried to talk Willie into reporting it, but he said David was a soldier and we should all cut him some slack this once. Willie served too. His whole family did. Willie said sometimes you see things that screw with you, and hopefully, David would work it out."

"Did Willie ever talk to David about the attack?"

"No. We left the rig the next day and David was killed a couple days after."

"But that's not the only time David lost his temper?"

Charlie shook his head. "It was the only time he got physical, but he yelled at people a lot. Sometimes he'd sit out on the deck and just stare across the Gulf. I could see his lips moving, but wasn't nobody out there with him." He gave her a sheepish look. "Don't tell anyone I said it, but it kinda creeped me out."

"Yeah, I can see that." Since her first conversation with Emma, Shaye had found the case chock-full of creepy. "So there's nothing else you can tell me about David's past, no other friends or family that he mentioned?"

"Nah. I mostly kept quiet around him. I always had this feeling he was going to blow someday, you know? That thing with Willie confirmed it."

"I appreciate you taking the time to talk to me." She pulled out her card and handed it to Charlie. "If you think of anything that might help, please give me a call."

He nodded and rose from the chair. He stuffed the card in his jeans pocket and headed out of the room, pausing at the door. "I hope you catch the guy," he said. "I only met Emma once, but she seemed like a nice lady."

"Thanks." Shaye looked down at her notes. Time to ask Greta where to find the cousin Ron.

CHAPTER ELEVEN

Corrine knocked on the front door of the apartment, then listened for any movement inside. The call had come late in the afternoon, but the woman had sounded frantic, and the distant sound of a child screaming had Corrine as concerned as the caller. The woman refused to give her name but said she was visiting a friend at this address and the baby had been screaming like that for over an hour.

It was common for callers to request anonymity. Getting labeled a snitch could lead to harsh consequences in some of the areas Corrine worked. She knocked again, but still nothing. Maybe the mother had returned and left with the infant. Or maybe she'd suffocated him and was hiding inside. Corrine sighed. She'd seen both.

She twisted the doorknob and was surprised when it turned easily in her hand. The door popped open a bit. "Is anyone home? My name is Corrine. I need to talk to whoever lives here."

She waited several seconds, but no one answered. Cracking the door another couple of inches, she peered inside and frowned. Something was wrong. She pushed the door open and stepped into the apartment. Most of the places she entered were sparse with belongings. The people she dealt with didn't have much, but this apartment was completely empty except for a couple of faded food wrappers on the floor near the window.

She stepped over to the kitchen and ran a finger across the counter. The layer of dust it contained would take weeks, if not months, to accumulate. She pulled out her phone and checked the address again. This was the right place, and the number on the door matched the unit number she'd taken from the caller. But she was certain that no one had lived here in some time.

There were five other units on the third floor, so she exited the apartment and knocked on the door across the hall. Silence. A strange feeling came over her and she twisted the doorknob. The door popped open and she found herself looking into another abandoned apartment. A chill ran through her. She released the doorknob and whirled around.

At the end of the hall, the apartment door across from the stairs creaked open. Her chest constricted and she struggled to take in air. The building didn't have a fire escape, and the third floor was too high to risk a jump. The only way out was that staircase. She pulled Mace from her purse and hurried down the hall for the stairs, her gaze fixed on the apartment across the hall. When she reached the stairs, she was almost at a run.

She was so focused on the apartment across the hall that she never heard the man come out of the apartment next to the stairs. When she took her first step down the stairs, hands slammed against her shoulders and sent her hurtling forward. She crashed midway down the stairs, her right shoulder and head smashing into the old wooden steps. She tried to grab hold of something, but couldn't get a good grasp on anything.

She flipped over again and again and finally crumpled to a stop on the second-floor landing. Pain shot through her right arm and shoulder, and her ankle throbbed. A shadow passed over her and she looked up, her vision blurred. She blinked, trying to clear her eyes, and moved her left arm across the floor, desperately searching for the Mace she'd dropped on the way down.

When the shadow bent over her, she screamed. A boot connected with her temple and it felt as if her head exploded. Then everything went black.

Ron Duhon was on a seven-day on, seven-day off schedule, and as Shaye's luck would have it, he happened to be on the off portion. He agreed to meet with her at a coffee shop, claiming his girlfriend was sick and he didn't want to disturb her by having Shaye come to his apartment. Shaye took down the address, thanked Greta for all her help, and headed out of the oil company, her notes tucked under her arm.

She'd talked to five other employees who had worked semi-regularly with David, but none of them had been able to add anything to what she'd already learned from Charlie.

None of them expressed as much dislike for David as Charlie had, but they all agreed that David had a temper and it was best to stay out of his way when he was in a foul mood. A couple said they were surprised to learn that he'd taken his anger out on Emma, as David appeared to really care about her, but then rage was an unpredictable thing. All five expressed some level of shock over the way things went down, but all of them seemed to think Emma had done the right thing and were sorry she'd been put in that position.

As Shaye drove to the café, she struggled to get a handle on David Grange. Certainly suffering or even witnessing atrocities shaped a person, and PTSD was common for people who had experienced something traumatic, but she was still having trouble reconciling the person Emma described before he went to Iraq with the person who had returned. What had happened while he was overseas that could force him that quickly into a complete one-eighty?

The people she really needed to talk to were those who served with David, but Emma didn't know any of their names, and the military sure as hell wasn't going to hand her over a list of what amounted to suspects. If this Ron was really David's cousin, then maybe he'd have another avenue for her to run down.

The coffee shop was in the Tremé, tucked between an apartment building and an art shop. Shaye entered the shop and looked around, almost doing a double take when she spotted the man who had to be Ron, sitting in the back corner. He looked up at her and she waved, then headed over to him. As she got closer, the differences between him and David emerged. Ron's cheekbones weren't as prominent as David's and his jaw wasn't as square, but they looked enough alike that Ron could have passed for David, especially in moonlight. The build was the same, and the haircut and color matched the photos she'd seen.

"Ron Duhon?" Shaye asked as she stepped up to the table.

"Yeah. You the PI?"

She pulled out a chair and sat down across from him. "I'm Shaye. Thanks for meeting me."

"No problem. You said this is about David?"

"Yes. I'm trying to get some information on him—his friends, family, past. I understand you were cousins."

Ron shook his head. "Nah. I mean, that's what I said to get him the interview, but I didn't know the guy."

"Then why would you vouch for him as family?"

"Lots of people are looking for work, especially with more of the military guys coming home. I had a buddy from high school who served with David. He said David needed a job in New Orleans and asked if I'd help him out."

"That was kinda risky, wasn't it?"

He frowned. "I didn't think so when I did it. I mean, my buddy vouched for him. David was military and his wife was a nurse. I did eight years serving, so I figured he was a good dude and could use a break."

"Uh-huh, and how did that turn out for you?"

"Not so well. I caught some crap from the other guys over the way David acted. Sometimes he was cool, but other times, he could be a real asshole to work with. Sorry for the cussing, but I don't really have a better word for it."

"That's okay. I've already heard that description a time or two today."

"I bet."

"Did David ever mention any other family besides Emma?"

Ron shook his head. "He didn't talk about much personal stuff, just about cars sometimes. When he was feeling sociable."

"Can you tell me how to contact this high school buddy of yours?"

"Man, I don't know. I don't want to get him in trouble. He was just trying to help the guy out. He didn't know the dude was going to lose it like he did."

"No one could have known that, and no one is responsible for David's actions but David."

"I guess so. His name is Paul Schaffer. I don't have his number. He called from the base. I think he was being deployed again, though."

"He's from New Orleans?"

"Natchez."

"Does he live on base when he's stateside?"

He shook his head. "Sorry. I didn't ask. We're not close or anything. He just calls me up when he's in town and we have a couple beers."

Shaye made a note of the name in her phone. "You

know if he's planning a beer call anytime soon?"

"I doubt it. Like I said, I think he's back over. Not sure I'd go this time, anyway."

"Why not?"

"There was some things David said…talking about stuff they did overseas."

"Like what?"

"He never gave me any details. The hints were bad enough. I got the impression the other guys in the unit were happy when the tour was over and David left."

Shaye frowned. Emma said David changed after his last tour, so whatever caused his shift in personality had happened while he was in Iraq. Ron seemed to be verifying that idea. Maybe this Paul had gotten him into things he couldn't handle once the dust cleared and the bombs stopped exploding.

"Do you need me for anything else?" Ron asked. "I need to get my girlfriend some cough medicine…"

"No, we're good. Thanks for meeting me." She handed him her card. "If you can think of anything else or anyone else who might know more about David, please give me a call."

"Sure." He shoved the card in his pocket and headed out of the café.

Shaye watched as he walked past the window of the café, hands shoved in his pockets, shoulders hunched, a slight limp favoring his right leg. He was the only person she'd interviewed who hadn't asked her why she wanted information on David. It was odd, but then someone from the oil and gas company had probably called to warn him.

She placed some money on the table and gathered her stuff. Time to head back home and try to track down Paul Schaffer. His was the only name she had that linked to David's time in the military. Hopefully, Schaffer would be stateside and have some answers.

Her phone rang as she exited the café. She didn't recognize the number.

"This is Shaye Archer."

"Ms. Archer, this is Sergeant Boyd with the New Orleans Police Department."

Shaye's hands tightened on the phone. Something had happened to Emma. Shaye hadn't worked quickly enough and the stalker had gotten to her.

"What happened? Is Emma all right?"

"I don't know an Emma, Ms. Archer. Your mother has been in an accident. She's in New Orleans General."

Her entire body went rigid and her breath exited in a whoosh. "Is she all right? What happened?"

"She's in with the doctor now. I'd rather discuss this in person."

"Of course. I'm on my way."

She broke into a run for her car and pulled away from the curb, tires squealing. For the moment, speed limits and red lights were suggestions. She was careful not to put anyone else in danger, but broke the law at least ten times before she jolted to a stop in the emergency room parking lot. She jumped out of her car and ran through the double doors, sliding the last two feet into the reception desk.

"I'm Shaye Archer. My mother, Corrine, was in an accident?"

A tall, stocky young man wearing a police uniform exited the emergency room doors and approached her. "Ms. Archer? I'm Sergeant Boyd."

"Where's my mother?"

"This way." He motioned her down the hall and they hurried into a room.

Corrine was lying in the hospital bed, an IV in her arm. Her face was puffy with scratches down the side and bruises already forming on her cheeks. Her lip was busted, and dried blood clung to her chin. Her eyes were closed and her breathing so shallow that if it weren't for the monitors, Shaye wouldn't have been certain she was breathing at all.

A doctor with a chart standing next to the bed looked over as they entered. "You must be Ms. Archer's daughter. I'm Dr. Stabler."

"Yes." Shaye hurried over to the bed, her heart clenching. The injuries looked even worse up close. "Is she all right? What happened?"

"I don't know exactly what happened," Dr. Stabler said. "Only that she took a fall down the stairs in an abandoned building. Her injuries are consistent with a hard fall. She has a couple of bruised ribs and a slight concussion. She's going to feel pretty bad for several days, and the ribs will bother her for a lot longer, but she's going to be fine."

The breath Shaye had been holding escaped and she

felt her knees buckle. She clutched the bed railing to steady herself. "Is she unconscious?"

"No. She's sleeping, probably her body's way of getting past the pain. I want to keep her here tonight for sure and run tests again tomorrow. Then I can assess when she can leave."

"Can I stay here with her?"

Dr. Stabler glanced at Sergeant Boyd, then looked back at her. "We don't usually allow overnight visitors in the emergency room, but in this case, I think we can make an exception."

"Thank you!" Relief washed through Shaye. If they hadn't allowed her to stay in Corrine's room, she would have spent the entire night pacing the emergency room lobby. Making the exception was easier on everyone.

"I'm going to make my rounds," Dr. Stabler said, "but I'll check back in before I leave."

Shaye nodded. As soon as the door closed behind the doctor, Shaye whirled around and locked her gaze on Sergeant Boyd. "What the hell is going on? The police don't answer calls for slip-and-falls."

"No ma'am. We got a call from the paramedics on the scene. They said your mother had bruises on her shoulders and they thought she might have been pushed."

"Who found her?"

"A couple of painters who were supposed to start work in the building next week, stopping by to get an estimate for supplies. Someone ran past them and knocked one of them down when they walked inside. They heard moaning and found your mother on the second-floor landing. I have officers going through the building now, but so far, it's clean except for your mom's footprints and boot prints in the dust."

"Did the painters get a good look at the guy?"

"Unfortunately no. The entry faces east, so it was too dim to make out anything of relevance. They put him at six feet or so and stocky, but that's all they could give us. We got her name from her license, and she had an 'in case of emergency' card in her wallet with your name and number."

"Wait a minute." Shaye turned to stare at the officer. "They didn't steal her wallet?"

"No. Her wallet contained her license, the emergency contact card, one credit card, and forty dollars in cash. Her purse contained the wallet, her cell phone, car keys, lip balm, and one of those eyeglass cleaning cloths. Do you know of anything that might be missing?"

Shaye blew out a breath, trying to clear her mind and concentrate on what the officer asked. "She carried very light on the job, but she always had a can of Mace."

Sergeant Boyd nodded. "The detectives found one on the staircase, but it hadn't been used."

"He got the jump on her."

"Most likely."

Shaye ran one hand over the top of her head. "Why was my mother in an empty building?"

"Her office said she got a call late this afternoon. A baby was screaming in the background and the caller claimed that had been going on for hours. She went to do a site check."

"Did she get the address wrong?"

"Not according to your mother. I spoke with her briefly when I first got to the hospital. She was still a bit unclear on some of the details, but she said the address was in her cell phone. I checked the notes and it was a match for where she was found. All calls on the agency hotline are recorded and they pulled the tape and verified she took it down correctly."

Shaye sucked in a breath. "Then that means…"

"Someone lured her into the building to attack her."

"Oh God." Shaye stumbled back from the bed and sat in a chair over to the side.

"Have you traced the call?"

He nodded. "Made from a disposable cell phone, paid for with cash at one of the hole-in-the-wall retailers with no cameras."

"So you've got nothing."

"I've already contacted her supervisor and asked for a list of people who might be holding a grudge against your mother, but given her line of work, I'm anticipating more than a couple of names. Can you think of anyone? Someone she might have mentioned at home? Someone she was scared of?"

Shaye shook her head. "Nothing that stands out from the norm. There's always someone angry. Someone convinced the state is out to get them even though they're horrible parents. But she hasn't mentioned anyone in particular. Not recently, anyway."

"Has she seemed different lately? More watchful? Worried?"

"No," she said, hesitating a bit before answering.

"You don't sound convinced."

Damn. The sergeant didn't miss much.

"She has been more worried lately, but it's because I moved out into my own place this week."

Sergeant Boyd's expression changed from concerned to understanding. "My youngest moved out two weeks ago. My wife was inconsolable for days. She probably used up all his cell phone minutes in the first week."

Shaye managed a smile. "So you're saying this is normal? How long does it last?"

"Until one of you dies." Sergeant Boyd frowned. "I'm sorry. That probably wasn't the right thing to say given the situation."

"Don't worry about it. Is there anything I can do to help?"

"Just take care of yourself and your mother. My captain has instructed us to leave a guard until we have a better handle on things. I'll be here for the next hour or so, then Deputy Crocker will take over until morning."

"Thank you." The relief Shaye felt knowing that the police would maintain a presence at the hospital was bittersweet. If Corrine had been anyone else, it would have been unlikely that they'd receive this kind of security detail, but the heir to Archer Manufacturing and daughter of a state senator tended to get things outside the norm. Even without asking.

As Sergeant Boyd left the room, Shaye rose from the chair and went to stand next to the bed. Corrine's face was drained of color, and the blood and bruises stood out like neon against her pale skin. Shaye reached up and gently brushed Corrine's bangs back from her forehead. The lump was pronounced and already dark purple. Shaye said a quick prayer that Dr. Stabler was right with his diagnosis. That knot looked bad. At minimum, her mother was going to have a killer headache when she woke up.

Corrine stirred and her eyes popped open. She glanced wildly around before her gaze locked on Shaye and the panic subsided. "Shaye. Thank God! For a moment, I wasn't sure where I was." Corrine lifted one hand, then groaned and let it drop back onto the bed.

"Try not to move," Shaye said. "Your ribs are messed up, so any movement is going to hurt." Shaye pressed the button to call the nurse. "Can you tell me what happened?"

"I think so. A policeman asked me earlier, but some of it was fuzzy."

"That's because you have a concussion. Do you remember more now?

"I went to a site call, but when I got there, it was all wrong. The apartment was empty. They were all empty. Then I saw the door open for an apartment at the end of the hall across from the stairwell, and I knew someone was there."

Corrine's eyes widened and she gripped Shaye's hand. "I pulled out my Mace and ran for the stairs. I thought I'd beaten him, but he fooled me. He wasn't in the apartment with the open door. He was in the one next to the stairs. He pushed me down the stairs. I hit my head and my vision blurred. Then he was standing over me. I believe he kicked me. I think that's when everything went black."

Corrine squeezed Shaye's fingers tighter and tighter as she talked, and Shaye felt her anger build that someone had put her mother through this. "Can you describe him?"

"No." Corrine's face contorted in frustration. "Damn it. He was too blurry. Tall, stocky, and a hoodie, but everything was blurry and gray."

"Please don't let it stress you. It will only make your head hurt more. The police are investigating. They'll get him."

A nurse walked into the room and Shaye moved back from the bed so she could check Corrine's vitals. "Things look good considering, Ms. Archer," the nurse said. "Does your head hurt? Your ribs?"

"Honestly," Corrine said, "I'm not sure there's a place on me that doesn't hurt. I'm too old to go falling down stairs."

The nurse smiled. "You're still young and vibrant. Trust me, none of us were made to tumble around the way you did. Dr. Stabler gave me instructions for a painkiller when you awakened." She pulled a bottle out of her pocket, gave Corrine a white pill, and poured her a glass of water. "This should make you feel better and help you sleep."

Corrine swallowed the pill and closed her eyes. The nurse turned to Shaye. "She'll go to sleep quickly. If she awakens again, let me know."

Shaye nodded and moved closer to the bed after the nurse left. Corrine opened her eyes. "I'm tired, but I'm afraid to sleep. Every time I open my eyes, I'm afraid I'll see him standing over me again."

"Don't worry. I'm going to be sitting right here, and Sergeant Boyd is right outside your door. No one is going to stand over you here except me and medical personnel."

Corrine forced a smile, her swollen lips making it look more like a grimace. "Have I told you what a great daughter you are?"

"Maybe a time or two." Shaye leaned over and kissed Corrine on her forehead. "Get some rest. I'll be right here."

Corrine shifted a little and closed her eyes. In no time at all, her breathing was rhythmic. Shaye stood there watching her sleep and mulling over everything Corrine and Sergeant Boyd had told her. Something was nagging at her, but she couldn't put her finger on what. The phone call to Corrine's office, the empty building, the painters...the purse!

That was it.

She hurried over to the table against the wall, opened Corrine's purse, and dumped the contents on the table. Wallet, phone, lip balm, keys...where was it? She flipped the purse back over and peered inside, opening the side pocket. And that's where she found it. Not an eyeglass cleaning cloth like Sergeant Boyd thought, because Corrine didn't wear glasses.

It was a decorator's swatch.

Shaye's hand closed around the cloth, making a fist. It

wasn't Corrine's job that had put her at risk. It was Shaye's. Her disguise hadn't fooled the stalker, and he was letting her know that not only did he know who she was, he knew how to get to her.

Fear, rage, and guilt coursed through her. When she'd taken this case, she'd never imagined that it might put those close to her at risk, not even as she'd started to understand more about the stalker's fixation. How had he figured it out? Had he followed Shaye to her apartment? Since she'd first met with Emma, Shaye had been extra careful when driving, more observant about the cars surrounding her.

She shook her head. The only way he could have followed her home is if he'd made himself invisible. Which meant he'd discovered her identity some other way. How much more did he know?

And how was she supposed to explain to her mother that all of this was her fault?

CHAPTER TWELVE

Emma dashed into the emergency room and stopped at the nurse's station, trying to talk and catch her breath at the same time. "Corrine Archer? Is she here?"

The nurse checked her computer screen. "She's in room seven, but—"

Emma didn't wait for her to finish the sentence. As soon as she heard the room number, she dashed through the emergency room doors and down the hall for room seven. Her pulse quickened when she saw the policeman sitting at the door outside of the room. He rose when she approached.

"I'm sorry, ma'am," the officer said, "but I'm going to have to see your credentials."

"Of course." She pulled her identification out of her pocket and presented it to the officer. "Can you tell me if Shaye is with her mother?"

The officer handed back her identification and narrowed his eyes at her. "You know the Archers?"

"Yes. I mean, I know Corrine from working with some of her wards, and I know Shaye from, well, from recently hiring her to look into a problem of mine. Is Corrine okay?"

"You should probably ask yourself."

"Of course. Thank you." She cracked the door open and peered inside, then sucked in a breath as she saw Corrine, so pale and bruised.

Shaye sat in a chair next to the bed and must have heard her intake of breath, because her eyes flew open. Her gaze locked on Emma and she jumped up from her chair. Emma rushed over. "What happened? Is she all right?"

"She answered a distress call for an infant," Shaye said, "but when she got there, the building was empty, and someone attacked her. She fell down the stairs and he clocked her in the head."

"Oh my God! What did the doctor say?"

"Bruised ribs, a concussion, and the general knocks from the tumble. She'll be sore and have a headache, but should be all right. He's going to do more tests tomorrow."

"Thank God. That's good. I mean, not good in the big scheme of things, but good considering."

Shaye nodded. "Some painters showed up to measure. If they hadn't interrupted whatever he had planned…"

Emma shuddered and crossed her arms across her chest. "Could she identify him? Has she been awake?"

"She's been awake, but her vision was too blurry to see him, and the painters didn't get a good look either given the bad lighting."

"Damn. I know, given her job, she probably isn't popular with a lot of people, but this seems sort of extreme."

"Yeah, I thought so too, until I realized it wasn't about her job." Shaye held out her hand, exposing a square of cloth with jagged edges. "I found this in her purse."

Emma frowned. "I don't understand…"

"It's a decorator's swatch."

"No!" Emma's hand flew over her mouth and she took a step back, as if the cloth were going to attack her. "Oh, Shaye, I am so sorry. I never thought…you have to stop now. Stop working the case."

"And leave you with no one? I don't think so."

"But you never signed up for this, and your mother definitely didn't. If anything happened to either of you, I don't know how I'd be able to live with myself."

"Nothing is going to happen," Shaye assured her. "My mother will go home to top-of-the-line security and given who she is, probably a police guard."

"But you won't."

"I'll probably stay with her for a while—at least until she's able to move around well."

Emma shook her head. "It's not good enough. As long as you leave Corrine's house to work on my case, you're still at risk. You see firsthand what he's capable of. Why is this happening?"

"I don't know, but I'm going to find out." Shaye placed her hand on Emma's arm. "I mean that. I'm going to figure this out."

"What about the cops?" Emma said. "You have the decorator's swatch. Corrine was attacked and it was planned. Surely they can't ignore all that."

"No. They won't ignore it."

Emma studied Shaye. "You don't sound convinced."

"I'm convinced they'll investigate Corrine's attack. I just don't know if they'll agree with our take on why. My mother makes a lot of enemies with her work. This thing with your stalker is a big unknown and a leap."

"That he would go from me to your mother?"

Shaye nodded.

"Damn it. He's got us right where he wants us. We know it's him, but other people might not believe us. The people we *need* to believe us might not."

"Don't worry about the police. I'll handle that end of things. Just worry about yourself. Did you have any problems changing hotels?"

Emma shook her head. "I drove around for a while. No one could have followed me without me noticing."

"Good. Did you sleep?"

Shaye's worry was genuine, and Emma considered lying because the last thing she wanted to do was give the young investigator something else to be concerned about. But she knew the dark circles under her eyes were a dead giveaway.

"Not really," Emma said.

"I know it's hard, but try to get as much rest as you can. I need you strong. Is everything else all right? No more problems with the car? No random items appearing? No old acquaintances contacting you out of the blue?"

Emma frowned. "Not really. I mean, when I got to the hospital today, I ran into a guy I dated through high school, but he was carrying flowers, so he must have been here to see a patient."

"Why did you end the relationship?"

"I got my scholarship in Dallas and he was staying here. And I wasn't invested in the relationship enough to attempt a long-distance thing."

"And he was okay with that?"

Emma hesitated. "He was hurt, at first, but by the end of summer, he seemed fine. We hung out at parties a couple times and he helped me pack to move. We lost touch the first year of school—you know how busy it is— but I can't imagine our meeting was anything but coincidence."

"Probably. What's his name?"

"Stephen Moore. His family is a fairly prominent one...his father is an attorney."

Shaye nodded. "I know the family a little by reputation. They've been involved in some of Corrine's charity events. Did he ask you out?"

"No. I mean, not really. He gave me his card and told me to give him a call sometime so that we could catch up."

"I'm trying to place him, but can't. What does he look like?"

"Funny you should ask. That was one of the things that surprised me a little. He didn't look like he did in high school. He used to have longer light brown hair that swept back on the sides sorta wavy—the preppy boy look. Now his hair is maybe a half inch long and a lot darker. But then that happens with age, right?"

"Lots of times," Shaye agreed. "I can't remember him, but then, I've met so many people at Corrine's events, there's no way I could recall them all."

Emma frowned. "You don't think…"

"I'm sure it's fine. He acted normal, right?"

"Yeah. He seemed surprised to see me. Told me he was sorry about what happened with David. I imagine he saw it on the news along with everyone else in New Orleans. He seemed like he did in high school. Older, but the same."

"Good. Let me know if anyone else surfaces."

Emma nodded and looked over at Corrine. "Does she need anything?"

"The nurse gave her pain meds and said she'd probably sleep for a while."

"Okay, but if you need anything, have them page me. I'll be on until eleven."

Shaye nodded and Emma exited the room. So many thoughts ran through her mind that it made her head ache. That night when she was hiding in the secret room, she'd thought nothing could be worse than the fear and terror she felt looking through that hole in the wall and seeing something—someone—that couldn't possibly be. But this slow, deliberate attack on her and now Shaye and her mother was like picking at a scab with alcohol-soaked fingers.

Who could possibly hate her so much that they would go to all this trouble? And why? Over her killing David? That didn't make sense. David didn't have anyone close enough to him to go to such an extreme. No family. No close friends. At least, that's what he'd said, and she'd seen no indication that he was lying.

But then, she'd seen no indication about a bunch of things.

He flipped back the lever and removed the third mouse from the trap. There was never a shortage of vermin here. That's what Mama had always said, but then, to Mama, everything was vermin, even if it walked on two legs. He dropped the mouse in the bucket with the other two and rubbed his ankle before rising. It always ached when it rained, along with his shoulder and hands. Damaged bones didn't much like the rain and humidity in New Orleans.

Maybe when this was over, he'd leave. This time for good. He'd almost gotten away once, but then the pull of Mama brought him back home.

Home.

It was supposed to mean something good. But home had never been good for him. Because Mama was there.

There to remind him every day of his failure as a man. There to remind him every day that women weren't to be trusted. There to remind him that if he didn't listen to Mama, he'd turn out to be a loser like his dad.

A dead loser.

He picked up the bucket and headed out of the shack.

There was work to be done. The private investigator would be suitably distracted with her mother. If he wanted to, he could take Emma tonight and leave New Orleans tomorrow. But then all the fun would be over.

He smiled and started whistling.

Maybe just a little while longer.

CHAPTER THIRTEEN

Emma wasn't sure how she did it, but she managed to finish her shift without falling apart or falling asleep. More importantly, all her patients received the care they deserved despite her inability to think about one thing for more than a minute at a time. She covered her mouth with her left hand and yawned while clocking out with her right.

"You're still not sleeping." Clara's voice sounded behind her and she jumped.

She turned around to see the older woman studying her. "What's got you so jumpy?"

"Nothing. Everything. Corrine Archer was admitted to the ER today. Someone attacked her."

Clara nodded. "I heard as soon as I came on shift. Dropped by for a peek, but didn't want to disturb her or her daughter. They were both dozing." She narrowed her eyes at Emma. "It's upsetting, but with the kind of work Corrine does, I'm surprised something like this hasn't happened before now. You want to tell me what's really bothering you?"

"It's my fault!" Emma blurted it out before she could change her mind.

"Unless you pushed Corrine down those stairs, I don't see how."

Emma glanced over as another nurse entered the break room. She motioned Clara away from the computer and waited until the other nurse had finished clocking in and left before speaking again. "It's because I hired Shaye."

She told Clara about Shaye's visit to the house and her disguise, then about the decorator's swatch in Corrine's purse.

Clara's eyes widened and Emma could tell she was unnerved. "You're going to tell the police about this, right?"

"It's not for me to tell."

"The hell it isn't! You've got to give them information so they can get this guy."

"What information do I have? That the same guy the police don't think is stalking me is the person who set up Corrine? Besides, if I tell the police something, they'll go straight to Corrine with the information."

"You're darn right they will. You want to tell me why they shouldn't?"

"They should, but that puts Shaye in a really bad position, and I can't do that. I've already brought enough trouble to her."

Clara's expression cleared in understanding. "Shaye doesn't want Corrine to know her attack was about her taking your case."

"She didn't come right out and say it, but if you were Shaye, would you want Corrine to know?"

"If I intended on sticking with the job, I suppose not. But Corrine needs to know that she's still in danger."

"Given her injuries, she's not going anywhere for a week or better. Shaye assured me that Corrine's house is like Fort Knox and she'd have a guard. But if she knew Shaye was in danger…"

"She'd try to help because when it comes to Shaye, Corrine has no boundaries," Clara finished and sighed. "I know you're right, but it feels wrong."

"I'm going to try again to get Shaye to tell the police."

"I think that's a good idea. I don't suppose you can convince her to drop your case. Not that I'm wanting you without support, mind you, but I think we both know this man after you is too big a problem for someone as inexperienced as Shaye to handle."

"Don't you think I know that? I already tried to talk her out of it, but she insists on sticking in. She claims that at this point, her pulling back probably wouldn't change things."

Clara frowned. "She may be right. You're not dealing with a normal mind. Whoever is doing this is very disturbed. He may not stop until he feels his house is clean."

Emma shook her head, frustration overwhelming her. "I just wish I knew why. Why is all of this happening?"

Clara leaned over and gave her a quick hug. "I think when we know the answer to that question, we'll know who he is. You be safe. And do your best to get some sleep. Are you still at the hotel?"

"Yes." Emma didn't go into changing hotels and the incident with her car. Clara was already worried enough.

Clara nodded. "I'm praying for you. Hard. And I believe you're going to be fine. You've just got to stay strong."

"I will. And thank you. If you're praying, then I know God's listening."

"Really? How is that?"

Emma gave her a small smile. "He'd be afraid not to."

Clara smiled. "You get out of here and get some rest."

Emma headed down the hall for the security office to get Jeremy. He must have been watching the hallway monitor because he was waiting for her at the door. "You ready to go home, Ms. Frederick?"

It wasn't home. At this point, Emma wasn't certain anything ever would be again.

"Yep," she said. "You ready to escort me to my car?"

"I am always ready for the company of a lovely lady. Just don't tell my wife."

Emma smiled. "You're wonderful for a girl's ego. Let's do this."

They headed out the emergency room doors and across the parking lot. Emma had parked as close as possible, but the handicapped spots and those designated for emergency personnel took up a good portion of the front of the lot. Her car was midway down under a light post. The lot was well lit, but the surrounding area wasn't. Danger might be lurking in the shadows of the hedges lining the right side, in the spot on the sidewalk where illumination from the streetlights didn't quite meet, across the street in the half-empty building.

She crossed her arms over her chest and shivered. It was at least ninety degrees out and humid, but she couldn't ward off the chill that ran through her. And she knew without a doubt that his eyes were on her. Somewhere in the dark. Close enough to see her.

Her pulse ticked up a notch and she increased her pace. Jeremy fell in step with her, not saying a word. Emma saw him scanning the parking lot, the sidewalk, the street. Looking for the threat that she knew was there but that remained hidden.

She practically ran the last ten feet to her car, but drew up short when she realized something was on the ground in the shadows right in front of the driver's side door. Jeremy grabbed her arm to keep her from moving forward and pulled out his flashlight.

When the light hit the three mice with no eyes, Emma screamed.

He lowered the night-vision binoculars and smiled. Emma thought she was being smart, parking in the open lot instead of the employee garage, but nothing was going to stop him from his mission. And the old man with her just made him laugh. The way he practically shoved her in the car and sent her away from the hospital, then took a picture of the mice with his phone, like that was going to matter to anyone except the woman he'd just scared half to death.

The old man was no match for him. Both of them combined were no match for him.

All of Emma's efforts—changing hotels, hiring a detective, parking in different places—were a waste of time. Emma couldn't make a move that he hadn't already anticipated. She wasn't clever enough. Wasn't cunning enough. Not like him.

The things he'd gotten away with were a testament to his prowess. He was the superior being. Mama may not have thought so when they were kids, but she had no choice but to think so now. He'd show her. He would never be a loser like his daddy.

At first, he'd thought Emma was different. That maybe Mama had been wrong about some women, but Emma had turned out to be just like all the others. Only caring about herself. Never satisfied until she'd ruined a man's life. She'd ruined David's, and she'd gotten off scot-free. But the legal system wasn't the only way to get justice.

Hell, it wasn't even the best way.

Emma pulled into the valet drive at the hotel and practically threw her keys at the young man before running inside. She could hear him calling after her as she ran down the hallway to the elevators. She knew she was supposed to give him her room number, but she was afraid that if she attempted to talk, she'd have a nervous breakdown right on the spot. She needed to get to her room, behind a lock and a dead bolt.

The elevator seemed to take forever, but at least it was empty. If anyone even looked at her for longer than a second, she wouldn't be able to handle it. She knew he was there. Had known it the instant she stepped foot outside of the hospital. Why hadn't she gone back inside? She could have slept in the break room. It had a little cubby with cots in case staff had to stay over and needed to catch some shut-eye. Why did she let Jeremy put her into her car?

Her entire body felt as if it were covered in something vile. Like his eyes were still on every inch of her. She knew it wasn't possible—not here in the hotel—but she couldn't shake the feeling from the parking lot.

The elevator chimed and opened and she bolted out of it, running down the hall for her room. She fumbled with the card and dropped it twice, cursed, then finally managed to get the door open. She shoved her shoulder against it so hard that she yelped and stumbled inside, pushing the door shut behind her and drawing the dead bolt.

She dumped her purse on the bed and pulled out her aunt's pistol, checking the magazine. It was loaded and one round was chambered. The guy at the gun range had told her it was dangerous to carry with a chambered round, but Emma figured it was even more dangerous to need the time to chamber a round if a stalker was after you. The gun was holstered and her purse was locked inside her locker at work. The risk of an accidental discharge was minor. The risk of coming face-to-face with her stalker grew every minute.

Still gripping the pistol, she headed into the bathroom. She placed the pistol on the counter and pulled off her clothes, letting them drop onto the cold tile floor. She turned on the hot water in the sink, dropped a towel onto the floor in front of her, then stepped on it. She grabbed her loofah from her travel bag and soaked it with the scalding water, then began to scrub her skin. A shower or bath was too risky. Not enough time to respond if he managed to gain entry into the room, but she couldn't take that layer of filth that his gaze had put on her skin.

She rubbed and soaked and rubbed and soaked at a frantic rate until every square inch of her body had been scrubbed clean. The light burn was preferable to the itching she'd felt before. Finally, she dropped the loofah into the sink. As she looked up, she saw her reflection in the mirror. Her skin was mottled red from head to toe. Some patches were darker than others, but not a single square inch of unmarked white remained. She let out a single cry and grabbed the pistol, then sank onto the floor and sobbed.

CHAPTER FOURTEEN

She heard footsteps on the stone steps and knew it was the man. Without thinking, she backed into the corner, as if hiding in the shadows would somehow protect her. The door swung open and the light blazed in, blinding her. She threw her hand over her face, peering through her fingers, trying to see what the man was doing.

And she saw the red dress.

No! The silent scream tore through her and she tried to shrink into the wall.

"It's Samhain," the man said as he moved closer.

She cowered down, praying the man would leave. That was the bad dress. Horrible things happened when she was forced to wear it. Things she didn't understand. Things that made her scream in pain.

She looked up as he leaned over her, the needle poised in his right hand.

"Time to become beautiful," he said before he plunged the needle into her arm.

Shaye jolted awake in the dimly lit room, momentarily panicking until she realized where she was. She glanced at her watch and couldn't believe it. Almost 8:00 a.m. Between doctors, nurses, and the occasional police guard drop-in, it had been a hectic night. Eleonore had arrived about thirty minutes after Shaye, ready to raise hell and call up the National Guard. Shaye had talked her off the ledge—a turn of events she found rather ironic—and finally convinced the psychiatrist that both of them could not share the one uncomfortable chair in hospital room and that Corrine would need someone at home with her the next day. Someone who could listen to her for hours at a time because there would be no end to the complaining once Corrine was at home and got indignant over the whole thing. Eleonore would have her hands full.

At some point, the room traffic died down, and when Shaye dozed off, the nurse must have turned off the overhead light. Now the lights above Corrine's bed and light emitting from the monitors were the only things illuminating the room.

Shaye rose from her chair to check on Corrine and was relieved to see her mother's chest rising and falling naturally. The bruises had darkened overnight, leaving her perfect white skin marred, something that would plague Corrine until the bruises went away. Her mother always insisted on looking her best. She wouldn't leave the house without makeup or with her hair in a ponytail. Shaye assumed it was a carryover from the way Corrine's mother had raised her. She had to assume because Audrey Archer had passed away when Corrine was not yet a teenager, so Shaye had never met her. But through Corrine's stories, she almost felt she knew her.

Corrine stirred and her eyes fluttered open. She looked

confused at first, but then her gaze locked on Shaye. "I forgot where I was for a moment," she said. "How long have I been out?"

"It's almost eight a.m., so quite a while. How do you feel?"

"Like I fell down a flight of stairs. You know, I did this when I was twelve and I don't recall it hurting that bad then."

"I hear that's what happens when you get old." Shaye struggled not to smile.

"Old? Old! We're practically the same generation."

"Uh-huh. Keep telling yourself that."

"Shaye Archer!" Corrine stared at her in dismay. Finally, Shaye couldn't hold it any longer and the grin she'd been holding in broke through.

"Shame on you," Corrine said, "picking on me when I'm hooked to machines. You just wait until I get out of here."

Shaye laughed and pressed the call button for the nurse. "How about we find out when that will be?"

Corrine's mouth quivered and she smiled, then she put her fingers on her cheeks. "Oh, that smarts. How bad is it?"

"The truth?"

"No, I want you to lie to me so I can be even more upset when I look in a mirror."

"It's not pretty, but I don't think anything will scar."

"Give me a mirror."

"Now?"

"Yes, now."

"Okay," Shaye said as she dug a compact out of her purse, "but don't say I didn't warn you." She opened the compact and handed it to Corrine.

Corrine held up the mirror and her eyes widened. She turned her head from side to side, studying the damage, then clicked the compact shut and handed it back to Shaye. "It's not as bad as I feared, but makeup is not going to cover this."

"I could get you a ski mask. Quite fashionable among skiers and criminals."

"They're horrible for your hair. I think I'll just deal with people asking me 'how does the other guy look?' for a couple of weeks."

A nurse walked into the room and smiled. "Make sure you tell them he looks worse," she said.

Shaye moved away from the bed as the nurse checked out Corrine. "You look good for a woman starting fights in abandoned buildings. I'm going to send the doctor in."

"Thank you," Corrine said as the nurse left. She looked up at Shaye. "I want out of here."

"I know you do, but you have to listen to the doctor. That's what you always told me."

"How did you grow up to be such a nag?"

"I had a good teacher. As soon as the doctor gives you clearance, you'll be lounging on the couch at home, driving Eleonore crazy."

"Eleonore?"

"She insists that staying with you during the day is how she can help most. Grandfather will be back from China sometime this afternoon, and he'll be stopping by. I'll be there tonight."

"And today?"

"I have to work. I need to get answers for Emma before…"

Corrine frowned. "Before something worse happens to her than happened to me."

Guilt rocked Shaye. The only reason Corrine lay here in that hospital bed was because of Shaye's case. Logic told her she wasn't responsible for the actions of a madman, but in her mind, it didn't lessen her culpability. If she hadn't taken the case, Corrine wouldn't be in danger. Even worse, she was hiding the reason for the attack from Corrine, and even though it was for her own good, Shaye had her own reasons for keeping the information secret. All Shaye wanted to do was help Emma, but she still felt selfish for hiding things.

Maybe because deep down, she knew that helping Emma also helped herself. Proved that she could do the job she so desperately wanted to excel at. Proved that she could find answers when the police had given up. She held in a sigh. In a couple of days, she had created weeks of issues to talk over with Eleonore. The woman was probably going to have to double her sessions.

Shaye placed her hand on Corrine's arm. "The first thing I'm going to do this morning is talk with a detective about Emma's situation. I might have enough evidence now to get the police involved."

Corrine's relief was apparent. "Thank God."

"It's not a sure thing, so don't celebrate yet. But I'm trying to shift the responsibility where it belongs as soon as I can."

"Is Emma okay?"

"Honestly, no. She's exhausted, terrified, and probably hasn't slept one good hour in weeks. I don't know how much longer she can hold up."

"If I can do anything, let me know. We have facilities for women...if she needs somewhere to get off radar for a while."

Shaye leaned over and kissed her forehead. "Have I told you lately how much I love you?"

Corrine smiled. "Probably, but I'm always happy to hear it some more." She sobered. "You be careful, Shaye. None of us are exempt from violence. You know that better than anyone. I just got a harsh reminder."

"I'm taking every possible precaution." *Except dropping the case.*

Corrine nodded but didn't look convinced. Shaye didn't blame her.

She wasn't convinced, either.

Emma jumped up, banging her elbow into something hard and immovable. She panicked for a moment before she realized she was on the floor in her hotel room bathroom and that immovable object that had just assaulted her was the cabinet. She rubbed her elbow, then pushed herself up from the floor. Her clothes and the towels were still scattered across the tile where she'd dropped them the night before. She picked her watch up from the counter and stared at it in disbelief. It was almost 8:00 a.m.

She'd slept on that floor all night.

That explained the catch in her neck and tugging she felt in her lower back. She was in good shape, but maintaining one sleeping position for hours on cold, hard tile would put a strain on anyone's physical fitness. She rolled her head around and her neck popped, relieving tension all the way down her spine.

She looked at herself in the mirror and almost didn't recognize the woman looking back at her. Her normally light skin was completely devoid of color, and her eyes were sunken into her head, dark circles surrounding them. She'd lost weight and her already-thin cheeks were starting to look gaunt.

I can't continue like this.

She walked to the bed and removed some clothes from her suitcase. As soon as she was dressed, she grabbed her cell phone. The police couldn't or wouldn't help her. Shaye was doing her best, but she was up against something she had no experience with. It was time to take the one action she'd been putting off.

"This is Patty," the Realtor answered on the second ring.

"Oh," Emma said, surprised that Patty answered. "Hi. This is Emma. I was going to leave you a message but looks like you're up and going."

"I keep trying to sleep in, but sometimes my body won't cooperate."

Instantly, Emma felt guilty for her earlier mental whining about being sore. Patty lived with far harder conditions, and it would only get worse, not better. "I got the name of a therapist from one of the other nurses. She has a niece with MS and says it's really helped improve her gait."

"Really? Thank you. I'm always willing to try new things. You never know what my body might respond to."

"Well, let's hope this therapist is one of those things that works." Emma pulled the card from her wallet. "Let me give you her information. Can you write it down?"

"Sure. I'm at my desk. Go ahead."

Emma read the business card, then rushed forward with the real reason for her call. "I want you to list the house now. I know I could make more on the sale if I did the improvements, but I don't think I can live there long enough to manage everything. I need to move on. As soon as possible."

"Of course you do. The way you've handled things has amazed me. Most people would have crumbled, but you've stayed strong and working."

"Working is what's kept me going."

"I get that. I feel the same way. Don't worry about the house. I have plenty of pictures that we took for the before and after. I'll get the listing ready and will let you know as soon as it's posted. I don't think you'll have to wait long for an offer. In fact, I expect you'll have multiple offers. Will you be home later so I can drop by and get a key, or can I get it now?"

"Actually, I'm not home right now. I headed out early to take care of errands and I work this afternoon. Can we do it tomorrow?"

"Of course. Whenever you have the availability, let me know. I'll hold off posting the listing until I get the lockbox on, but I'll pass the information around my office and to a couple of clients of mine who are looking in the area. It might be sold before I get a key."

"That would be awesome. Thanks, Patty. I'll call you later today or tomorrow morning and let you know when we can meet."

"Great. And thanks for the therapist information."

Emma shoved the phone in her jeans pocket and grabbed her purse. Her stomach rumbled and she felt slightly dizzy. First things first, she needed to eat. She grabbed her laptop. While she was having breakfast, she'd start researching the market for nursing jobs in other states. Maybe she'd start with California. Or even Alaska.

Anywhere far away from Louisiana.

CHAPTER FIFTEEN

Jackson frowned at the two news vans parked in front of the police station. Men with cameras and wiring walked around, hooking up equipment. Two reporters he recognized from the morning news stood as assistants attached earpieces onto them. He drove past and parked around back and entered through the rear door. "What's with the circus up front?" he asked the desk sergeant.

"Senator Archer's daughter was attacked yesterday evening."

"Corrine Archer? Is she all right?"

"Word is she's pretty banged up, but not life-threatening."

"Who's lead?"

"Boyd got the call yesterday, but given the political angle, I'm sure it will be pushed up to a senior detective as soon as the chief is filled in."

Jackson nodded. The sergeant was right. Pierce Archer was a senator and one of the richest men in the state. Nothing but the best would be good enough for his daughter's investigation. Which left Jackson totally out of the running as long as he was saddled to Vincent.

The sergeant shook his head. "It's a darn shame it happened to Corrine. She's a class act. You know she's a social worker, right?"

"Yeah. I met her daughter the other day. They seem like good people."

"The best. Back in the day, Susan and I fostered kids. Too old for it now, but Corrine was a big support to us then."

"Really?" Jackson's respect for the old sergeant went up a couple more notches. "I didn't know that. That's a great thing to do. Not many can handle it."

"We weren't sure we could at first, but after a while, you learn how to manage things. We couldn't have kids ourselves, but we ended up with some in the long run. Had eight over the years. Two of them we got to adopt. The other six are still in touch, though. All of them are doing good. Either in college or working decent jobs."

"Can't ask for much more than that."

"No. If they're paying their own way, not hurting other people, and not in jail, I consider them a success story. But then Susan always said I set the bar too low."

"How can that be? You married her."

The sergeant laughed. "I'm going to use that one on her next time she trots that statement out." The phone rang and the sergeant reached for it. Jackson gave him a wave and headed over to his desk. A stack of paperwork awaited him—his and Vincent's. Not that it mattered. It didn't require much effort to document next to nothing, and that's what Vincent specialized in.

Jackson reached for the first folder and brought up the database to start logging the information. He'd been at it an hour when he saw Sergeant Boyd cross the street, pausing long enough to weave through the reporters. Jackson watched as he entered the building and headed straight for the break room. He grabbed his coffee cup and headed that way, hoping to catch Boyd alone.

He was in luck. Boyd was pouring a cup of coffee and nodded at Jackson as he entered. He looked like he hadn't slept well.

"I heard you got the call on Corrine Archer's attack yesterday," Jackson said. "Is she all right?"

Boyd took a drink of his coffee and nodded. "She's banged up and has a slight concussion, but she should be able to go home today."

"What happened?"

"Somebody faked a call to her office, claiming a baby was in distress. Corrine went to the location given, but the building was empty. When she realized she'd been tricked, she tried to get away, but he shoved her down the stairs, then gave her a good kick in the head. A couple of painters showed up to measure for the renovations and chased him off. They called 911 and I got the nod."

Jackson shook his head. "I know social workers make enemies, but that seems rather elaborate."

"Yeah, that's what I thought. Whoever did it was clever enough to close all the apartment doors and clean up the lobby and hallway enough to make it look occupied. On the surface, it looked like any other rathole apartment building that she might walk into. It wasn't until she opened the doors and saw the apartments were empty that she realized something was wrong."

"You heading the investigation?"

Boyd snorted. "No lowly sergeant is going to draw the investigation of the assault on Senator Archer's daughter. I'm sure it will be kicked up today. You interested?"

"Wouldn't matter if I was. Vincent won't take real work unless he has to."

"That's true enough."

"But I wish I could. I met Corrine's daughter the other day. She's a nice girl."

Boyd nodded. "I talked with her some at the hospital last night. Seems a class act, like her mother. Maybe a little tougher. Has a bit of an edge to her."

Jackson held in a smile. Corrine's attack must have had Shaye off her game, because there was no "bit of" about her edge. Shaye's edges were sharp enough to cut glass. "Well, hopefully, it's wrapped up soon. The last thing we need is some loon targeting social workers. Hard enough to keep good people in those jobs to begin with."

"Yeah. I've gotta go bring the chief up to date. Wish me luck."

Jackson gave him a nod and Boyd left the break room, looking more anxious than Jackson had ever seen the young sergeant appear before. But then, he was being called to his boss's boss's boss's office to explain an attack on one of New Orleans's favorite natives and the daughter of one of the most powerful and wealthy men in the state. Jackson could only imagine how stressful that conversation would be. The chief wasn't exactly known for his calm demeanor. He'd take the attack on Corrine as a personal insult to him, the police, the department of social services, the city, the state, and maybe even the universe.

Jackson exited out of the break room and saw Vincent strolling across the department, a good hour late. Jackson headed across the room and before he could talk himself out of it, stopped at Vincent's desk. "Did you hear about the attack on Senator Archer's daughter?"

Vincent flopped into his chair and looked up at Jackson. "Is that what all the hoopla is about outside?"

Jackson nodded. "Boyd took the call yesterday but he won't get the case, not given the vic. I was thinking maybe we could ask for it."

"The hell you were! The last thing I want to do is spend my time answering directly to a politician. Bad enough we're usually answering to them indirectly. I don't need a single bit of information to already know that everything about that case stinks. Too many suspects, for starters. Want to run down a list for me of every enemy our good senator has and combine that with the list of people who lost their kids and wouldn't mind taking a shot at a social worker? We'd be investigating half the city, and that's a conservative estimate."

"It would be a big feather in your cap, though. Think about it. With a recommendation from Senator Archer, you could take your pick of cush security work when you retired."

Vincent frowned, and Jackson could tell he was considering the benefit of a more luxurious retirement against the requirement of actually working. Laziness must have won out, because he shook his head. "I got plenty to retire on. Anything gained wouldn't be worth the headache. Take my word on that, Jackson. You're young and don't know shit about how things work. You'll get your chance to tangle with politicos soon enough, but not as long as I'm on the ride with you."

Jackson didn't bother to launch another argument. It was clear Vincent's mind was made up. He nodded and headed back to his desk to shuffle more paperwork, his frustration starting to get the better of him. At first, he'd been simply bored with the lack of work, then he'd grown aggravated with Vincent's laziness and his unchecked ability to hold Jackson back. Now he was simply getting angry, and sooner or later, everything would come to a head.

His cell phone rang and when he saw Shaye's name come up on the display, he grabbed it and took off for the break room again. He had left Shaye a message the day before, wanting to talk to her about what he'd managed to find on David Grange, but he couldn't imagine she was calling about David. Not with her mother in the hospital.

When he was far enough away from Vincent, he pressed the screen and answered the call.

"I need to talk to you," Shaye said. "Can you get away to meet?"

"When?"

"Thirty minutes. The same café."

"I'll be there," he said, not even caring if Vincent bitched about him taking off again. He slipped the phone into his pocket and went back to his desk to grab his keys.

"Where are you going?" Vincent asked.

"I've got an errand to run."

"You've got paperwork to do."

"And it will take me twenty minutes. When you have some real work for us, give me a call. I'll be back later."

A couple of detectives with desks nearby raised their eyebrows, but no one was stupid enough to comment. They all knew Vincent was slacking, but he had seniority. Without waiting for a response, Jackson turned around and headed for the back exit, already wondering why Shaye wanted to meet. He had a gut feeling that she knew something about her mother's attack that Boyd didn't.

Something that might narrow the suspects down from half the city to a handful.

Emma pulled on her scrubs and ran a comb through her hair. She'd ordered a huge breakfast and managed to eat at least two bites of everything. Given that her last meal had been lunch the day before, it still wasn't enough, but it was all her nervous stomach could handle. While she struggled through breakfast, she'd planned her escape. San Diego had a slew of open nursing positions, and a good amount for private practices, not just hospitals. If she was going to fade into the sunset, then she needed to change everything, not just her location.

She had enough money to get to California and live off of for several months. A beach house was out of the question; a studio apartment was within reach. As soon as the house sold, she'd have enough money to get a small place there or pick up and go somewhere else.

Her cell phone rang and she checked the display. It was the hospital. She answered the call, expecting to hear her supervisor asking her to work another double, but it was Jeremy.

"Ms. Frederick, this is Jeremy. Are you all right?"

The worry was so apparent in Jeremy's voice that Emma instantly felt bad that she hadn't contacted the security guard sooner. He'd shoved her into her car the night before and practically yelled at her to leave. She'd followed his instructions and never looked back, but that meant Jeremy was left standing in the parking lot wondering what the hell was going on.

"I'm okay," she said. "I'm sorry about last night. I didn't mean to scare you."

"Wasn't you that caused the problem. Those mice didn't blind themselves and stroll across the parking lot to die next to your car. I figure there's things about it I don't understand, but I didn't have to know all the details to see you were terrified."

"Yes, I was. Am."

"I know you're scheduled today, but I didn't know if you'd come in. I wanted to let you know I reviewed the security footage of the parking lot."

Emma clutched her phone. "Did you see him?"

"Yes. But he was wearing a hoodie and he never looked toward the camera. He walked across the parking lot to your car, his head down, and sometimes turned away from the cameras at an angle. He knew they were there."

Damn it! Another dead end.

"I figure you're going to the police, right?" Jeremy asked. "I know it's not much, but at least I can show them proof that someone did it deliberately."

"Of course. Thank you, Jeremy. I'll be sure and let them know."

"This guy…he's a piece of bad work."

"Yes, he is."

"You be careful. If you come in today, you park up front with the ambulances, okay? I'll see to it that no one has a problem with it."

Emma's eyes teared up at Jeremy's kindness. "Thank you so much. I'll see you soon."

She hung up before she started crying. So many people were worried about her and doing the most they could to help. It was heartening and overwhelming at the same time. Even worse, it was frightening. Her stalker had already gone after Shaye for helping her. What if he went after Jeremy next?

That couldn't happen.

She stuffed her pistol and cell phone into her purse and headed downstairs to the valet. "I'm sorry," she said to the young man at the valet station. "I wasn't feeling well last night and forgot to wait for a ticket when I left my car."

"That's okay, ma'am," the valet said. "The manager recognized it. I'll get it for you right away."

"Thank you."

The young man hurried off and Emma waited anxiously for her vehicle, a million thoughts rolling through her head. So many things to do, and all of them needed to be done now. She had to get organized. Get a plan and get out of New Orleans.

Her car stopped in front of her and the valet got out and handed her the keys. She gave him a tip and hopped inside, but when she went to put her purse on the passenger's seat, she realized it wasn't empty. In the middle of the seat was a bracelet. She let out a cry and the valet knocked on her window.

"Are you all right?" the valet asked.

Emma put the car in gear and squealed away, leaving the stunned valet staring after her. As she pulled out of the garage, she rolled down the window, grabbed the bracelet, and flung it into the street. Even though it was only in her hand for seconds, it felt as if the metal burned her skin. She screeched to a stop at a red light and yanked her cell phone out of her purse. Shaye answered on the first ring.

"He found me again," Emma said. "He left a bracelet he gave me for my birthday on the front seat of my car. And that's not the worst of it."

Emma told Shaye about the mice in the parking lot the night before. With every word she uttered, her breathing grew faster until she was about to hyperventilate. Finally, she finished and sucked in a giant breath, trying to bring as much oxygen as possible into her body. Her vision blurred momentarily and she eased up on the accelerator, then it cleared again.

"Please stay calm," Shaye said, "especially while you're driving. I know how frightening all this is, and I don't blame you for being scared. I'm scared too, but we're going to figure this out."

Emma didn't doubt Shaye's sincerity at all, but her hope that anyone could help her was rapidly vanishing. "How did he find me again? I was careful this time. I'm sure no one followed me when I checked in. Even last night, when I was ready to explode, I drove around the city twice before going back to the hotel."

"I have an idea about that. When he found you at the repair shop in Bywater, I had my suspicions, but now I'm almost positive."

"Positive of what?"

"He put a GPS on your car. That's how he always knows where you are."

Emma felt her back and neck tighten. It was something she'd never considered, but it explained so much. And completely destroyed her idea of getting away. Unless she abandoned the car here and flew to San Diego, he'd just track her right to her front door again. Her breathing increased again as wave after wave of hopelessness came over her.

"I can't get away," Emma said. "I was going to leave tomorrow. Drive across the country and start over, but he's taken that option away as well."

"I think I can help with that, but I can't do anything until tomorrow."

"Yes, of course. You've got to take care of your mother. I understand." Given that Corrine's attacker was almost certainly Emma's stalker, she couldn't expect Shaye to keep working on her case. Not today, anyway, but she couldn't help the feeling of abandonment and helplessness that she felt. In her entire life, she'd never felt so alone.

"It's not that. I have a line on a guy David served with on his last tour in Iraq. He's the one who called in a favor to get David his job at the petroleum company. I'm hoping he knows something that helps make some sense of all of this, but I've got to make a drive to Fort Polk to track him down. It's not the sort of conversation I want to have over the phone. You learn more when you can watch someone while they talk. And if he doesn't know I'm coming, he can't prepare."

Immediately, Emma felt guilty for assuming that Shaye had abandoned her, even though she wouldn't blame her one bit if she did. But as long as Shaye was still working, Emma still held on to a small ray of hope. Given the extremity of her situation and Shaye's lack of experience, Emma was probably hoping for a miracle, but that didn't matter. She had to have something to latch onto or the thin thread that held her sanity in the balance would snap in two.

"How is Corrine?" Emma asked.

"Feeling well enough to complain. They'll send her home later today. Her best friend will stay with her until my grandfather arrives. And I'll stay at her house tonight. I'm more worried about you. You're going to need to change hotels again. If you'll call and have the hotel pack your things, I'll pick them up after I get back. You can take a taxi to another hotel tonight and I'll bring your things to you tomorrow morning."

It was a good plan. She could catch a taxi at the front entrance of the hospital. That way, if he was watching her car, he wouldn't see her leave. But even the thought of arriving at another hotel in the middle of the night had her anxiety increasing. "I think I'm going to stay at the hospital tonight. There's a room off the break room with cots for staff to use if we get caught working a double or staying for a specific patient."

"That's good. You'll be safe at the hospital. Tomorrow morning you can either take a taxi and meet me at a new hotel or I can pick you up. Either way, maybe you'll finally get a decent night's sleep."

"Maybe." Emma had all but given up the idea of a good night's sleep, but maybe Shaye was right. If she was tucked away in the hospital staff lounge, with Jeremy watching over the security monitors, she would be safe. It wasn't a good long-term plan, but for one night, it might be the best plan she could come up with.

"I'm about to leave to meet with a New Orleans police detective."

"Do you think they'll believe me now?"

"I think he does already. Hopefully, we can make something happen."

"Yeah."

Hopefully.

Shaye put the cell phone on her dresser and stared out her bedroom window into the alley. Her hands were sweaty and her pulse elevated. Most people couldn't possibly imagine the horror that Emma was experiencing. They couldn't understand how terrified she was. How desperate.

But Shaye understood all too well.

She pulled on a fresh shirt and hurried into the bathroom to give her teeth and hair a brush. She checked her watch and cursed because there was no way she would make her meeting with Jackson on time. She grabbed her car keys and hurried out of her apartment. When she'd set the meeting time with Jackson, she'd barely given herself time to get from the hospital back to her apartment for a change of clothes, but she wanted to talk to him as soon as possible and then get on the road to Fort Polk.

He'd left her a message the night before, but with everything that happened, she hadn't checked her phone until after midnight. Given what she'd found in Corrine's purse and what Emma had just told her, Shaye was more desperate than ever for information on David Grange and hoped Jackson had come up with some hard information on David's past. Aside from the Paul Schaffer lead, all she'd managed to do so far was verify things that she already suspected or that Emma had told her. Someone had to know more. And she was going to find him.

Traffic was light, and she made the drive to the café in less time than she originally figured. Only five minutes late. Not too bad. She parked at the curb a half block away and hurried into the café. Jackson was already seated at the back corner table, a black coffee in front of him and a latte in front of the chair across from him. Shaye wasn't sure if he was returning the favor from their last meeting or showing her that he also paid attention. Either way, she appreciated the drink and the efficiency.

"Thanks for the coffee," she said as she slid onto the chair. "I haven't stopped long enough to grab a cup this morning and I'm hovering somewhere between comatose and desperate."

"Been there a few times myself. How's your mother?"

She wasn't really surprised that he knew about the attack on Corrine. Reporters had shown up at the hospital shortly after she'd arrived, and it had taken police threats to get them out of the building and onto the sidewalk where they belonged. They'd hung around for another hour or two, but finally cleared out, most likely when they found out her grandfather was in China on Archer Manufacturing business and couldn't get back to New Orleans until this afternoon.

"She's fine, considering. She'll have a heck of a headache, but the bruised ribs will probably be the worst."

Jackson nodded. "You don't realize how much you use your stomach until you have abdominal damage."

"That's the truth."

Jackson stared at her for several seconds. "I hope this meeting is about the message I left you last night…"

"But you don't think it is."

He shook his head. "I guess I don't. The timing of Corrine's attack is a little too convenient. Given her work and your grandfather's status, I know there's probably a hundred other options, but I wondered if it all hadn't run together."

"It's that coincidence thing again. I didn't like it either, and the whole time Sergeant Boyd was telling me what he knew, then afterward when Corrine told me what had happened, I wondered. Then I got confirmation."

Shaye told him about the decorator's swatch in Corrine's purse and her disguise when she visited Emma's house. "No way that was an accident. Her credit cards and cash were in place. He didn't take anything. He left the swatch."

Jackson's expression darkened. "That's not good."

"I know it's him. But why Corrine? Why not go after me?"

"Maybe he's showing you how smart he is. Maybe he's attacking you at your weak spot. My best guess is because he wants to scare you."

"Like he's scaring Emma."

"Yes and no. You've gotten in his way. He controls situations through fear. I think he's trying to scare you away. It's a sick, twisted game he's playing. The problem is, he's making all the rules, and you don't get to pick if you play."

Shaye blew out a breath. "You warned me that he'd come after anyone he perceived as getting in the way of his fun."

"Yeah, well, sometimes I hate it when I'm right."

"I know the feeling. Unfortunately, there's way more going on than just the attack on my mother." Shaye told him about the mice and the bracelet. "He's getting more brazen. The security guard said his face never shows on camera, but he's got footage of a man leaving those mice. Surely that's enough evidence for the police to do something."

"Wow." Jackson leaned back in his chair. "That is some serious sick shit. What the hell happens to a person to make them that way?"

"I'm not sure we want to know."

"Yeah, well, I think that's plenty for the police to take her complaint seriously. Of course, they have the same limitations we do in locating the perpetrator, so while I definitely encourage Emma to report everything, I don't know how much it will change things. As least in the immediate future."

"I know I'm still her best hope to get information, but maybe if they assign someone to her case, I can turn over what I've got so far and someone more qualified can take over."

"You're doing a fine job. I mean that."

Shaye felt a light blush creep up her cheeks. "Thank you."

"You have a good mind for these things, and you're a

good judge of character. That goes a long way to being a good investigator. That being said, I wish you'd never taken this case. It's not exactly the kind of thing you should be cutting your teeth on."

"I know. It's turned out to be something I never anticipated, but I can't back out now. Emma needs me, and if I'm being honest, I want to be part of getting this guy. Especially now."

Jackson nodded. "Now that it's personal."

"Yeah." Shaye blew out a breath. "The thing is, I know David isn't the stalker, but I can't help but feel that it all circles back around to him. I talked to people at his job yesterday, but no one had much insight other than they thought he was creepy. One guy gave me the name of someone who served with David his last tour in Iraq. He's still enlisted and stationed at Fort Polk. I'm going to try to run him down today. Did you find anything?"

"Not much. The Social Security number didn't pop on employment records until he enlisted, so a little over eight years ago, but his age comes up as twenty-six, so that's about right if he enlisted at eighteen."

"What about birth records?"

"Nothing so far, but it didn't sound like he came from a family with resources, so it could have been a home birth."

"Or he's not from here at all. We can't take anything David told Emma as the gospel."

"That thought crossed my mind as well."

Shaye sighed. "I'm getting nowhere. He knows

everything and I know nothing."

"It certainly seems that way, but it's not exactly true. You have a lead on the guy who served with him. Maybe he will know something. And I'll keep looking. I can check records throughout the entire state. It just may take a while."

"I really appreciate it." She shook her head, trying to make sense of all the moving pieces, and then remembered her conversation last night with Emma in her mother's hospital room. "Something else. Emma said an old boyfriend of hers from high school, Stephen Moore, was at the hospital yesterday." She repeated Emma's story to Jackson.

"Doesn't sound suspicious," Jackson said.

"Not on the surface, but I don't like the timing. Also, I lied to Emma and said I couldn't place him even though he'd taken part in some of Corrine's charity events."

"Now I'm fascinated. Why did you lie?"

"Because of something Emma said about his appearance. I asked her to describe him, to make sure I was thinking of the right guy, but the description Emma gave was completely different from the way he looked in high school. Emma said so herself. I'm certain I know who he is and what he used to look like, but now…"

"What does he look like now?"

"David Grange."

Jackson whistled.

"I don't think Emma has latched onto that yet, but from long, wavy, light brown locks to military short and dark is a strange choice for a guy to make, especially when I'm going to hazard a guess that it's not the best look for him."

"When was the last time you saw him?"

"A couple of months ago, and he looked like he always did."

Jackson nodded. "You don't have any reason to suspect a connection with the old boyfriend and David, do you?"

"No. Nothing like that."

"Soooooo, maybe he wants back in with Emma, saw pics of David on the news, and thinks she has a type?"

"Maybe. I don't know exactly, but again, it's the timing that doesn't feel right."

"Okay. Do you want me to pay him a visit?"

"Oh! You can do that? I mean, without an official reason?"

"It doesn't have to be official. I could just drop by and have a chat with the man…see if I can get a feel for him."

Shaye tapped her finger on the table. On one hand, since she'd be at Fort Polk, she'd love the help, but on the other hand, she didn't want Jackson doing her job, especially when it might compromise his own. On the third hand, she might have a hard time questioning Stephen herself since he knew who she was. "I don't want you to get into trouble."

"So I won't get into trouble. What's he going to do? Call and complain to my boss that I spoke to him?"

"He might. He's an attorney."

"Shit. That means I have to be polite."

Shaye smiled. "Probably a good idea. If you don't mind doing it, I have to admit, it would really help me out. I don't know how long I'll be at Fort Polk, and I really want to move on Moore as quickly as possible, if for no other reason than to eliminate him from the suspect list."

"You mean the suspect list with no names on it."

She sighed. "Yeah, that one. I don't suppose there's any chance you could get assigned to my mother's case?"

"Not as long as I'm chained to Vincent. I suggested he ask for the assignment this morning and he acted like I'd just discharged my weapon in the men's room. It's probably just as well. If you got me, he'd be lead, so you're probably better off with someone else. Given your grandfather's, uh, prominence, the best detectives will be assigned to the case."

"But the best detectives don't know what we know. I suppose I'll have to tell them. Do you think it will do any good?"

"I think at this point, you stand a better chance of being taken seriously than before. He messed up by attacking Corrine. I have no doubt he did it to force you to back off, but I don't think he thought clearly about what kind of resources the family name would pull." Jackson shook his head. "And then it could be he's so cocky he doesn't care."

"Or the game's almost over."

"Yeah, I didn't want to say that one."

"I'm not foolish, Jackson," she said quietly. "I may be

young and lack investigative experience on criminal matters, but I'm no stranger to evil."

He studied her for several seconds, and she could tell he was debating whether or not to say whatever was on his mind. Talking must have won out because he finally said, "I reviewed your file. I hope you don't mind."

She'd known he would. He needed to know enough about her before he could trust the information she provided him. There was plenty of general crazy in New Orleans, and there was no future in wasting time on the outrageous theories they came up with. Still, it always bothered her on some level that people had access to such intimate details about her life. Basically, that they knew as much as she did. It made her feel as if she were sitting at the table in her underwear, all her scars laid bare for observation. And speculation.

His expression shifted from expectant to contrite. "You do mind. I'm sorry. I shouldn't have said anything."

"No. It's all right. You're not the first and you'll never be the last. Besides, you wouldn't be much of a detective if you took me at face value and didn't check up on me."

"True. But it's got to be hard...the most private things about your life being so public."

"There was a media circus at first. Corrine taking custody of me made it a bigger deal than it would have normally been, but it was worth it. If not for Corrine, I wouldn't have a normal life. She knew exactly what I needed and had the resources to provide it. Without her, I'm not sure I'd even be here."

"Oh, you'd be here. You're a fighter. That much is obvious. But you might not be as pleasant."

She smiled. "You think I'm pleasant? That might be a first."

He grinned. "I'm around cops and criminals all day long. The bar isn't all that high."

"You really know how to flatter a girl."

He sobered and looked down at his coffee, then back up at her. "Have you ever thought about looking into things…for yourself, I mean?"

Shaye considered his question before answering. Not because she didn't know the answer, but because she wasn't sure it was something she was ready to share with anyone else.

But if not now, when?

She'd been keeping it all in, talking openly only to Eleonore, and it got harder every day to keep the wall around her erect. Maybe it was time to let her guard down. Time to start trusting that the world contained more good people in it than her mother and her psychiatrist.

"I think about it every day," she said. "Unanswered questions are the reason I wanted to be a PI."

"But?"

"But I'm not sure I'm ready for the answers."

He nodded. "Well, when you are, and if you want some help, I'm available."

The sincerity in his words was so clear, and a warm feeling passed over Shaye. Aside from family, medical personnel, and a few choice others, she'd never felt that people really wanted to help her. Instead, she felt they'd wanted to gawk at her like those people who slowed to look at car accidents. Jackson was different from anyone she'd met before. He looked at her like a real person, an individual. Everyone else saw the girl with the missing past, the poor abused victim, Corrine Archer's daughter, or Pierce Archer's granddaughter. It was a good feeling to be seen as only Shaye, but also one she wasn't quite comfortable with.

"Thank you," she said.

He must have sensed her discomfort because he changed the subject. "But first, we solve the mystery of David Grange."

Guilt nagged at Shaye and she couldn't help launching one more protest, no matter how feeble. "I can't even begin to tell you how much I appreciate your help, but promise me you won't do anything to jeopardize your job. I wouldn't be able to live with the guilt."

"I promise I'll be very sneaky, but I want to do this. I was there the night Emma killed David. I saw what it did to her. I want answers for her as much as you do, and more importantly, I want this sick bastard behind bars so that he can never do this to anyone else."

"Then I guess we better get to work."

CHAPTER SIXTEEN

It took Jackson less than a minute to locate the law office where Stephen Moore worked and only double that time to flash his badge at the dour receptionist and get a pass through even though she'd made it clear that Mr. Moore talked only to people with scheduled appointments. The walk down the hallway to Moore's office took less than ten seconds, but he was sure Mrs. Dour had called to warn him, because Moore was already standing behind his desk, looking a bit anxious, when Jackson stepped inside.

As Jackson approached the desk, Moore moved to the side and extended his hand. "Stephen Moore. Mary said you're with the police?"

"Yes." Jackson flashed his badge, but didn't give Moore long enough to zero in on his name. If he could get out of here without Moore knowing who he was, that was probably for the best. He'd done some background checking before he'd driven to the law office. He knew Moore specialized in corporate law, which meant he spent his days making a lot of money getting corporations off for crappy things that corporations tended to do. Moore had the money, the family backing, and the business connections needed to cause problems for him if he weren't careful.

Moore motioned to the chair in front of his desk and took a seat behind it, clearly uncomfortable with Jackson's silence. Jackson took a seat and studied Moore for a couple more seconds before speaking. "Do you know Emma Frederick?"

"I, uh, yes. I knew her in high school, that is."

"But you don't know her now?"

"We haven't been in touch for some years."

Jackson nodded, glancing around the room. He pointed to a framed photo of Moore and Emma displayed on a credenza. There were other pictures of Moore and older people, probably his parents, but no other pictures of women. And based on the photo, Moore had definitely changed his appearance. The man sitting in front of him barely resembled the younger version in the photos.

"You haven't seen her in years, but you still keep a picture of her?" Jackson asked.

"She was a wonderful girl, and we had some good times. I prefer to surround myself with positive items rather than impersonal vases and such."

"Sure. I bet the new girlfriend doesn't feel as positive about those pictures though, right?"

Moore's ears reddened. "I'm not seeing anyone seriously right now. How can I help you, Detective?"

Got a bit of a rise out of him with that one.

Stephen Moore wasn't the harmless innocent that he tried to portray. There was a temper in there. "Ms.

Frederick is having a bit of trouble," Jackson said.

"I'm sorry to hear that, but I don't practice criminal law."

"She doesn't need a lawyer. She needs the man who's stalking her to stop."

Moore's eyes widened. "I...I don't understand. Why are you talking to me?"

Jackson held in a smirk. A person with no guilty feelings would have launched into sympathy or a rant about violence and society. Moore had gone straight to "why me?" "I understand you visited Ms. Frederick at the hospital yesterday."

"No. I mean, I did see her at the hospital yesterday, but I went there to visit someone else."

"Who?"

"A former client."

"Do you always bring flowers to former clients who are in the hospital?"

"If I liked them, I do."

"Uh-huh. So you just happened to go see this client at the same time that Ms. Frederick was coming on to her shift?"

"I guess so. I don't understand what you're getting at."

Jackson smiled. "Nothing, really. We're just talking to everyone who's seen Ms. Frederick recently to see if they have any idea who might be harassing her."

Moore's eyes narrowed for a split second, then his expression went completely blank. He knew Jackson was fishing and he wasn't taking the bait. "I'm afraid I can't help you with that," Moore said. "Until today, I haven't seen Emma since the day she moved to Dallas. I wasn't even aware she'd moved back to New Orleans until I saw the news story about the situation with her husband."

"But you didn't get in touch with her then."

"No. I thought about it, but I ultimately decided that it would be intrusive and she needed time with those closest to her."

"That was considerate of you." Jackson rose from his chair. "Thanks for your time, Mr. Moore. If you can think of anything that could help Ms. Frederick, please give us a call."

Jackson could feel Moore's eyes on him as he exited the office, but the lawyer never uttered a word. Jackson supposed he could have asked Moore where he was the night before when someone placed the mice beside Emma's car, but he knew the answer would be "in bed." That's what any intelligent person would say, whether or not it was the truth. A lawyer, criminal or no, would know that with certainty.

The money, connections, and lawyer thing made Moore a difficult nut to crack. To get information on the man would require skill, cleverness, and some possible sneakiness. Jackson was capable of all three, and would gladly incorporate them to get what he needed. He pushed open the door to the law office and stepped out onto the sidewalk. Jackson may not have gotten much out of Moore, but he suspected Shaye's intuition was right about one thing: the man's interest in Emma Frederick hadn't gone away.

Shaye knocked on the barracks door and waited. The drive had seemed twice as long as it actually was. Even worse, all that time to think had yielded no revelations, so all she accomplished was a sore lower back and the discovery that her SUV rattled a bit at high speeds, and she needed to take it in for service. Her anxiety level seemed to have crept up with every mile. If she didn't find out something useful, then it would be an entire day wasted, and something told her she didn't have much time left before the stalker made his final move.

The door opened and a guy who'd clearly been asleep looked out at her. "Yeah?" he said.

"I'm looking for Paul Schaffer," she said. "Is he here?"

The young man shook his head. "Paul shipped out today."

Shaye didn't even bother to try to hide her disappointment. "I don't suppose there's any way I could contact him."

"Not until he's at base camp," the young man said. "Sorry."

"What the hell are you talking about?" Another soldier yanked open the door and stared out at Shaye. "Paul leave you high and dry? The last thing that dude needs is a kid or something."

Shaye felt a blush creep up her neck, and she pulled

her identification from her wallet. "I just want to see if he can give me some information on someone he served with."

The second soldier leaned over to see the ID while the first one turned around and shuffled off. "PI? That's cool. Who's the guy you're asking about?"

"David Grange. Do you know him?"

"Nah. But if you're looking for Paul, you'll probably find him at the bar."

Her pulse quickened. "He's not deployed?"

"He was supposed to be, but he got this tooth that went so bad his eye was swollen shut. He had surgery yesterday so he couldn't ship today."

"And you think he's at the bar, why?"

"Thing hurt like hell but the docs aren't big on handing out painkillers. I listened to him moan and complain half the night. I figure he went straight for a bottle of whiskey as soon as the doors opened. Freedom Bar. Just down the street from the base."

"Thank you."

"No problem." He winked at her and shut the door. Shaye headed back to her SUV and drove out of the base.

The Freedom Bar was easy to find and didn't appear to have many patrons. She suspected that drastically changed as night approached. Lucky for her, Paul should be easy to find. The bar had the windows covered with thick shades, and she blinked a couple times to focus in the dim light. A soldier occupied a single table at the back of the bar. The right side of his face was puffy and his right eye was swollen.

She walked up to his table. "Is that dentist recommended?"

He looked up at her, clutching a glass of whiskey in his right hand and a handful of peanuts in his left. "Depends on who's asking. You the dentist police?"

"You're Paul Schaffer, right?" She pulled out her identification and his eyes widened. "Mind if I take a seat?"

"Go ahead," he said, but he didn't sound sure at all. "What's this about?"

"I'm trying to get some background information for a client."

"On me?"

"No. On David Grange."

Paul's expression darkened and he shook his head. "I don't have anything to say about David Grange."

"Why not?"

"Because can't no good come of it."

Shaye studied him a bit as he picked at a napkin, shredding the end of it. He was definitely worried. Time to find out about what.

"Good or not," Shaye said, "that's the job I'm here to do."

Paul lifted his eyes to hers. "What's he done?"

Shaye was momentarily taken aback. "You don't know?"

He shook his head.

"Last month, David's wife killed him."

Paul's eyes widened and there was no mistaking his

expression. His shock was real. But there was something else Shaye saw in the look he gave her. Something that didn't quite make sense.

Relief.

"Wow," he said. "Is she going to prison or something?"

"No. It was self-defense."

He didn't seem remotely surprised at that revelation.

"I'm surprised no one told you," Shaye said.

Paul shrugged. "David wasn't exactly the friendly sort. When he finished his last tour and left, I doubt he asked for anyone's phone number. I'm certain no one asked for his."

Shaye frowned. "See, that confuses me. Because my understanding is that you helped David get his job in New Orleans."

"Whoever told you that lied. I haven't had anything to do with David since we left Iraq. I damned sure wouldn't vouch for him. Who said I did?"

Shaye had no idea what was going on, but this meeting wasn't going anything at all like she'd figured it would. Paul seemed to be negating everything Ron said, but why would Ron lie? What could possibly be in it for him?

"Ron Duhon," she said, watching Paul closely to gauge his reaction.

It didn't take a genius to figure out what he was thinking. Paul scowled and his face flushed red. He slammed his glass down on the table and the bartender looked over at them. "Sorry, man," Paul said and the man went back to wiping down the bar.

"I take it you don't like Ron either?" she asked.

"Ron…David…same person."

Shaye froze. That wasn't possible. Sure, they looked a lot alike, but David Grange was dead and Ron Duhon was very much alive. "I don't understand."

"Look, we were all in the same unit in Iraq. Most of us had served together before, but David was new. Ron and I are from the same town and our moms are best friends, but I never liked him. He was always an outsider in high school, the weirdo, you know? And that didn't change any here. But for whatever reason, he latched onto David and the two of them got tight."

"They didn't seem like the type to become friends?"

"No one seemed like the type to be friends with Ron. But after shit happened, well, we all realized David was just as screwed up as Ron. Hell, maybe Ron could see it in him 'cause he's just as messed up."

"What happened?"

Paul glanced over at the bartender and shook his head. "I don't want to talk about it. Don't matter now. David's dead and Ron's done with his time in. As far as I'm concerned, that makes both of them dead. I gotta tell you, I'm not the least bit unhappy about it."

Paul's jaw was set in a hard line. Whatever he knew, he wasn't about to part with it. Not simply because she asked. But maybe, if he knew why she was asking, his conscience wouldn't let him keep the secret.

"I told you David's wife killed him," she said. "He came back from Iraq different than before. Abusive to

Emma. She cut ties with him, but he didn't take the hint from her or the legal system. He started stalking her. The day she killed him, he broke into her house. The police have no doubt he was there to kill her."

"Why are you telling me this? What difference does it make why he hit on his wife? The dude's dead and gone and good riddance."

"He's dead but not exactly gone."

"What the hell are you talking about?"

"Someone is stalking Emma, and leaving her keepsakes from her dead husband."

Paul sat up straight. "And you think it's me? I haven't been off base for the last month except to come to this bar, the gas station, and the grocery store. Ask anyone."

"I never said it was you. But it was someone who knew David well. Otherwise, why go after Emma?"

"I don't know, and I don't want to know. Look, I'm sorry for his wife, but I don't want anything to do with this."

"Too late. Ron Duhon dropped you right in the middle of it. Any idea why?"

"Because he's a psycho? Because he's the one stalking that woman and he's covering his own ass?"

Shaye studied Paul as he talked, but she couldn't see any indication that he was lying. All she saw was anger, indignation, and fear. It was the fear that worried her.

"Look," she said. "Tell me what you know, and as long as you're being straight with me, I promise I'll go away and never come back."

He stared at her for several seconds, clearly weighing the pros and cons. Finally, he said, "You gotta understand, I didn't see anything myself. None of us did."

He reached for the package of cigarettes sitting on the table and lit one up. He puffed quickly several times, then leaned toward her. "We got a tip that there was a store of stolen US weapons in a village just outside of our base camp. Our unit went in. We identified the structure and had it surrounded. David and Ron were closest to the structure, but no one was supposed to breach until we got the signal."

"But they went in anyway."

Paul nodded and puffed on the cigarette again. "We didn't know at first. Not for a while. We were all holding position, waiting for orders. There wasn't any gunfire—nothing to signal that they had breached the structure. When we finally got the signal to move, they didn't respond."

"So you assumed they'd been flanked?"

"Yeah. We rushed in from all sides and threw tear gas into the structure, then we entered."

Paul downed the rest of his whiskey, his hand shaking as he placed the glass back on the table. "The intel was wrong. The structure was a family home."

"The gas would only immobilize them, right?" Shaye asked, not understanding why he was so upset.

Paul stared down at the table. "They'd been slaughtered. The mother and father and all four kids, including an infant. They were tied to chairs and tortured, cuts all over their bodies, and their eyes..." He choked up.

"Their eyes had been gouged out. Every one of them."

He looked up at her as he delivered the last sentence, and Shaye felt her stomach roll as she thought about the infant. What kind of monster could do such a thing?

"You're saying David and Ron did that?"

"The blood was fresh. There were two blankets on the floor covered with it."

"They wore them to protect their clothes?"

Paul nodded. "But they both had blood on their boots. I don't know if anyone else noticed. I glanced down and saw and when I looked up, David was staring at me with that dead look he'd get. His eyes would turn dark and lifeless, like a snake, and he'd stare at you until you wanted to crawl out of your own skin to get away. He knew I knew. I could feel it. Maybe the others felt it too."

Paul shook his head. "Either way. None of us ever said a word. Not to command. Not to each other. We reported what we found when we returned to base, and command put it down to roving bands of thieves that were in the area."

"But you don't think that's what happened."

"No ma'am. David and Ron are what happened. I'm as sure of that as I am that you're sitting here in front of me. And that's why I said I don't want anything to do with your investigation. I haven't had a good night's sleep since that day. Every time I close my eyes, I see that family, then that dead-eyed look from David. I'd take ten bad teeth over one of those dreams."

Shaye's heart clenched at Paul's words. She understood

all too well how nightmares could destroy your waking life. "Have you talked to someone? Everything you say is confidential."

"No. Plenty of guys around here tried it. I didn't see it do any good for them. Probably not going to for me. You know, I thought I'd seen bad things in Iraq…really horrible stuff. And then I saw that."

He looked directly at her. "I looked right in the face of pure evil. And the worst part is, it wasn't the enemy."

CHAPTER SEVENTEEN

As soon as she got into her car, Shaye pulled out her cell phone. Her conversation with Paul had completely unnerved her. At first, she'd convinced herself he was making it up to throw her off track, but no way could he fake the suffering she'd seen when he'd told her about the nightmares. Paul had some deep issues to work out, and she hoped he'd get the help he needed before it was too late.

The thing that nagged at her as she pulled out of the parking lot was why Ron had given her Paul's name in the first place. But then she'd remembered that Paul was supposed to ship out today, and Ron would probably have known that through his mother. Throwing out Paul's name was an easy way to get her focus on someone else and someone she would have had a hard time contacting for days at least, if not longer.

Paul also confirmed that he'd never visited Ron in New Orleans, which Shaye had figured once she'd heard the Iraq story. Basically, everything Ron said was a lie. At least, that's the way it looked to Shaye. Of the two, Paul was the more believable. In fact, Shaye would bet her nine years of therapy that Paul was telling the truth. Ron, on the other hand, had dished out the lies so easily and without a change in behavior. All signs pointed to Ron as the stalker. He looked enough like David for people to be mistaken, even a traumatized Emma could have gotten it wrong in the dark, with only a sliver of moonlight to illuminate his face.

Ron thought putting her on Paul's scent would buy him time. Days, or possibly weeks. He hadn't counted on a bad tooth keeping Paul available for Shaye to question. He didn't know his time had just expired.

She pulled up Ron's number but didn't press it.

It probably wasn't smart to confront a sociopath.

But Ron didn't know that she'd talked to Paul, and Paul certainly wasn't going to let that secret out. He'd already promised her he wouldn't tell anyone they'd spoken and never wanted to hear the names Ron Duhon and David Grange again. What she needed was a picture. If she could arrange another meeting with Ron, she could establish herself across the street behind a car and snap a shot of him. Then she could hunt down Hustle and see if he could ID Ron as the man who'd given him the scarf.

That should be enough to get the police to question Ron. She bit her lower lip. Shouldn't it?

Before she could change her mind, she pressed Ron's phone number.

You have reached a number that has been disconnected or is no longer in service...

What the hell? She hung up and checked the number

in her history. That was definitely the one she'd used to call Ron the day before. She hit the number again. A couple seconds later, the message repeated.

She scrolled down and found the number for Wellman Oil and Gas and dialed. Greta answered the phone.

"Hi, this is Shaye Archer. I talked to some of your employees a couple days ago."

"Of course, Ms. Archer," Greta said. "What can I help you with?"

"I tried to reach Ron Duhon, but his cell phone has been disconnected. Did he provide you with a new number?"

"No. I'm afraid Mr. Duhon is no longer employed by Wellman Oil and Gas."

"Can you tell me why?"

"He called yesterday and said he had another job and wouldn't be back. The crew manager was fit to be tied, as Ron was supposed to go offshore tomorrow."

"Did he say where he was going?"

"I'm sorry, but no."

"Would you mind giving me his home address?"

"Not at all. Let me look it up." Greta was silent for a couple seconds, then gave Shaye the address.

"Thank you," Shaye said.

"No problem. Have a great day!"

Shaye tossed her cell phone onto the passenger's seat. As soon as she hit Interstate 49, she pressed the accelerator down, hurtling her SUV forward. The four-and-half-hour drive stretched in front of her like an eternity. Ron already had a day's jump on her, and now he was getting another. Another day to cover his tracks, plant more misdirection, set up alibis.

Or finish the job.

Eleonore inched forward across the bedroom until Corrine made it to her sitting room couch and sank onto the overstuffed cushions. "You're hovering," Corrine said as she looked up at Eleonore.

"I have a medical degree. When our friends are injured we're required to hover. I'm pretty sure I took an oath."

Corrine smiled. "I'm fine. Really. As long as I don't have to sprint. If that need arises, just go ahead and shoot me."

Eleonore walked over to the bar and pulled out a bottle of whiskey. She poured Corrine a shot and handed it to her. "That should take the edge off."

Corrine took the shot and glanced over at the bar. "I'll have Marie move everything to the pantry."

"Please don't go to any trouble. I'm not an addict looking for a fix. Me and your whiskey are safe."

"You're sure?" Corrine already felt bad enough that Shaye's treatment had kicked Eleonore off the wagon. She didn't want to tempt her further. Not that she knew much about Eleonore's trouble with alcohol. Her friend rarely mentioned it and had never provided details.

Eleonore sat on a chair next to her and sighed. "Look,

I had a drinking problem before, but I'm not your average alcoholic. It's not something I crave all the time, never was. It's a crutch, just like food or drugs or church or whatever else people use to escape reality for a bit. That's an explanation, not an excuse, by the way. And this time, it won't get out of control."

"How can you be sure?"

"Simple. Because my tastes have improved, and I'm lazy and cheap."

"I don't understand."

"I never liked wine or beer—scotch was always my drink of choice, and I've found that I can't stomach even a sip of the cheap stuff. Carlin's Beverages is the closest place that carries the brand I like, and it's a five-mile drive across the middle of the city. Besides, have you seen the price on a good bottle of scotch? Good Lord, I almost fainted."

Corrine smiled. Eleonore always made light of things, especially when she knew they'd weigh on Corrine, but this time, Corrine decided she could take her friend at her word. Eleonore might hedge on some things, but she had never outright lied to Corrine. If her friend said she could handle it, then Corrine had no doubt Eleonore thought she could.

She downed the shot and handed the glass back to Eleonore. "Normally, I would say it's too early, but since I've been sitting in that awful hospital bed all morning, and my back and ribs are killing me, I'm going to say make it a double."

"Didn't the hospital give you something for pain?"

"Yeah, advice. They told me to take some aspirin."

Eleonore gave her a disgusted look. "Aspirin? What is their problem?"

"Too many addicts faking back injuries to scam drugs is my guess."

"You're a social worker who was pushed down a flight of stairs while you were doing your job. Hardly an addict looking for a fix."

"Two social workers were arrested last week for dealing drugs to case parents. Want to take a guess where they got the drugs?"

"Jesus H. Christ." Eleonore pulled a pad of paper out of her purse and scribbled on it. "This is the big advantage of being a medical doctor rather than a psychologist. I'll give this to your housekeeper to get filled, and don't let the pain get too bad before you take one."

"Thanks."

Eleonore cocked her head to the side and studied Corrine for several seconds. "Have you considered a job with less risk?"

"Now you sound like my father."

"A successful man who has never been shoved down a flight of stairs."

"If some of his business competitors got the chance, that could change."

"Touché. Look, I see this as a wake-up call. Things are changing. Every day this city gets more dangerous than the day before. People care less and hold grudges more. You walked into an abandoned building alone on the basis of an anonymous phone call. If those painters hadn't shown up… I'm not saying you should quit. I know what the job means to you, but I think you need to stop taking some of the risks you do."

"I know. I've thought about little else all day. This wasn't the first time someone's taken a swipe at me. You know that, but it's the first time it was calculated. Most of the lumps I've taken have been due to emotional outbursts while I was conducting an on-site visit."

Eleonore nodded. "Not premeditation."

Corrine locked her gaze on Eleonore's. "Don't tell anyone, especially Shaye, but this scared the shit out of me. When he was standing over me, I knew with absolute certainty that I was going to die." Tears welled and she rubbed her nose with her finger. "Now all I can think is 'what if.'"

Eleonore reached over and put her hand on Corrine's arm. "Me too, honey. Me too."

Shaye pulled up in front of the apartment building and parked. She pulled her nine-millimeter out of her purse and tucked it in her waistband under her shirt. After talking with Paul, she knew what Ron was capable of. No way was he getting the jump on her while she struggled to pull her gun out of her purse. She wasn't about to be that evening news story.

As she walked up the sidewalk to the building, she questioned, once again, the insanity of what she was doing.

What was she going to say to Ron if he was there? *Hi, I talked to Paul and you're a psycho?* And how was she supposed to get a picture of him standing in front of him? Her current plan was to ascertain Ron was home, ask a couple of innocuous follow-up questions, then wait across the street for Ron to leave the apartment. Her camera was always in her car and the telephoto lens she had would make Ron look like he was standing in front of her, even from a half block away.

The building had three breezeways with the apartment doors off of them that dead-ended at the back of the building. The end of the first breezeway was where Ron's apartment was located. As she walked down the breezeway, she realize how isolated she was. The apartments contained no windows on the front facing the breezeway, and the angle of the building made her passage invisible to anyone except another person in the same stretch. Essentially, she was in a tunnel with one exit and no view to outsiders.

She stopped in front of the apartment door and put her ear up against it, trying to hear if there was any sound of movement inside. A television blared a *Law & Order* rerun, but she couldn't hear anything else. Still, the television indicated someone was probably present.

She rapped on the door and waited, her hands hovering near her waistband. Several seconds later, the door swung open and a young, petite woman with long brown hair and a fading shiner on her right eye looked out at her.

"Can I help you?" the woman asked.

"I'm looking for Ron Duhon. Are you his girlfriend?"

The girl shot her a derisive look. "Hell, no, I'm not his girlfriend. You think I stick with guys that punch me in the face? I kicked his ass to the curb a week ago."

"Did Ron do that?" Shaye pointed to her eye.

"Yep. I told him to consider it his eviction notice. He was never on the lease anyway."

"But he used to live here?"

"If you want to call it that. He worked offshore most of the time. When he was in town, he showered here. Slept here sometimes, but spent most of his time in French Quarter dives waving dollars at cheap whores. I shoulda kicked him out before he hit me."

"Do you have any idea where he's staying now?"

"Nowhere that I know of. He came by here yesterday to get the last of his things. Said he had a job with a pipeline in Alaska and was leaving tomorrow. Good riddance, I say."

Shaye's mind raced. The new job matched what Ron said when he gave notice at the oil company, but she couldn't work up the same "good riddance" sentiment as Ron's ex. No way would he leave town without finishing the job. And for all Shaye knew, that might mean cleaning house—Emma, Shaye, Corrine, and the girl standing in front of her.

Indecision coursed through her as her mind weighed the pros and cons of giving the girl information. What if she was lying and in on it with Ron? The black eye was real, but she could have gotten it from someone else. What if the girlfriend changed her mind and took him back? She'd probably tell him everything Shaye told her.

What if he kills her?

That one question outweighed all the risks. No way was Shaye living with this woman's death on her conscience. She pulled out her identification and showed it to the girl. "You might be in danger. Can I please come in and talk to you?"

The girl's eyes widened and she stared at Shaye as if waiting for the punch line. When none was forthcoming, she stepped back and nodded. Shaye walked into the apartment, praying she was doing the right thing.

CHAPTER EIGHTEEN

Emma poured herself another cup of coffee and checked her cell phone for the hundredth time. She was breaking the rules by having it on her during her shift, but she was beyond caring. As soon as her boss arrived in the morning, she was resigning anyway, and with no notice. If anyone wanted to put remarks in her permanent file for that decision, then so be it. Better a mark on her employment record than an obituary in the local paper.

It had seemed impossible, but after Shaye's phone call on her way back from Fort Polk, Emma had been more nervous than ever. The story the soldier had told Shaye horrified her, but at the same time explained so much. Maybe David had suffered some sort of mental break. Maybe this Ron was the source.

Maybe Ron was her stalker, getting revenge on Emma for killing his ally.

Ron made as much sense as anyone else, and Shaye seemed to think he was capable. She'd told Emma her plan to contact Ron again with the hope of getting a photo that the skater kid could identify. It sounded like a good idea, except for the part where Shaye was essentially going to willingly put herself in front of a crazy man. Emma had tried to talk her out of it, but Shaye had insisted that they needed something to give the police so they'd pick Ron up. Even if they couldn't hold him for long, it would buy Emma time to get out of town without being observed.

Emma couldn't argue with Shaye's reasoning, but didn't like the young woman taking such risks. Shaye had promised to meet Ron in a public place and call Emma the moment she had the photo. Emma had been obsessing over her silent phone ever since. Shaye should have made it back to New Orleans over an hour ago. Where was she? Why hadn't she called?

Every time Emma started to dial Shaye's number, a range of thoughts went through her mind from "she's checking on her mother" to "what if Shaye's phone rings while she's sneaking up on Ron for a picture and he catches her?" So far, she'd ended up sliding the phone back into her pocket, deciding the risk to Shaye was too great.

If she was being honest with herself, Emma also felt guilty. After her conversation with the detective that morning, Shaye had called her, trying to convince her to go to the police with all the evidence they had so far. It wasn't that Emma had found fault in Shaye's arguments, but the truth was, after she'd discovered the bracelet, she'd driven straight to the hospital and hidden in the break room until her shift started, too afraid to leave.

She'd tried calling the police, but the person who'd taken her call hadn't been helpful at all, insisting that she had to come to the police station to file a report. Emma supposed she could have tried harder to get an officer dispatched to the hospital to take a statement, but given the prejudice the police already seemed to have against her, she simply didn't want the hassle. She promised herself she'd go in tomorrow, right after she gave her notice.

Her phone vibrated in her hand and she jerked, spilling coffee onto her hand. She gasped as the hot liquid scorched her skin and immediately tossed the Styrofoam cup into the garbage. As she turned on the cold water in the sink, she checked the display and saw it was Shaye. She shoved her burned hand under the cool stream and answered the call.

"Are you all right?" Emma asked.

"Yes," Shaye said. "I'm sorry I couldn't call sooner."

"Did you get the picture?"

"No. Ron's disappeared."

Emma stiffened. "What?"

"He quit his job with no notice and his girlfriend kicked him out a week ago for slapping her around. He picked up his clothes yesterday and told her he had a new job in Alaska."

"What do you think that means?"

"I don't know for sure, but I'm worried it means he's about to flee New Orleans."

Emma clutched the phone, her voice catching. "He…he won't leave as long as I'm alive."

"That's the part that worries me. Are you staying at the hospital tonight?"

"Yes."

"Good. I'm going to contact the cop I talked to earlier

and see what he can do about Ron. I filled the girlfriend in on everything, and she's going to file charges tomorrow. At least the cops will go looking for him then. Maybe by the time they find him, I'll have something for them to use to hold him."

"If they pick him up, how long can they hold him?"

"Forty-eight hours. Then they have to charge him or let him walk."

Emma blew out a breath. Forty-eight hours wasn't a lot of time, but it might be enough to hand over her house to Patty, do something about her car situation, and get the hell out of New Orleans.

"I'm quitting my job tomorrow morning," Emma said. "I need to meet Patty sometime tomorrow to give her a house key and pack up some of my stuff, but I'm leaving."

"I don't blame you. I'll collect your stuff at the hotel tomorrow morning and take you to your house to meet Patty. Then we'll deal with your car situation."

"None of that falls in your job description."

"I work for you. Keeping you safe seems like a good way to spend my time and *your* money."

Emma smiled. "I guess I can't argue with that. I'm glad I met you, Shaye. For so many reasons, but mostly because I'd lost faith in people. You and some others have brought it back."

"When we feel surrounded by evil," Shaye said quietly, "it's easy to forget that the world also has good, but it's there. We both have to keep believing that."

A sliver of peace ran through Emma. If after

everything Shaye had been through, she was able to have a positive outlook, then Emma could too. Maybe not today, or tomorrow, but sometime, when this was all behind her. It gave her hope for the future, something she'd lost sight of.

"Go look after your mother," Emma said. "This mess will be waiting for both of us tomorrow."

"I will. Don't leave the hospital for any reason, and tell that security guard friend of yours to keep watch for a man who looks similar to David."

"I'll show him a picture of David. He's keeping watch."

"Good. Stay safe, Emma."

Emma ended the call and slipped her phone back into her scrubs. Ron's disappearance was frightening on so many levels, but she couldn't help feeling a tiny bit elated that they'd finally identified her stalker. He had a face and a name and most importantly, a connection to David. The connection that had been missing since the beginning.

An end was in sight. All she had to do was stay alive until Ron was behind bars.

Shaye directed her SUV toward the Garden District and called Jackson. He answered on the first ring.

"You got a minute?" she asked.

"I've got all the time you need. Did you find out anything at Fort Polk?"

She filled him in on her visit with Paul, Ron's disappearing act, and the cooperation of his now terrified ex-girlfriend. "Is it enough to pick him up?"

"If the girlfriend makes the complaint, sure. Assuming we can find him."

"Yeah, that's the part that concerns me. I don't necessarily believe he's headed to Alaska, but I do believe he's leaving town, just not before he finishes the job."

"Where is Emma?"

Shaye pulled to a stop at a red light. "At work now, and she's going to stay at the hospital until morning. They have some sort of employee room with cots in case they're stuck overnight with a patient."

"Good. That's probably the safest place she could be right now, in New Orleans, anyway."

"That's what I thought. Did you get anything on Stephen Moore?"

"Yeah, in fact, I was just about to call you," he said. "I paid Moore a visit." He filled her in on what he'd discovered.

Shaye frowned. If she weren't set on Ron being the stalker, Moore would definitely fill some of the slots. "I still think Ron's our guy, but it sounds like Moore could become a problem or even be part of the problem. Maybe everything that's been happening wasn't the result of only one person."

"It's possible. Given what Schaffer told you about Ron and David, I agree that he's probably the stalker, but I think Moore's definitely capable of slipping across the line of legal and illegal, assuming he hasn't already. At least now he's on notice. Sometimes that's all it takes to get someone to back off."

"I hope you're right," Shaye said. "Did you turn up anything else on David?"

"Unfortunately, no. The man seemed to have materialized at age eighteen."

"Which makes things all that more suspicious."

"I get the feeling that this entire thing goes so much deeper than it appears. Way before his military service even."

Shaye had shared the same feeling for a while now. The fact that Jackson felt the same way only confirmed her belief. "I know. The more I learn, the more I feel like I'm just scratching the surface. Everything I've found so far is awful..." She cut off her sentence before she admitted something she wasn't willing to share with someone she barely knew.

"You're almost afraid of the answer," Jackson finished. "So am I."

A feeling of relief and something else entirely swept through her. She frowned, trying to put her finger on it, and suddenly realized it was a connection. She felt a bond with Jackson that she had never felt for anyone but Corrine and Eleonore. It wasn't as strong, but it was there—troubling and scary as hell.

She shook her head, refocusing on the case. There was plenty of time to work out her personal issues when Ron was behind bars and Emma could go on with her life. Right now, the only thing that mattered was finding Ron before he took his final shot at Emma.

"I'm pulling into my mom's house, so I've got to get off the phone."

"No problem. If the girlfriend shows tomorrow like she says she's going to, I'll let you know what happens. I'll try to get on the case, but unfortunately, I don't have much pull on those things."

His frustration was so evident, and Shaye felt sorry for the position he was in. She had known from the moment she started her college job with a detective agency that she would never be able to work for someone else. The agency she worked for was one of the largest in the city, with fifteen investigators on staff and tons of cases moving through the office. Between her three-year stint there and listening to Corrine's tales of bureaucratic job horror, Shaye was certain she needed to own her own business, preferably one that required a single employee—her.

"I appreciate anything you can manage," Shaye said. "I know your hands are tied."

"Thank you. And Shaye?"

"Yeah?"

"Don't let down your guard. He might come after you as part of his farewell tour."

Shaye hung up the phone and pulled up to the electric gate in front of her mother's home, noting the unmarked police car parked across the street. She punched in the code and the gate slid back, allowing her to drive through, then closed silently behind her. Eleonore's silver Mercedes was in the middle of the circular drive with Pierce's black Aston Martin slotted behind her.

Shaye sighed. She wasn't in the mood to deal with all of them at one time, but given the situation, she supposed it couldn't be avoided. On the upside, given that he'd just spent a day on an airplane, Pierce wouldn't stay long, and Eleonore had been on duty all day. Surely she'd be ready to escape to a hot shower and her favorite recliner.

Shaye let herself in the front door and heard the chattering upstairs coming from the direction of her mother's bedroom. She took the stairs two at a time and found all three of them in Corrine's sitting room. Her grandfather gave her a broad smile as soon as she entered the room, and she went over to give him a hug. If an ad agency had needed a model for the successful businessman look, Pierce would have been a shoo-in. At fifty-nine, he was fit and tanned, and the silver running through his black hair seemed to make women swoon. But then with his power and pocketbook, he could sport a purple mullet and women would still chase him. So far, Corrine's mother was the only one who'd ever caught him.

"I hear you've taken on your first client?" he said.

"Yes," Shaye said. The one-word answer was intentional. The more Pierce knew about her work, the more he would badger her to take a position at Archer Manufacturing. Some boring, unfulfilling nightmare that would pay her too much and have everyone else resenting her. No thanks.

"I guess you did enough insurance work for the other

agency, so you know the ropes."

She nodded, then glanced over at Corrine and Eleonore, who both shook their heads. Clearly, the three of them were on the same page as to how much information Pierce needed about the women in his life.

"I still want you to be careful," Pierce said. "This situation with your mother concerns me. I've always worried that she'd be targeted by one of my enemies or one of those crazy people she deals with. It's going to take a magician to sort it out."

"I'm sure the police are doing all that they can," Shaye said, struggling with the weight of everything that she suspected and that the police didn't know.

"Damn right they are. And after I meet with the captain tomorrow, they'll be doing even more."

Corrine stared at him in dismay. "Dad, please don't go down there raising hell. The police have been wonderful, and I don't want special treatment. Other people in New Orleans have had crimes committed against them as well. They're all important."

Pierce turned around to look down at Corrine. "Not as important as you are to me." He leaned over and kissed her cheek. "I promise not to embarrass you, but I'm still paying them a visit. Eleonore, always a pleasure seeing you." He gave Shaye a hug. "Good luck with that case. Call me if you need anything."

"I will," Shaye said. "Thanks."

Pierce smiled at them and exited the room. As soon as they heard the front door close behind him, Shaye plopped down on the couch next to Corrine and they all relaxed.

"I love him to death," Corrine said, "but he's a stubborn and exhausting man."

"With only one child, who was attacked by a maniac," Eleonore said, "but I don't disagree with either sentiment."

"I take it no one told him I'm not working an insurance case?" Shaye asked.

"Good God, no," Corrine said. "The three of us would never hear the end of it. And believe me, he'd hold all of us responsible. He'd never believe for a minute that you're just as stubborn as he is and wouldn't take good advice from Jesus himself if it was contrary to what you wanted to do."

"So true," Eleonore said. "On all counts."

Shaye snorted. "My grandfather is an amateur nagger compared to the two of you."

"I take issue with that," Eleonore said. "Psychiatrists do not nag. We're licensed to tell you the best way to live your life. You people just refuse to listen." She rose from the couch. "Since the next shift has arrived, I'm going to take off. I hear a hot bath and leftover lasagna calling my name. Walk me out, Shaye, and we'll coordinate our schedules for tomorrow."

"I don't need a babysitter," Corrine griped. "I have a security guard, courtesy of my dad, two policemen in an unmarked car circling the block, and a maid. Besides, this place is wired up better than Fort Knox."

"Uh-huh," Eleonore said, and waved Shaye toward the door.

Shaye followed Eleonore downstairs, but instead of

heading for the front door, Eleonore walked straight through the entry and headed for the kitchen at the back of the house.

"Is everything all right?" Shaye asked, worried that Corrine wasn't doing as well as she seemed to be.

Eleonore stopped walking and whipped around to look her straight in the eyes. "You tell me."

"What...I don't understand."

"There's something you're not telling us. Your mother may have missed that flash of guilt on your face earlier, but I didn't."

Crap. Shaye had tried hard to keep up her pleasant facade, but she should have known Eleonore would catch even the slightest blip. "There is something bothering me, but I'll only speak about it in a professional capacity."

Eleonore narrowed her eyes. "Your profession or mine?"

"Yours."

"Shit."

"Take it or leave it."

Eleonore knew exactly what Shaye was up to. If Shaye gave her information patient to psychiatrist, nothing she said could be repeated, not even to Corrine. So the choice was to know what Shaye was hiding but not be able to tell anyone, or not know at all.

"This goes against all my better judgment," Eleonore said, "but consider us in session. Lay it on me."

Shaye told Eleonore about the fabric swatch she'd found in Corrine's purse.

"Damn it!" Eleonore exploded. "You're telling me the man stalking your client did this to your mother?"

"I think so. But I can't tell her," Shaye said. "If she knew, she'd insist I quit the case, and you know I can't do that. Emma needs my help. When I refused to quit, mother would insist on helping, and that could get us all killed."

"Like you're experienced with stalkers? Shaye, this man is terrorizing a woman, and I can only assume his ultimate goal is to kill her. You're not qualified to deal with that any more than Corrine is."

"I'm not dealing with it alone. There's a cop helping me, and besides, I'm pretty sure I've figured out who the stalker is. If everything goes right tomorrow, the police will pick him up for questioning. By that time, I think I'll have enough evidence for them to hold him."

Shaye deliberately left out the fact that Ron was in the wind and that even if his ex-girlfriend filed a report on him, the police might not be able to find him. Those details would only make Eleonore worry more. If the cops couldn't find Ron tomorrow, then she'd consider telling Corrine the truth.

"How can you be sure you've got the right guy?" Eleonore asked.

Shaye gave Eleonore a rundown of Ron and his military past with David. Eleonore's expression grew grim.

"You're talking about sociopaths," Eleonore said.

"I know. Even if I hadn't studied them in school, we've talked about them enough for me to recognize the signs."

Eleonore reached out to grab her hand. "Promise me you won't take any risks. Promise me that you'll carry that pistol of yours everywhere. And promise me you won't hesitate to blow that son of a bitch away if there's even an ice cube's chance in hell that he can get to you."

Shaye squeezed her hand. "I promise."

CHAPTER NINETEEN

Emma clocked out, then filled a cup with water and sank into a chair in the break room. The shift had felt twice as long as normal. She knew it was because of anxiety and exhaustion, but she'd kept putting on a smile, checking blood pressure, making notes, and reminding herself that this was the last time she'd be making rounds for a while. After tonight, she planned on taking some time off to get her head on straight. Her patients deserved the best she was capable of, and even though she had been competent on the job the entire time, she knew her interaction with patients wasn't up to her personal standards.

She reached into her pocket and pulled out the prescription bottle for the sleeping pills she'd been prescribed after David had…gone. She'd taken them two nights in a row and had some of the best sleep ever, but then she'd gotten that being-watched feeling and had become afraid to sleep that soundly. Tonight, though, she was in the safest place possible. The longer she went without sleeping, the weaker her body got. And if things went really wrong, she'd need that body.

She poured one of the pills into her palm and slipped

the bottle back into her pocket. Indecision plagued her. Could she risk taking the medication? Could she risk another night of no sleep? Earlier on shift, she'd had to sit down because her vision was starting to blur. If she didn't rest, would she even be capable of leaving New Orleans tomorrow?

It was that last thought that made her mind up. Before she could change it again, she popped the pill in her mouth and took a swig of water. She was halfway through the rest of the cup when the door opened and Clara came in. She took one glance at Emma and frowned. "Don't tell me you're working a double again."

"No. I just clocked out. I promise."

"Good." Clara walked over and gave her a critical look. "Those bags under your eyes are going to have to file for their own zip code if you don't get some rest."

"I have a feeling I'll get some tonight."

"I talked to Jeremy earlier this evening. He told me about what happened last night. You changed hotels, right? Is the new one better?"

"Not exactly. Actually, I'm going to sleep here tonight. I just…I don't feel safe anywhere but here."

"Oh honey." Clara put her hand on Emma's shoulder and squeezed. "I wish there were something I could do. If staying here makes you feel better, then do it. I'll check in on you when I go on break."

"Thank you."

"You hang in there. This is all going to be all right. You'll see."

Emma nodded as Clara left the room, hoping the senior nurse was right. She pushed herself up from the table, tossed her cup in the trash can, and went through the back door on the break room and into the sleeping area. No other staff members were using the room tonight, at least not yet. She stuck her purse under the bed in the back corner and lay down on top of the mattress, not even bothering with a blanket.

She was asleep before her head ever hit the pillow.

Clara eased the door open to the patient's room and stepped inside. Miss Melody, a tough old bird who'd broken her hip, waved at her, clutching her signature pink lip gloss, as she stepped inside.

"Why aren't you sleeping?" Clara asked. Miss Melody might be tough, but in addition to her broken hip, she had an iffy heart, which was why she was lounging in intensive care instead of a regular room.

"Been sleeping darn near all day. A person's not supposed to spend that much time unconscious unless they're dead."

Clara smiled. "That's always the way it is when a body's sick, isn't it? You sleep all day, then you're awake all night when there's nothing good to watch on television."

"If those cheapos at the hospital would get cable that wouldn't be a problem. They've got reruns on older than I am."

Clara put the blood pressure band on Miss Melody and took out her stethoscope. Miss Melody sat still and silent while Clara checked her vitals and made a note on her chart. Her blood pressure was a little high, but that was normal given the circumstances. "Is your hip hurting you?" Clara asked.

Miss Melody waved a hand in dismissal. "I've had corns that hurt worse."

"Well, if there's anything I can do for you, just push that button."

"Unless you got Netflix in your scrubs, I'll have to rough it."

Clara laughed. "At least try to get some rest. Your body heals while you're sleeping, so you'll get out of here faster."

"Hmmm. I may have to think on that one."

"I'll be back later to check on you." Clara exited the room and headed back to the nurse's station. Miss Melody was the last patient in her rotation, so it was paperwork time until she had to start the next set of rounds. She was halfway down the hall when she veered off to the left, deciding to take a short detour past the break room.

The break room was empty, and she slipped through the back door to the sleeping area. It took a couple of seconds for her eyes to adjust to the dim light, but she finally spotted Emma on the bed in the back corner curled up in a ball. She eased a blanket out of one of the storage lockers and covered Emma with it before leaving.

Clara had tried not to get too much into Emma's

business, but the reality was, she was worried about the young nurse. Truth be told, Emma was in worse shape than some of the patients in her charge. Her body would only last so much longer before it collapsed. Either way, the bad guy won. If only there were something she could do. The older she got, the more she decided the world was becoming filled with crazy people.

Sweet little Emma with a stalker…some psycho attacking Corrine Archer…it was as if someone had declared a war against good. If Clara were thirty years younger, she'd be tempted to break heads. She was an educated woman with a solid professional history, but her life hadn't started out that great. Growing up in the Ninth Ward, people cultivated all kinds of skill sets. She hadn't needed any of them since the day she moved out of her mother's shack and into the dorm room at college, courtesy of a full scholarship, but that didn't mean she'd forgotten how to handle bad people.

He watched the hospital parking lot from the rooftop across the street. Her car was still there, but he knew she was no longer on shift. He'd called earlier pretending to be a police officer, and the receptionist confirmed that Emma had clocked out for the night. But almost an hour later and still no sign of her. If she got caught up talking to a staff member, she might be ten or fifteen minutes late leaving, but an hour was something else entirely.

She might have taken a taxi. From his position, he had a clear view of the front entrance of the hospital, and he was fairly sure he hadn't seen a taxi pull through. He might be mistaken, but something told him he wasn't. He thought back to the time he'd spent in the hospital for a broken wrist. Of all his injuries, it was the only time he'd actually gone to the hospital, but then, he'd been an adult and able to choose.

There had been a shooting at a bar that night and several people were brought in with gunshot wounds. He'd heard the surgeon who'd tended to them talking to the nurse outside his room, saying that he was going to stay the night so that he was available in case any of the patients needed him. That must mean the hospital had a place for staff to stay the night if they needed to. It made sense if they were handling a critical situation.

He was quite certain Emma wasn't handling anything critical, not in a work capacity, but he'd bet anything that she was somewhere inside the hospital, utilizing that space set aside for personnel to stay the night. She thought she was being sneaky, but he was never far behind. This time was no different. Emma couldn't hide from him. And he had one more card to play before the finale. With the private investigator out of the way, probably hovering over her rich, beloved mother, Emma was all alone again. And that was just the way he wanted her.

He scurried down the fire escape and up the alley to the hospital parking lot. The smoking area was off to the side, hidden from view of hospital windows and shielded from the parking lot by a tall hedge. At first, he'd been a little surprised that health professionals chose a habit like smoking, but then he supposed everyone had to have their outlet.

A couple minutes ago, an ambulance had returned to the hospital and he'd seen one of the paramedics head for the smoking area, already removing the black uniform shirt he wore over a white undershirt, trying to get a momentary break from the awful humidity. The other had remained in the ambulance and was slumped down in his seat, eyes closed, and probably wouldn't stir unless a call came in.

He pulled his hoodie up and crept down the side of the hedge, careful to keep the security cameras from getting a good shot of his face. When he stepped through the hedge and into the tiny smoking area, the young paramedic looked up at him in surprise.

"Dude," the paramedic said, "you scared me for a minute there."

He glanced over and saw the shirt draped over a nearby hedge and held in a smile. "Sorry about that. I don't suppose I could bum a cigarette?"

"Sure." The paramedic reached into his pocket. "There's been wild dogs roaming the alleys around here. We brought two people in last night who'd been bitten. Crazy shit."

The paramedic pulled a cigarette out of the pack and looked back up.

He grabbed the paramedic by his hair and before the man could even utter a cry, sliced his throat from side to side. Blood spurted out from the cut and he pushed the paramedic backward before it got on him. The paramedic clutched his throat with both hands, blood pouring between his fingers, choked sputtering sounds coming from his throat.

He watched as he fell backward off the bench and lay there on the ground still gurgling until finally, his hands went limp and slid away from the incision. His eyes were wide open, frozen in that horrified look people got when they knew they were about to die. His mouth was open as well, as if he were trying to let out one final cry.

The eyes.

The eyes looked at him.

Judging him. Mocking him. Even in death.

He stepped across the bench and bent over, shoving his knife into the eye socket. He pressed down until the eyeball popped out with a sickening *pop*, then repeated the process on the other side. He gathered the eyeballs and threw them toward the dumpster behind him. Alley cats needed dinner, too.

He stepped back and studied his handiwork. It was the first time he'd managed a clean cut through the neck. It was an efficient way to kill someone but not an interesting one. It was all over too soon. Not enough suffering. Not enough time to contemplate all the bad decisions one had made.

Like marrying Emma.

Anger and loathing flared up inside him as he thought about David dying like this. Cut so cleanly and deeply that he didn't have a chance to finish what he'd started. Caught by surprise by a whore. But that was okay. Emma would pay for what she did to David. She'd pay for not dying like she was supposed to. But first, he'd make her wish she'd died that night instead of David.

He pulled off his hoodie and used it to wipe the blood off his knife and hands. Then he threw it in the Dumpster and grabbed the paramedic's shirt off the hedge and pulled it on. It was a little tight—the paramedic wasn't as toned as he was—but it was good enough to get by. Good enough that no one would look twice. He pulled a ball cap from his back pocket and pulled it on. He knew how to avoid security cameras.

The receptionist barely glanced at him as he walked into the emergency room lobby and headed through the double doors. He walked past the empty rooms designated for emergencies and followed the hallway to the intensive care wing. David had told him that's where Emma worked, so he knew she was somewhere nearby. He looked down one hallway but saw only patient rooms. On the next hallway, he hit the jackpot.

He pushed open the door to the break room and walked inside, barely holding in a smile when he saw the room was empty. At the back of the room was another door. He hurried to it and pushed it open, peering inside. The light from the break room streaming through the door opening was the only light available, but it was enough for him to catch sight of her.

His jaw clenched involuntarily when he saw her sleeping. That wouldn't do at all. He wanted her awake and terrified. Resting was out of the question.

Voices sounded in the hall, and he jumped back from the doorway and hurried over to the cooler. When the nurses entered the room, he gave them a nod and exited the room with a cup of water. He could still hear them chattering as he walked down the hall.

He needed a distraction—something that got them mobilized in one location long enough for him to get to Emma without being caught. He turned down the hallway that contained the intensive care patients and headed to the last room. He pushed open the door and peered inside, smiling when he saw it was occupied by an old woman. He pulled on gloves as he walked over to the bed and glanced at her chart. Melody Pitre. A broken hip was about to be the least of her worries.

He stepped closer to the front of the bed and eased one of the pillows from beneath her head. She didn't even stir. The lack of challenge was almost disappointing, but then Melody Pitre wasn't really a target. She was simply a tool.

Leaning over the bed, he shoved the pillow down onto her face. Immediately, she started thrashing, and he was surprised at her strength. He could feel her fingernails digging into his hands as she pulled at his fingers. If not for the gloves, he had no doubt she had the strength to break the skin. He pressed harder, and after ten more seconds of struggling, she went still. The heart monitor set off an alarm and he dropped the pillow on the floor next to the bed and fled the room.

He ran toward the hallway to the break room and slipped into the janitor's closet. Seconds later, he heard a rush of footsteps as the nurses ran past. He waited a couple more seconds, then slipped out of the closet and hurried for the break room. As he'd expected, the room was empty, but he knew that could quickly change.

A few minutes—that's all he could risk.

But that's all he needed.

CHAPTER TWENTY

Clara picked up Miss Melody's hand one more time, checking her pulse. It was faint but steady. She blew out a breath. This had been a close one. More than one time while they worked on her, Clara had been afraid that Miss Melody was never going to see Netflix again. They'd all been relieved when they got a pulse. Until she was conscious, they had no way of knowing how much damage, if any, had been caused, but she was alive. Right now, that was all that mattered.

Clara stepped back from the bed and reached for the pillow that had gotten kicked under the bed while they were working on Miss Melody. She'd get a new pillowcase from the linen closet. She looked down at Miss Melody once more and frowned. What in the world had happened? Clara had checked on the senior just thirty minutes before. Nothing in her vitals had indicated that her heart was under any more stress than normal.

The doctor had dismissed it as the stress of the hip surgery and Miss Melody's weak heart, but Clara couldn't help but feel that something was off. From a medical standpoint, the doctor's assessment was sound. From

Clara's decades of experience standpoint, the doctor's assessment was missing something.

She shook her head and pulled the pillowcase off the pillow. A flash of color on the white cloth caught her eye and she lifted the case up to get a closer look. Her breath caught in her throat when she saw the pink lips impressed onto the pillowcase.

Mrs. Melody's heart hadn't given out on her. Someone had tried to smother her.

Shaye!

Still clutching the pillowcase, Clara ran out of the room, an irrational panic coursing through her. *Miss Melody is a patient and no relation to Shaye*, she reminded herself as she raced to the break room. *There's no reason for Emma's stalker to attack a patient like he did Corrine*. But every awful thing Emma had told her ran through Clara's mind, and the logical argument didn't cause her panic to subside.

She hurried across the break room and pushed open the back door, the light from the break room illuminating the sleeping area. Emma was still curled up on the back bed, but in the dim light, Clara couldn't tell if she was breathing. She tossed the pillowcase on a table next to the door and grabbed a box of tissue and crammed it under the door to prop it open. She stepped into the room, peering into the dark corners, praying that no one lurked in the shadows.

Please, Lord, let her be all right, she prayed as she inched across the floor.

When she reached the bed, she leaned over and looked

at Emma's chest, but it was too dark for her to see if she was breathing. She hated to startle her, but seeing no other choice, she reached down and placed her fingers on Emma's neck. She choked back a cry of relief when she felt it beating strong beneath her fingertips.

She backed out of the room, grabbing the pillowcase before she pulled the door shut behind her. As soon as the door clicked shut, she sank into a chair, silently willing her racing heart to slow. She took several deep breaths and blew them out slowly. Emma was safe and that was a blessing. But someone had tried to kill Miss Melody.

She needed to call the police.

"Unit 718. Come in."

Mike Phillips jolted awake and banged his elbow on the steering wheel of the ambulance. "Damn it!" He grabbed the radio. "This is unit 718."

"Car accident at the corner of Esplanade and Burgundy."

Mike glanced over at the passenger's seat and shook his head when he saw it was empty. "My partner is taking a restroom break. Can you send another unit?"

"10-4."

Mike glanced at his watch and cursed again. He'd been asleep for over thirty minutes. If he didn't get a grip, he was going to end up losing his job. And God only knew that with a newborn daughter and a girlfriend who had an aversion to working, someone had to make a paycheck. He shoved the door open and stepped out of the ambulance to go find Drew. He was probably smoking again. How any one human being could smoke that much, Mike would never know. Not to mention that Drew had to spend a rent payment on cigarettes.

Mike yawned and stretched his arms over his head. He wouldn't even care if Amy never got a job if she'd bother to pull her weight around the apartment. But every morning when he got home, it was a wreck, and that was the case even before she had the baby. Now he spent all day tending to a screaming colicky infant because Amy claimed she needed to sleep. What the hell did she think he was—a vampire? Tomorrow night was his night off, but swear to God, if he didn't get some sleep tomorrow, he was going to tell Amy he had to work and check into a motel. Let her go a day or two without any sleep and see how it felt.

"Yo, Drew!" Mike yelled as he stepped around the hedge that blocked the smoking area from the parking lot.

He glanced around the benches but didn't see his partner anywhere. Maybe he hadn't lied when he told dispatch Drew was in the john. As he turned around to leave, an ear-splitting wail filled the air. He whipped around and saw an alley cat on top of one of the benches, his tail flickering. A second later, he jumped off the bench and the sounds of a cat fight filled the air. Mike frowned and headed over to the bench. Alley cats usually scattered when people came around, but these two hadn't even noticed he was there.

"What's the matter, you two?" he asked as he stopped at the bench and peered over. "You fighting over some hot pussy?" He laughed at his own joke, then focused on the lump that the cats were poised on.

And screamed.

Clara had just reached the reception desk when a paramedic ran into the emergency room, yelling incoherently. His eyes were wide open, all color was drained from his face, and his entire body shook.

"He's in shock," Clara said. "Call for backup."

She tossed the pillowcase on the reception desk and ran over to the paramedic, scanning his body for injury. "What's wrong, Mike? Where is Drew?"

"Dead!" Mike screamed. "He's dead!"

Two nurses ran into the lobby and looked at Clara, clearly out of their element. "Take him to a room and get him calmed down." She looked at the receptionist. "Call Jeremy and tell him to meet me out front. And then call the police and tell them that someone tried to murder a patient."

The girl paled. "Yes, ma'am." She grabbed the phone. Clara could hear her shaky voice summoning Jeremy as she walked outside.

She looked across the parking lot and spotted Mike's ambulance. Nothing appeared out of place except that Drew was nowhere in sight. The young paramedic was never without a pack of cigarettes in his pocket. If he wasn't inside the hospital, he was probably in the smoking area. The door behind her swung open and Jeremy hurried outside.

"What's going on?" he asked.

"One of the paramedics came inside in shock, screaming that the other boy was dead. And someone tried to kill one of my patients."

"What?" Jeremy stared at her as if she'd lost her mind.

"You heard me. Now pull out that gun of yours and let's go see if we can find Drew. He may need medical attention." Clara took off down the sidewalk, pleased that her voice sounded strong, because the truth was, she was scared shitless. During her career, she'd seen all manner of violence, but always sometime after it had occurred. She hadn't been on-site for any of the evil men perpetrated against one another since she'd left the Ninth Ward.

Jeremy strode next to her, gripping his pistol and casting glances her way. She knew he was confused, but he was also a good man and he'd known her forever.

"You all right?" she asked him.

"I'm a little confused, but if you think something's wrong, then I'm betting something's wrong. You really think something happened to Drew?"

"I think Mike was in shock, and in the five years he's worked this hospital, I've never even seen him lift an eyebrow."

Jeremy nodded. He knew Mike as well as she did. He was efficient and focused to the point of appearing callous.

Clara was already bracing herself for whatever had sent him over the edge that way. It had to be bad beyond imagination.

They walked around the hedges into the smoking area and alley cats raced from behind a park bench and scattered around them. Clara's heart dropped and she slowed as she approached the bench. Jeremy pulled out his flashlight and shone it over the bench, but the moonlight had been enough for Clara to see what had done Mike in. It damned near did her in as well.

Her hand flew up over her mouth and she took a step back, bumping into Jeremy.

"Sweet Jesus," Jeremy said.

Panic coursed through Clara, setting every nerve ending in her body on edge. Her stomach rolled and a wave of dizziness washed over her. "We've got to get the police. Something horrible is going on here."

Jeremy nodded and silently backed away from the bench. Clara paused long enough to say a silent prayer for Drew, then spun around and practically ran back to the hospital.

With every pounding footstep, she tried to make sense of the irrational.

And failed.

CHAPTER TWENTY-ONE

Emma awakened to the sound of commotion in the break room. So many voices, and all of them talking at once. It sounded more like a college dorm room than a hospital. She pushed herself up a bit, trying to make out the muddled words. Her head felt as if it were stuffed with cotton. She looked at her watch and blinked several times, trying to focus on the time. Damned sleeping pill.

Six a.m.

Too early for the day shift. So why all the racket? She struggled up to a sitting position and frowned. The noise level was that of a party, but the tone of the voices was all wrong—high-pitched and strained. Something was wrong.

The door opened and Clara stuck her head inside. "You're awake?"

"Sorta. What's going on out there?"

"Give me a minute." Clara closed the door and Emma heard her giving orders to the staff.

Orders that included the police?

Emma stiffened. Surely she'd heard wrong. The medicine was messing everything up. A second later, Clara came into the room, and one look at the senior nurse's face and Emma knew something was horribly wrong.

"What happened?"

"Someone attacked Miss Melody last night."

"Oh no! Is she all right?"

"She's still unconscious but stable."

"Thank God. Who attacked her? How did he get in?"

"He killed one of the paramedics and took his shirt."

Emma sucked in a breath, her head spinning. "He killed a…oh my God. Why would anyone want to hurt Melody?"

Clara shook her head. "The police are questioning everyone on shift last night but they're not giving out any information."

"Do you know anything about her?"

"Personal you mean?"

Emma nodded.

"What little bit I know I told the police. I know she's got money. Her clothes are tailor-made and the jewelry she was wearing when they brought her in isn't the kind you buy from a case. She was arguing with someone on the phone this morning about money. When I told her not to take calls that upset her, she told me her nephew was the most useless human God had ever created."

"You think he tried to kill her to get her money?"

"I'd hate to think it, but it happens more and more these days."

"That's awful. I can't believe it."

"It's hard to. I mean, you hear such things on the news but you never really think…" Clara looked at Emma. "But then, you know that better than most of us." She gave Emma's shoulder a squeeze. "I've got to make rounds. Why don't you try to get another couple hours?"

"Yeah, maybe," Emma said but she knew there was no way in hell she'd be able to sleep after what Clara had told her. She'd slept here thinking it was safe. She had no doubt Melody had felt the same, but look what had happened. If someone killed a paramedic just to get his hands on Melody's money, there was no reason her stalker couldn't do the same.

A chill ran through her and she crossed her arms across her chest. She'd even taken a sleeping pill. Stupid! She couldn't remember lying down, much less anything that had happened while she was asleep. Not a single noise or movement. Not even a dream. She may as well have been under anesthesia.

She reached for the lamp next to the bed and turned the switch on, the small light casting a decent glow across the room. She threw the covers off her legs and felt something slip on her finger. She lifted her left hand and barely managed to cover her mouth with her right hand before she screamed.

The wedding band that had once fit perfectly sat loosely on her now-thinner ring finger. It glittered in the lamplight, mocking her with every glint.

She bolted from the bed and ran into the attached bathroom. She barely made it to the toilet before retching. Over and over she heaved, until her chest and back ached. Finally, she yanked the ring off and dropped it into the toilet, then flushed it away. Her finger still tingled from where the ring had rested as if saying no matter what she did, she couldn't erase her past.

She jumped up from the floor and hurried to the sink. The medicine cabinet next to it contained basic bathroom supplies. Fumbling through the items, she located a wire brush and alcohol. She poured the alcohol onto her hand and began scrubbing.

"I have to make it go away," she said as she ran the wire back and forth and around her finger.

She didn't even stop when it started bleeding.

Shaye burst into the emergency room and rushed up to the reception desk. "I'm looking for Clara Mandeville."

"I'm sorry, but Ms. Mandeville can't be disturbed." The young woman looked completely rattled.

"My name is Shaye Archer. Ms. Mandeville asked me to come."

The girl's eyes widened. "Oh, Ms. Archer. Yes!" She grabbed the phone and spoke to someone, then hung up. "Ms. Mandeville is in intensive care room seven. Down the hallway and to the right."

"Thank you," Shaye said as she rushed through the doors and down the hall. Clara had refused to give Shaye details with her early-morning phone call. She'd simply said that Shaye needed to get to the hospital right away. That Emma needed her. The cop cars in the parking lot hadn't done anything to decrease her fear.

The only redeeming part was that if Emma needed her, then that meant she was alive. At least, Shaye assumed that meant Emma was alive. But what if the worst had happened and Clara didn't want to tell her over the phone? She'd literally pulled on clothes as she ran out of Corrine's house. Her mother was still asleep, thank goodness, and the housekeeper assured Shaye she'd keep watch on her until Eleonore arrived. Then Shaye had broken at least ten major traffic laws on the drive over.

She skidded around the corner to the critical care hall and burst into room seven. Emma sat on the edge of a hospital bed, Clara standing in front of her, wrapping her hand. Another nurse held a tray with bandages.

"Are you all right?" Shaye asked as she walked up. "What happened? Why are the police here?"

Emma stared at the wall in front of them, not even acknowledging Shaye's presence. Her eyes were red and swollen. Her skin was pale and she looked several years older than she had the day before. Clara motioned to the nurse to finish wrapping Emma's hand and headed out of the room and across the hall to a vacant room.

As soon as she closed the door behind them, Clara gripped Shaye's shoulders and looked her up and down. "It is so good to see you, child. It's been too long."

Shaye nodded, but couldn't meet Clara's gaze. She'd always had good intentions of visiting Clara, but she'd spent so much time in the hospital, and all of it associated with negative things. She'd wanted to put it all behind her, and unfortunately, Clara had gotten lumped in with that part of her life. "I wanted to visit you but…"

"Oh honey, I understand. Sometimes a person's got to pick a day to start their life over and never look back. I did it once myself and never regretted it for a moment. I'm proud of what you've accomplished, and I'm glad you're helping Emma."

Shaye sniffed. "Thank you. It means a lot. Really."

Clara nodded. "It was a bad one here last night."

"What happened?"

"A man killed a paramedic outside and stole his uniform to get in here. He suffocated another patient."

"Oh my God. Is the patient all right?"

"She's been unconscious but she's starting to stir. We won't know the extent of the damage, if any, until later."

"What does this have to do with Emma? Why is she in shock?"

"At first, I didn't think it had anything to do with Emma. The patient is a wealthy woman who recently cut a lazy nephew off the money train. I figured it was him behind it. Then I went back to the break room to check on Emma and that's when I found her scrubbing her knuckles. When I tried to get her to stop, she took a swipe at me. Said she had to get the evil off."

"The evil?"

"Took me a while to get it out of her. That man…if you can even call him that, killed that paramedic and suffocated that poor old lady to get at Emma."

"How can you be sure?"

"For starters, the paramedic's eyes were cut out. Jeremy didn't see the face when we found Drew, but when the police told him about it this morning when they questioned us, he flipped and told them about the mice."

Shaye's hand involuntarily flew up to cover her mouth.

"Soon as I heard that, I hustled back to the break room, and that's when Emma told me about the ring." Clara looked visibly ill.

"What ring?"

"When Emma woke up this morning, she was wearing her wedding band. The one she swore she'd thrown away."

She had to get the evil off.

"Oh my God." Shaye's stomach rolled. "She thought she'd be safe here."

"Everyone thought she'd be safe here. How could anyone predict something like this? Even if someone had suggested it, no one would have believed it could happen."

"Did Emma talk to the police?"

Clara nodded. "She came around enough to talk to them, and she managed to get the story out. It was when she found out about the paramedic that she went over the edge again."

"Do they believe her now?"

"They seemed a bit skeptical, but with a dead paramedic, a patient who was attacked, and Jeremy's story of the mice, they seemed to come around. It probably would have been better if Emma hadn't flushed the ring, but I understand why she did. She told them about you, too. When they find out you're here, they're going to want to talk to you. I just figured you'd want to know what you were walking into."

"Yes. Thank you." Shaye blew out a breath. "What the hell is wrong with this guy?"

Clara shook her head. "I wish I knew. Maybe it's as simple as what Emma said—evil."

The door swung open and both of them jumped. Emma stepped inside, closing the door behind her. Color had flooded back into her skin, and instead of looking spaced out, Emma looked angry. "You said you could help me with my car situation?" she asked Shaye.

"Yes. I think so, but—"

"Can we do it now?" Emma asked. "I mean right now?"

"You can't leave the hospital right now," Clara said. "The police may need something and that…that thing is out there somewhere."

"That's exactly why I've got to leave," Emma said. "Not just the hospital. I'm leaving New Orleans. And I want to do it as soon as possible."

"But the police believe you now," Shaye said. "They'll be looking for Ron."

Clara's eyes widened. "You know who did this?"

"I have a damned good idea," Shaye said.

"What makes you think they'll find him?" Emma asked. "He killed a man last night and almost killed a patient, just to put that piece of gold on my hand. He'll do anything. And there's nothing anyone can do to stop him. I won't be safe until he's dead, not really. But the closest I can come is disappearing."

Shaye couldn't argue with her. The best thing Emma could do was leave New Orleans and do everything possible to cover her tracks. Without the benefit of the GPS tracking device that Shaye was fairly certain was on Emma's car, Ron would have no way to locate her short of searching the medical facilities in every city across the United States.

"Okay," Shaye said. "I'll call my friend and ask him to meet us right now. Go get your things."

"Thank you," Emma said and hurried out of the room.

"Are you sure you know what you're doing?" Clara asked.

"Not entirely," Shaye said, "but in this case, yes. I'm pretty sure the stalker put a GPS tracker on Emma's car. That's how he's been able to locate her even when she changed hotels."

"So she needs a new car, but it's Sunday."

"The friend I'm calling owns a used car lot and he owes me."

The "friend" was actually a former client at her previous job. While investigating him for insurance fraud, she'd discovered that his employees were the ones ripping off the insurance companies. He'd told her that any time she needed a favor involving automobiles, he would take care of it. She planned on holding him to his word.

Clara nodded. "I see what you're thinking."

"Yeah, it's all good except for the part where the police are going to have a stroke when they find out Emma left with me."

"I'll handle them. You just get Emma out of New Orleans."

"Absolutely."

CHAPTER TWENTY-TWO

Emma clutched the keys to her slightly used SUV and looked at Shaye. "I don't even know how to begin to thank you."

"No thanks are necessary. I'm glad I could help."

Emma glanced back at the car lot owner, who was staring at the SUV, a rueful look on his face. "I'm not so sure he is."

"Oh, I'll bet he's not losing any money. He's just not making any. I was thinking I could pick up your stuff at the hotel and meet you somewhere."

Emma was about to agree when her phone rang. She checked the display and frowned. "It's Mr. Abshire."

"Your nosy next-door neighbor?"

"Yeah." She answered the call and knew right away that something was wrong.

"Are you at home?" he asked, his voice elevated several octaves. "I knocked and knocked but you didn't answer."

"No, I'm not. What's wrong?"

"The street's full of police cars. They were in Mrs. Pearson's house, then they came to yours. When you didn't answer, they came to mine, asking if I knew where you were."

"They didn't tell you what's happening?"

"No. But I think you should come home."

Emma clutched the phone. It wasn't her home. Not anymore, but she'd never heard Henry sound so stressed. "Okay. I'm on my way."

She slipped the phone back into her pocket and told Shaye what Henry had said.

Shaye frowned. "I don't like it."

"I don't either, but if the street's full of cops, like Henry says, then nothing can happen, right?"

"I guess not, but I'm going with you. I'll be right behind you."

Relief coursed through Emma. "Thank God."

A million thoughts ran through Emma's mind as she drove to Algiers Point. Why had the police been inside Mrs. Pearson's house? Had she been robbed? But if that were the case, why wouldn't they tell Henry? Why fix on her? And why all the secrecy?

By the time she pulled down her street, she'd convinced herself that Henry was probably overreacting. He was always fretting about, getting dramatic over the way people parked and how people walked their dogs. This was going to turn out to be nothing.

Three police cars and an ambulance parked on the street in front of Emma's house changed her mind. The upbeat spirit she'd tried so hard to work up disappeared like vapor and her stomach churned. Something was seriously wrong. She pulled up behind one of the police cars and parked, Shaye pulling in behind her. Emma hesitated for a moment, then climbed out of her car and walked up the sidewalk with Shaye, fighting the panic that was starting to set in. Why was the ambulance here? Who was it for?

Two cops stood on the sidewalk in front of Mrs. Pearson's house next to the ambulance. As they approached, Emma looked over at the ambulance and was shocked to see Patty sitting there, an oxygen mask on her face. She rushed over to the Realtor.

"What happened?" Emma asked. "Are you all right?"

Patty nodded and held up a finger.

"A little more," the paramedic said to Patty.

"What happened?" Shaye asked the paramedic.

"I'm not completely sure. When we got here she was on the steps. Her breathing was so labored she was about to pass out, so I got her over here and got the mask on her."

Emma and Shaye looked over at the house and Shaye tapped Emma's arm when a young detective walked out. "That's Jackson, the detective I've been talking to."

Emma nodded. "I remember him. He came the night I…that night. He was kind."

Jackson's gaze locked on them and he gave them a brief nod.

"His partner must be here," Shaye said. "He's got seniority and from what I can tell, pretty much prevents Jackson from actually working."

"The fat older guy with nose hair and a widow's

peak?" Emma asked.

"That's probably the one."

"He wasn't kind. In fact, he was an asshole."

"Definitely the one."

"Emma," Patty wheezed and Emma and Shaye moved closer to her.

"Don't try to talk," Emma said. "You need to get your breathing right first."

"I'm okay," Patty insisted. "It was horrible. I've never...I didn't...Jesus, it's the worst thing I've ever seen."

Emma's pulse spiked. "What happened?"

"Mrs. Pearson's nephew called. They've been trying to reach her and she wasn't answering. She leaves a key with me when she goes out of town, in case something happens. She was supposed to pick it up yesterday, but when she never called, I figured she'd stayed longer with her new grandbaby. I didn't think... Oh my God." Patty burst into tears and the paramedic handed her a tissue.

"Someone killed her!" Patty blurted out. "And took her eyes. What kind of person would do that? I don't understand. She was such a nice lady, and she didn't have anything much of value. Why would someone hurt her?"

As soon as Patty said "eyes" Emma froze. No. It couldn't be. "I don't know why, Patty," Emma managed to force out. "I'm so sorry you found her. Is there anything I can do?"

Patty shook her head. "I just need to get my wind back and get home. I tensed so much my muscles are in knots."

"I can help with that, ma'am," the paramedic said.

"Shaye!" A man's voice sounded behind them and they turned around.

Jackson hurried up to them and motioned them to the side.

"Patty said Mrs. Pearson was killed," Emma said.

Jackson nodded and looked at Emma. "I heard there was trouble at the hospital last night. Detectives were waiting to talk to you this morning. They weren't happy to find out you'd split."

Emma felt her back and neck tighten. "I don't really care that they were unhappy. If the police had listened to me, Mrs. Pearson and that paramedic might still be alive."

"I know that," Jackson said. "I'm on your side, believe me, but you're going to have to talk to them. Your neighbor has probably been dead a couple of days, but with the eye thing...detectives have finally connected the dots and they all point back to you."

Emma felt tears well up in her eyes. Every time she thought she was going to finally escape, everything got worse. "Why Mrs. Pearson? It doesn't make any sense. We're neighbors but we're not particularly close."

Jackson nodded. "Nothing in the house was disturbed but I noticed footprints in the dust in the attic." He pointed at the small window on the front of the house near the roofline. "Right below that window. I think he was watching you from there."

Emma stared at the window, then looked across the street at her house. Her skin began to itch. "When does it end?"

"Soon," Jackson said. "Ron's girlfriend is at the precinct right now filing a complaint. I told the lead detective on the paramedic murder about the domestic abuse complaint and what Shaye found out about David and Ron serving together. They're looking for him. He's exposed now. It will be over soon."

Emma nodded. She could tell by his expression that Jackson was telling her the truth, and she wanted to believe him, but she'd invested too much hope in things that had never materialized, and she simply couldn't afford to any longer. She'd celebrate when Ron was behind bars. Not a moment before.

"What do you need me to do?" Emma asked.

"Can you come down to the police station now so we can get everything documented?" Jackson asked. "It will take a while and we have uncomfortable chairs and horrible coffee, but you'll be safe there."

"You make it sound so enticing," Emma said. "Once you have my statement can I leave? New Orleans, I mean?"

"Just leave us a way to contact you, and you're free to go wherever you'd like," Jackson said. "You're the victim here, Emma. If anyone tries to make things hard on you, remind them of that."

"Thank you," Emma said. "I know you've been helping Shaye."

"I'm afraid I wasn't much help. Shaye put the entire thing together."

Emma glanced over at Shaye, who looked slightly uncomfortable with the compliment. "I wouldn't have made it this far without her," Emma said.

"You're stronger than you think," Shaye said quietly.

"Then let's get this over with," Emma said. "Can we go now?"

"Absolutely. I assume you want to drive yourself and meet there?"

"Yes."

"Okay," Jackson said. "I'll go let my superior know I'm heading back to the station."

"Do you need me right now as well?" Shaye asked.

"We'll definitely need you, especially once we have Ron in custody. The DA will need your testimony to build the case against him, but it doesn't have to be today. If you need to get back to your mother…"

Shaye nodded agreement, but the expression on her face wasn't one of concern for her mother. No, Emma had seen that look before—like a dog with a bone. There was something Shaye wanted to get away and do, but Emma would bet anything that it had nothing to do with Corrine.

"Go straight to the station," Shaye said to Emma, "and call me when you leave." She looked at Jackson. "Can you send someone to pick up her things at the hotel while she's being questioned? I don't want her returning there. In case he's watching."

"I've got it covered," Jackson said.

"Thanks." Shaye gave Emma a quick hug and headed off down the sidewalk.

Jackson stared after her several seconds and Emma felt a tiny quiver in her stomach when she realized his interest in Shaye was deeper than this case. She wondered if Shaye had noticed, but guessed that she hadn't. A man would probably have to advertise in neon before Shaye paid attention. But still, a tiny sliver of happiness ran through her. Every day was an opportunity for something better. Maybe her horrible situation contained a silver lining after all, for Jackson and Shaye.

It was something she planned to daydream about on her long drive to California.

Only happy thoughts from now on. Even if they were about other people.

Shaye jumped in her SUV and took off. As she drove, she pulled out her cell phone. On the way to Emma's house, she'd received a call from Charlie Evans. She hadn't answered because she'd been on the phone with Eleonore, but he'd left a message that she'd listened to just as she'd pulled up to the curb at Emma's house.

She pressed Play on the message and Charlie's voice boomed over her truck speakers.

Hey, uh, this is Charlie Evans from Wellman Oil and Gas. You talked to me the other day about David. I thought of something I wanted to tell you. Anyway, I'm at home if you want to call.

She hit the Call button and Charlie answered on the first ring.

"This is Shaye Archer."

"Oh, yeah. I remembered something...I don't know

that it means anything, but you said to call…"

"You never know what might be important. What did you remember?"

"One night offshore, one of the engineers got real drunk and was acting a fool. We were all laughing at him and David said he was dumber than Dugas."

"Is Dugas another employee?"

"We ain't got a Dugas working here. I didn't think about it at the time because I got a cousin Toby that says the same thing, but then I remembered it and thought you might want to know."

Shaye frowned. If there was a point to Charlie's story, either he hadn't made it yet, or she had missed it entirely. "I'm not sure I understand."

"Shit. I'm not explaining it good at all. Dugas was a half-wit that lived in the place Toby grew up. The people that live there say it, but I don't see why David would know it, unless he was from there too or had been there at least."

Shaye's pulse quickened. "What's the town?"

"I don't know that it's a town, really. More like a spot in the road a couple miles from Port Sulphur. My cousin called it Hamet, but I ain't never seen it on a map."

"Port Sulphur…Highway 23?"

"Yeah, that's it."

"Thank you for telling me."

Shaye pulled into the nearest parking lot and used her phone for a quick Google maps search. No surprise when Hamet didn't pull up, but Port Sulphur was only a forty-five minute drive. She tossed her phone on the passenger seat, but when she went to put her SUV in gear, she stopped and reached for the phone again. This time, she searched "David Grange" and "Hamet."

Then she gasped.

Bayou News, June 2000
Hamet Boy Drowns

A ten-year-old boy from Hamet drowned last week. A local fisherman pulled the body out of the bayou and identified the boy as David Grange Jr., son of resident grocery store owner David Grange Sr. and wife Abigail Grange. The family could not be reached for comment.

The next link was an obituary for David Grange Sr. His death was one week after his son's drowning and no cause of death was given. The timing made Shaye wonder if it was suicide. Surely if there had been any indication of foul play, in either death, the police would have investigated. She did a search on the wife and came up with an address in Port Sulphur. No phone number, but then the questions she had weren't the kind you asked people over the phone.

She pulled out of the parking lot and headed the opposite direction of the city. Emma was safely tucked away at the police station and would soon be far away from New Orleans. The police were looking for Ron, and with any luck, he'd be behind bars soon. The worst was behind her client, but if Shaye could get Emma answers about the stranger she'd married, it would be the icing on the cake.

Not knowing was awful.

Like a slow-moving cancer silently eating away at you.

CHAPTER TWENTY-THREE

Jackson looked through the one-way window into the interrogation room as Detective Murphy took Emma's statement. For Emma's comfort, he wished he could have taken it himself, but between the information Shaye had been feeding him and what Emma told him before Murphy arrived, Jackson figured he was pretty much up to speed on everything relevant.

"Hell of a thing." The desk sergeant stepped up next to him. "That poor woman thought her problems were over when she killed that son of a bitch she was married to, and now this."

Jackson nodded. "It's an awful lot for one person to handle in a short span of time."

"I heard the attack on Corrine Archer might tie into this somehow. You know anything about that?"

"Yeah. Corrine's daughter is a PI. Emma hired Shaye to find her stalker because Vincent blew her off."

The sergeant shook his head. "I know our hands are usually tied until we have something viable, but it wouldn't have killed Vincent to look into it."

"It might have. He seems to think anything but driving

that desk will send him to an early grave."

The sergeant clapped him on the shoulder. "Hang in there. I know being saddled with Vincent is keeping you from doing the work you want to do, but it won't be forever. Vincent will retire or he'll be assigned another new guy. Either way, you'll be in the thick of it soon enough."

"I hope so," Jackson said as the sergeant headed down the hall for the front desk.

Jackson stared at Emma as she wiped tears from her eyes with her fingers. It didn't have to come to this. Emma should never have had to endure what she did the last six days. Shaye's mother shouldn't have been attacked. That poor old woman and the paramedic shouldn't be dead.

All because the police's hands were tied and Vincent was too lazy to check anyway.

His cell phone rang and he checked the display. "Shaye? Is something wrong?"

"No. Actually, I'm tracking down a lead on David Grange." She told him about Charlie's phone call and the news article. "I'm on my way to Port Sulphur to talk to the widow. If the man calling himself David Grange was from around there, maybe she'll recognize him."

"Wow." Jackson took a couple of seconds to process what Shaye had told him. "Are you sure you want to keep digging? The cops are combing the streets for Ron. The hunt is almost over."

"The hunt for the stalker is almost over, but Emma still doesn't know who she married and why he flipped on her. I know it won't change anything that's happened, but I think if I can get her some answers, it will help her move forward."

Because Jackson knew Shaye was speaking from experience, he couldn't find a solid argument to use to try to talk her out of her plan. "I get it. But be careful. That widow has had her share of tragedy, too. She might not want to talk."

"Then I'll find someone who will. I'll give you a call if I find something. Is Emma at the station?"

"She's giving her statement now."

"Good. Make sure she gets out of there safe. I don't want to hear from her again until she's at least a state away or Ron's behind bars."

Shaye disconnected and Jackson slipped his phone back in his pocket and frowned. Something about Shaye's trip to Port Sulphur was bothering him but he couldn't put his finger on why. Ron wasn't from Port Sulphur, or anywhere near there. Nor did they have any reason to think David had ever told him the truth about his own past. The likelihood of Shaye running across Ron was slim to none.

But still, the whole thing left him with a general feeling of unease. He'd feel better when Shaye was back in New Orleans, in residence at her mother's heavily secured home. At least until Ron was behind bars.

Traffic was practically nonexistent on the lone road to Port Sulphur, so Shaye managed the drive in less than forty minutes. Her cell phone service was sketchy, so it took her a bit to locate the widow's house, but finally, she pulled through an ornate entry and down a driveway lined with azalea bushes. The house was bigger than she would have thought she'd find in such a tiny place. Not as big as Corrine's, but the construction was solid and it was kept nicely. Owning a grocery store must be a lucrative business in Port Sulphur.

She parked in the middle of the circular drive and knocked on the massive hand-carved wooden door. About twenty seconds later, the door swung open and a sixtyish, heavyset Creole woman looked out at her. "Can I help you?" the woman asked.

"My name is Shaye Archer. I'm a private investigator from New Orleans and I'm trying to track some information for a client. I wondered if I could speak to Mrs. Grange."

The woman narrowed her eyes. "Mrs. Grange ain't got no business in New Orleans. No friends or family either. Can't imagine she could help you."

"I'm trying to get information on a man that I believe used to live in the area. I was hoping Mrs. Grange knew him."

"Mrs. Grange ain't left the house for almost fifteen years. Why you asking her?"

"Because the man I need information on has been using the name David Grange."

The woman's eyes widened. "What you mean, using the name?"

"He's been living, working, has a Social Security card, and even got married using the name David Grange. I've been trying to track him and information led me here. Imagine my surprise when I find out the real David Grange passed away when he was a boy."

"You think it's one of those identity theft things? I seen that on the news."

"I think it could be. That's why I'd like to talk to Mrs. Grange. See if she has any idea who might have had access to her son's information in order to use it."

The woman nodded and motioned her inside. "I'm Sissy. Been working for Mrs. Grange since she married. Worked for her mama before that."

Shaye stepped into the entry and glanced around. A huge circular staircase sat at the back of the entry, ornate iron spindles gleaming with polish. A formal living room was off to the left and looked like something out of an old picture book with its dated artwork and stiff and uncomfortable-looking furniture. To the right was a library, dark wooden bookcases covering every square inch of wall space. The carpets and decor in the entryway were as dated as the living room, and Shaye decided Sissy hadn't been exaggerating when she described Mrs. Grange as a hermit.

"You thinking it could be family?" Sissy asked. "None comes to visit, but I know she's got cousins and such. I always say trusting someone just because you related is a good way to get screwed."

"It certainly can be, and family would be the most logical explanation."

The woman looked at her again, her expression conflicted. "I suppose it wouldn't hurt for you to talk to her, but I gotta warn you, Mrs. Grange ain't been right since her boy passed. She sits in this house and stares out the window or at a wall and that's about it. Me and Mina manage to make her eat a couple times a day, but she don't do much else."

Shaye frowned. "Are you saying she doesn't speak?"

"She *can* speak, if that's what you're asking. She just doesn't. Told me one time there wasn't nothing worth saying."

It sounded to Shaye like Abigail Grange had checked out of life. She understood the desire. When Shaye had first gone to live with Corrine, she felt that way every second of every day. It didn't happen as often now, but sometimes, when the nightmares were the worst, the thought would pass through her mind.

Was it worth it?

So far, the answer had always been yes, and thankfully, it was getting easier to say it.

"I understand," Shaye said. "There's things in my past that I don't like to think about. I promise I'm not here to upset her."

Sissy studied her for several seconds. Something in Shaye's expression must have convinced the housekeeper of her sincerity because she nodded. "Come with me."

Shaye followed her down the hallway to the back of the house. At the end of the hallway, Sissy knocked lightly on a door, then opened it and stepped inside. "Mrs.

Grange. There's a lady here that needs to speak to you."

Shaye stepped to Sissy's side and got her first look at Abigail Grange, who sat in a rocking chair in front of a picture window. If someone had checked out of life, people often said they were a shadow of their former self. Abigail Grange didn't even have enough substance to be a shadow. Her pale skin was almost translucent and hung on her tiny frame like fabric. She looked over at them, her gaze seeming to go right through them and into the hall.

"Will you speak to her?" Sissy asked.

Abigail nodded, and Sissy motioned Shaye toward the window.

Shaye walked over to where Abigail sat and took a seat in a chair a couple feet away, not wanting to stand over her while they were talking. "Mrs. Grange, my name is Shaye Archer. I'm a private investigator from New Orleans. There's a man I've been trying to get information on who I think used to live in Hamet. He's been using your son's name."

Abigail looked perplexed. "Why would someone do that?"

Shaye reminded herself that Abigail had been out of society for a long time, and thus far, Shaye had yet to see a television. It was possible Abigail had never heard the term "identity theft."

"Sometimes," Shaye said, "people pretend to be someone else because they don't want anyone to know their true identity."

"Why would that bother a person?"

"The most common reason is because they're involved in criminal activity. They might be wanted for crimes under their real name, so they assume someone else's identity in order to hide from the law."

Abigail frowned. "And you think someone is using David's name for such a thing? Has the man you're looking for committed a crime?"

"The man in question is deceased, but he abused his wife. The question of his identity didn't come up until after his death, and his wife would like to know who she was really married to."

"Oh. I imagine that must be horrible for her."

Abigail's expression and voice were mildly sympathetic, but it was clear to Shaye that the woman wasn't completely in the conversation. More like she was drifting on the outside of it.

"Can you tell me your son's Social Security number, so I can verify if his identity is the one my client's husband was using?"

Abigail looked up at Sissy. "My small box, Sissy."

"Yes, ma'am," Sissy said and retrieved a jewelry box from her nightstand.

Abigail opened the jewelry box and her eyes filled with tears. She lifted a photo and stroked it with her finger, then handed it to Shaye. "My son."

Shaye took the photo and looked down at the smiling boy, holding up a large fish. He looked like his mother, or at least, like his mother would look if she had some weight and color to her and hadn't aged beyond her years. "He's beautiful," Shaye said, a lump forming in her throat. How awful it had to be to lose a child. She couldn't fathom losing someone she loved. In fact, it was something she deliberately avoided thinking about.

Abigail took the photo back and handed Shaye a Social Security card. Shaye checked the information she had stored in her phone, and her pulse ticked up a notch. It was a match to the employment records from Wellman Oil and Gas.

"Did you report your son's passing to the Social Security Administration?" Shaye asked.

"I thought the doctor did that," Abigail said.

Shaye looked over at Sissy, who shook her head. "Doc LaFleur is who she's talking about, but he wasn't no spring chicken and had his hands full just keeping people tended to. My guess is the paperwork never got filed."

Shaye nodded. If the SSA was never notified of David's passing, that explained how Emma's husband was able to use his identity. If he was from the area, he might have guessed that the death had never been reported. She pulled up a picture of the man calling himself David Grange and turned the phone to face Abigail.

"Do you recognize this man?"

Abigail took one look at the phone and wailed. "No!" She threw her hands up in front of her face as if she were being attacked. Her entire body shook as she sobbed.

"Mina!" Sissy yelled and ran over to Abigail, trying to calm her down.

Shaye jumped up from her chair, feeling completely

helpless as another woman rushed into the room and over to Abigail. The other woman pushed Sissy out of the way and grabbed Abigail's arms, speaking to her in a low, level voice. Sissy grabbed Shaye's arm and pulled her toward the door.

"You said you wouldn't upset her," Sissy said as she stomped down the hall.

Shaye practically jogged to keep up with the woman, still trying to process Abigail's unexpected reaction. Before she'd had her outburst, Shaye wouldn't have even thought her possible of such emotion. "I didn't mean to upset her. I don't even know why she's upset."

"What did you show her?"

Shaye held up her phone.

Sissy gasped and her hand flew over her mouth. She reached out and took the phone from Shaye, her hand shaking, and pulled it closer to her face. "Lord, Jesus. Is this the man? The man that stole David's identity?"

"Yes. You know him?"

Sissy turned the phone away and pushed it back at Shaye. "I never thought I'd see that face again. It's Jonathon Bourg. The last time I seen him he was no more than fifteen or sixteen, but I'd know that face anywhere."

"Why does he upset you and Abigail?"

"Because he killed David."

CHAPTER TWENTY-FOUR

Jackson left the interrogation window and headed back to his desk, but couldn't sit still. He ended up pacing the rows until Vincent yelled at him to sit down or go outside. He claimed Jackson was making him tired. Jackson figured he was probably telling the truth. The man was so inert, just watching someone else move probably exhausted him. He was just about to go outside and take a walk around the block when he heard Detective Reynolds take a call about Ron Duhon.

He lurked at the detective's desk until he hung up the phone. "Was that a tip on Ron Duhon?" Jackson asked.

"Yeah." Detective Reynolds grabbed his keys from his desk. "Is Murphy still taking the Frederick woman's statement?"

Jackson nodded.

Reynolds looked at him for several seconds, clearly contemplating something, then looked over at Vincent. "Hey, can I borrow Lamotte for this check? Murphy's tied up in interrogation."

Vincent waved a hand in dismissal. "Please. Get him out of here."

"Thanks," Jackson said as they exited the building. "What's the tip?"

"We circulated pictures of Ron this morning among our street contacts. One of them called in and said a maintenance worker saw Ron at the Midnight Moon motel. It will probably turn out to be nothing, but there's always a chance the worker got it right."

Jackson nodded. Chasing a long shot was better than stagnating at his desk.

Shaye struggled to maintain her cool, but was certain her expression was anything but composed. "But...the report said it was accidental."

Sissy nodded. "I think you best come with me. I'm gonna need a shot of bourbon. Maybe two."

Shaye followed Sissy down a side hallway and into a kitchen at the rear of the house. Like all the other rooms, this one was stuck in time as well. Sissy went straight for a locked cupboard on the far wall and removed a key from her pocket to unlock it. She pulled a bottle of bourbon out and placed it on the counter along with two glasses.

"We have to keep it locked or Abigail will help herself to a bottle," Sissy said as she poured. "Damn near killed herself with vodka once. That's when Mina and me started locking it up. Didn't want to remove it altogether as sometimes we slip a bit in Abigail's afternoon tea to help her sleep." She placed the glasses on the table and sat down. Shaye slipped into the chair across from her and noticed that Sissy's hand still shook as she took a big sip of the whiskey.

"Jonathon and Nathan Bourg was twins," Sissy said. "They lived in the swamp around Hamet with their mama, Helen. All the kids was supposed to go to school in Port Sulphur, but they didn't show half the time. I know it's the law and all, but I'm guessing the teachers was happier when they weren't there."

"Why's that?"

"They was what polite people call 'troubled,' but I think it went deeper than that." Sissy took another drink of the bourbon. "They used to come into town and sit on the bench outside the general store. They rarely had money, so they wasn't there to shop. They'd just sit there and stare at people with them black eyes. You didn't dare look back. Not if you wanted to sleep that night. It was like looking at a snake. Cold. Inhuman."

Twins! Shaye struggled to absorb and process what Sissy had told her. She knew Ron couldn't be Jonathon's twin. Ron's identity had been simple to verify, but if Jonathon had a brother, he could be Emma's stalker. Where they chasing the wrong guy? "What about their father?"

"As far as the townspeople knew, they wasn't one, but there was rumors." Sissy locked her gaze on Shaye. "What I'm about to tell you, I ain't never told another soul. Never intended to." She took a deep breath and blew it out. "I was walking home from Mrs. Godeaux's one night. That would be Mrs. Grange's mama. Mrs. Grange was nineteen at the time and had just gotten engaged to Mr. Grange.

"On nights when the moon wasn't out," Sissy continued, "I always walked down Main Street and then to my house—it's about a mile outside of town—but when the moon was full, sometimes I'd take the path along the bayou all the way home. There's something about moonlight on the water that makes a person calm after a hard day of work, and Mrs. Godeaux was not an easy woman to work for. Anyway, I was just outside of town when I heard a man and woman arguing up ahead of me. The woman was yelling at the man as how he couldn't lay with her and make babies then pretend it never happened. I couldn't hear what he said, his voice was too low, but whatever it was, she weren't happy about it. She told him that she didn't want his money and that one day he'd pay for treating her like trash."

"You didn't recognize the woman's voice?"

"No, but I didn't need to. Next thing I knew, I heard someone running on the path straight toward me. The man yelled for her to wait, but she kept going. I don't know why I did it, but I ducked into the bushes and watched until she ran by. It was Helen Bourg."

"Do you think the man was someone from Port Sulphur?"

"I know who the man was. I recognized his voice when he called after her. It was Mr. Grange."

"Oh no! Do you think Mrs. Grange knew?"

"I don't think Mr. Grange ever told her, if that's what

you're asking, but there was whispers. Helen wasn't exactly known for being a lady. Most of the boys round town had a go with her when she was a teen. Word was she got Mr. Grange drunk and had a go at him one night at a bonfire party when Mrs. Grange had the flu."

"You think she was trying to get pregnant by Mr. Grange?"

Sissy's eyebrows shot up. "I guess I hadn't thought about it that far, but I suppose it's possible. Given that she hadn't gotten pregnant before then, I guess she could have been trying to snag a savior. The Granges were the wealthiest family in the area."

"What about Helen's parents? Where were they while their daughter was running wild?"

"Her mama died when she was a little girl, maybe three or so. Her daddy…" Sissy swallowed and made the sign of the cross. "I don't like to speak ill of the dead, but there wasn't nothing nice about Randal Bourg. I ain't got no proof, but there was talk that he had his way with the girl himself, and he traded her to men he knew to pay off gambling debts."

Shaye's stomach rolled and she forced the nausea back. "How old?"

"Ten, maybe younger."

"Why didn't anyone do something?"

"Some of us called social services, but we didn't have no proof. They did one of those checks, but the girl said it weren't true. I guess they couldn't force a medical exam over gossip."

"Probably not," Shaye said, but it made her blood boil. No wonder Helen was off. No wonder her own children were troubled. "I'm guessing Mrs. Grange pretended she didn't hear any of the rumors and hoped Helen Bourg would go away. Did she?"

"Pretty much. She never made no scene or nothing. Just disappeared into the swamp. Came into town to get her welfare checks every month and buy some food, but that was it. Once the boys was ten or so, she sent them instead. Then Nathan died."

A guilty sense of relief passed over Shaye when she heard those words. Jonathon's twin couldn't be the stalker. They had gotten it right. Ron was the criminal. "How did he die?"

"Drowned. He had crab traps set up along the bayou that he worked. He sold the crabs to the grocery store. People here like 'em right out of the water. Anyway, it was right after one of those tropical storms came through leaving thunderstorms behind that it happened. The tide was running high and fast. Best anyone can figure, he slipped off the bank and got tangled in his lines and couldn't get out. By the time Jonathon found him, it was too late."

"I guess Helen came to town then."

"Once. She took one look at the body, turned around without saying a word, and headed right back to Hamet. Ain't no one set eyes on her since. People say Jonathon left when he was eighteen. Without Jonathon there to cash her checks, we thought we'd see Helen again, but she never surfaced."

"She might be dead."

Sissy nodded. "Dead or gone. Don't know that it makes a difference to anyone here, especially with what Jonathon did."

"Tell me about it."

"Jonathon was beside himself over Nathan's death. He went straight to the grocery store, still dripping wet from pulling Nathan's body out of the water, and lit into Mr. Grange. Told him it was all his fault. That if he took care of his responsibilities Nathan wouldn't have been crabbing in a storm for a couple of dollars. Told him he'd pay for what he'd done."

"What did Mr. Grange do?"

"I didn't see it myself, but my friend was there and said Mr. Grange just stood there looking horrified. Maybe because Jonathon was airing his dirty laundry in the store. Maybe because he was afraid of what people would tell Mrs. Grange. Maybe it was guilt over the way those boys had to live. Ain't nobody knows for sure."

Sissy sniffed and wiped her nose with her fingers. "About two weeks later, David Jr. drowned. He'd gone fishing like he always did, and when he didn't come home, Mr. Grange and a neighbor went looking for him. They pulled him out of the bayou a little ways down from his usual fishing hole. There was a crowd of people on Main Street when they brought the body in. That was my day off and I'd just come out of the drugstore. I watched as they carried his body into the doctor's office. Then I caught sight of him—Jonathon was standing across the street, watching them. He was smiling and I knew it was him. Just knew it."

"What did the doctor say?"

"He said it looked like an accident. Wasn't no bump on his head or anything else to indicate someone had struck the boy, but I ask you, how hard would it be to hold a sixty-pound child under water long enough to kill him? Jonathon was a big strong boy while David was slight like his mother."

Shaye sat back in her chair and blew out a breath. Sissy had provided the answer to so many questions, but one still remained—had Jonathon's childhood made him a monster or was he a born sociopath? Had he simply managed to fool Emma until he couldn't control it any longer? Or had he left Hamet and all his evil thoughts behind when he'd joined the military only for Ron Duhon to recognize him for what he really was and bring the monster back?

"I don't suppose you know where they lived?" Shaye asked. Someone in Hamet might have known Helen. Might have known more about the boys' childhood.

Sissy's eyes widened. "You ain't thinking of going into that swamp. No, ma'am. I can't let you do that. It's the house that bred evil out there. Ain't nothing good can come from disturbing things that's best left at rest."

"If I don't get answers for my client, *she* can't ever be at rest." Shaye leaned forward and looked Sissy directly in the eyes. "My client killed Jonathon. She thought she married one man and he turned out to be someone else. If I can tell her exactly who that someone else was and why, she'll know the truth about the man she married. The man who managed to convince an intelligent woman with a nursing degree that he was normal and sane, until he wasn't."

Sissy's expression instantly shifted from frightened to sympathetic. "Oh, that poor girl. I know she did right in killing him, but that's because I know the truth about Jonathon. Your client don't have that to fall back on."

Sissy stared at her for several seconds, clearly conflicted. Finally, she spoke. "I went to the house once a long time ago with some church ladies. We thought we'd bring Ms. Bourg some food and some clothes for the boys. She ran us off with a shotgun before we could even get out of the car. But I think I remember where it was. Maybe not exactly, but I can get you close."

Sissy reached over and put her hand on Shaye's arm. "And I'll pray. You're gonna need it."

CHAPTER TWENTY-FIVE

Emma splashed cold water on her face, then patted it dry with a paper towel. Giving her statement had been harder than she'd thought it would be. The numb feeling that had settled over her that morning had disappeared and with each sentence, it was as if she were living the horror all over again.

It's over. You can leave now.

She headed out of the restroom and to reception. That's what she had to keep reminding herself. Her luggage from the hotel was waiting for her at the reception desk and the SUV had a full tank of gas. There was nothing else to stop her from leaving. Hell, maybe she'd get to California, get on an airplane, and leave the country.

Without a passport.

Shit. She stopped in her tracks. She'd been so focused on leaving that she hadn't even considered the things she had to have in order to establish herself in another state. She had license and credit cards on her, but her passport and Social Security card were tucked away in her jewelry box in her bedroom. Along with her mother's wedding rings.

She hurried to reception. "I'm Emma Frederick. Is Jackson Lamotte available?"

"No ma'am. He left a couple minutes ago. Can I help you with something?"

"Are the police still at Mrs. Pearson's house? I need to get some things from my house across the street, and I'd feel better if they were there."

"Let me check." He made a quick phone call. "Two units are still on-site processing the crime scene. Best guess, they should be there another thirty minutes or so."

Emma bit her lower lip. She could always leave her house key at the police station and have Shaye go there later to collect her stuff. But she hated to ask the woman for another favor, and there was always the risk that someone would break in. She could get another passport or Social Security card, but her mother's wedding rings were priceless.

Damn it. Why hadn't she thought of them before now? If her mind wasn't crap, she would have gotten all this stuff the day she was at the house with Shaye.

The police are right across the street. It's broad daylight. You can call Shaye on your way and tell her what you're doing.

"Thanks." She grabbed her overnight bag and headed for her car before she changed her mind.

The motel manager flipped through the ring of keys, clearly agitated. "I don't know why you cops can't find something better to do than hassle honest businessmen."

Jackson glanced around the fleabag motel and smirked. "I'd be willing to bet that the only honest thing that's happened here in the last twenty-four hours was the two of us showing up."

The manager shot him a dirty look. "I should make you get a warrant."

"Go ahead," Reynolds said, "but when we get that warrant, we'll be sending a forensic team to inspect every square inch of this place. That includes your business records."

The manager stomped up the stairs and walked to a room at the far end of the building. "The guy paid in advance for three days. Said he was leaving town after that." The manager banged on the door. "It's the motel manager. I need you to open up."

They waited, but no sound came from the unit.

"Is there a back window or door?" Reynolds asked.

"No." The manager pointed at the door and window on the front of the unit. "You're looking at the only two ways in and out."

"Open it," Reynolds said, and pulled out his pistol, nodding to Jackson to do the same.

The manager opened the door and practically ran backward. Reynolds shoved the door open with his shoulder and moved inside, ready to fire, Jackson right behind him.

The smell hit them immediately, and they both flung their arms up over their nose and mouth. Reynolds headed for the bathroom and took a look inside.

"That's our guy," Reynolds said. He reached for his phone as he made tracks for the door.

Jackson pressed his arms tighter over his nose and mouth and stepped inside the tiny bathroom. He had to be sure, and one glance was all he needed. The body in the bathtub was definitely Ron Duhon. Jackson had never met the man before, but was certain he'd looked better. His body was slumped in the tub sideways, his legs hanging over the side. The band around his biceps and needle sticking out of his arm told Jackson almost everything he needed to know.

Still holding his breath, he grabbed a washcloth from the sink and stepped up to the bathtub. Leaning over, he grasped the man's hand with the washcloth and moved the wrist and fingers. They flexed, which meant rigor had already come and gone.

"What the hell are you doing?" Reynolds's voice boomed behind him.

Jackson dropped the washcloth and hurried out of the motel. When he reached the balcony, he expelled the breath he'd been holding and sucked in a huge gulp of hot air. "We were wrong," he gasped.

"Wrong? Are you crazy? That's Ron Duhon. I'd bet my badge on it."

Jackson nodded. "It's Ron Duhon, but he's been dead at least twenty-four hours."

"So?"

"That means he couldn't have killed that paramedic

last night at the hospital. He's not Emma Frederick's stalker."

"Fuck," Reynolds said.

Emma broke several speeding laws on the way to her house, but she didn't even care. As soon as she had taken care of this one last errand, she planned on breaking even more. In fact, she wasn't even going to consider doing the speed limit until she'd crossed the Louisiana state line into Texas. Then maybe she'd think about slowing down. Maybe.

She pulled up in front of Patty's house and hurried to the front door. Patty had still been talking to the police when Emma left earlier to give her statement. She had no idea if the Realtor had been transferred to the hospital or was back home, but she'd already decided to drop the key through her mail slot. That way, if Patty was resting, Emma wouldn't be the cause of her having to get up and answer the door. With Patty's condition, her breathing was a big concern, and the stress of the situation would probably have caused her muscles to knot.

She dropped the key through the mail slot and heard it *ping* on the tile entryway, then dashed back to her car and rounded the block to her own home. Two cop cars were still parked in front of Mrs. Pearson's house, but officers were getting into one of the cars as she parked. The officers from the second car were nowhere in sight, so Emma assumed they were still inside.

She hurried to the front door and let herself in, determined to get in and out before the cops left. She practically ran up the stairs to the bedroom and pulled open her nightstand. A single folder inside contained all her important documents. She'd always meant to rent a safe-deposit box for the items, but had never gotten around to it. A quick check determined that her Social Security card, birth certificate, and passport were inside. She placed the folder on the nightstand and pulled out a velvet-covered ring box. Her mother's wedding ring glittered inside. She slipped the box in her pocket and grabbed the folder.

Three blind mice. Three blind mice.

The whistling came from the doorway behind her.

Her breath caught in her throat and pain rocketed through her chest as if she'd been shot. It wasn't possible. The police were right outside. He wouldn't risk coming after her here. Not now.

The whistling stopped. "I knew you'd come home again."

Emma whirled around and gasped.

Three blind mice.

CHAPTER TWENTY-SIX

Shaye slowed to a stop and studied the rudimentary drawing Sissy had made for her. The problem she'd run into was that swamp roads weren't clearly marked. Instead, Sissy had indicated places to turn with landmarks like "tree split by lightning." A decade ago, those directions might have been stellar, but years of Gulf weather had made some of them a challenge to spot. She'd already encountered two dead ends and was about to turn around again.

Traipsing around the swamp with a paper drawing was a huge departure from GPS and Google Maps. But even if Hamet roads were visible on a satellite rendering, her phone service had been fading in and out ever since she left the highway.

Her phone buzzed and she saw it was a message from Emma.

Returning to my house to get passport, social security card, and my mother's wedding rings and to drop off house key to Patty. Police are still there.

Shaye frowned. She would have preferred if Emma had driven straight to the interstate and headed the opposite direction from her house, but if the police were still out front, then she would be all right. Ron wouldn't be foolish enough to turn up at his own murder scene, not in broad daylight.

Be careful.

She typed the message and hit Send, then sighed when service dropped again and the message remained unsent.

She put her SUV in reverse and tried one more time to locate three cypress trees at an intersection that formed a triangle. This was the last road, and it was proving to be the most elusive. After another ten minutes of driving around, she was almost ready to give up when she spotted two trees and what was left of a third to her right. She wheeled her SUV down the road and stopped to inspect the trees. It could be the set Sissy was talking about.

What the hell. She guided the SUV onto the dirt path. Worst case, she'd be turning around again. The path was filled with big holes, forcing her to inch along. The alternative would have been bouncing in and out of them so hard that it might cause physical damage, to her and the SUV. The brush on the side of the path grew closer and more dense until she could hear it scratching the outside of the truck.

The trees grew together overhead, forming a canopy over the path, and the farther she drove, the less light streamed through until it seemed more like dusk than afternoon. The tree limbs got lower and lower until she could hear moss running across the top of her SUV. Her headlights came on and she lifted her foot from the accelerator, slowing down to a crawl. The path was overgrown, but not so much that it appeared untraveled. If Helen had left when Jonathon did, someone had continued to come here afterward, at least for some time. Maybe not often, but often enough to keep the path from becoming completely grown over.

None of that did anything to diminish the creepiness of it all. The dark, mostly overgrown path with a canopy of trees and hanging moss looked like something out of a horror movie. The path made a sharp right and she guided the SUV around the corner, then slammed on the brakes as a shack appeared right in front of her. The SUV lurched and stopped only inches from the front porch.

If the path had looked like something out of a horror movie, the shack held the starring role. It was constructed of wood and tin. The wood was gray and rotting, the entire structure sagging on the right side. The tin was rusted and Shaye could see holes in the sheets that made up the roof.

The overwhelming desire to put her SUV in reverse and get the hell out of there washed over Shaye like a tidal wave. Sissy had been born in the swamps and held some old beliefs about haunts and such. Shaye didn't tend toward fanciful beliefs, but she couldn't argue with Sissy on this one. The house felt wrong. Oppressive.

Nothing good had happened here.

Given its condition, no one was living there, so a look around wouldn't hurt. If Helen was the last to live here, maybe there was a family photo left behind, something concrete she could show to Emma when she explained her mysterious husband's past. She reached for her purse and pulled out her nine-millimeter. The house may be devoid of people, but that didn't mean swamp creatures hadn't taken up residence, and many of them could be deadly, especially if they felt their home was threatened.

She left her headlights on, hoping to cast some light into the dark shack, but still grabbed her flashlight out of the glove box. She carefully chose her first step onto the dilapidated front porch. One wrong selection, and she'd go straight through to the ground. It wasn't the drop that concerned her, but the thought of rusty nails piercing her skin. There was a time in her life when she slathered on Neosporin like most women did body lotion. She had no desire to revisit that.

She paused in front of the windows to peer inside, but the grime on the glass prevented almost all of the glow from her headlights from entering the structure. In the dim light, it was difficult to make out anything inside except shadows. At least none of the shadows were moving. She continued to the door and found it contained no lock or even a doorknob. She pushed it open and stepped inside.

The front of the shack was one room that, based on the remnants of furniture, served as kitchen, living, and dining. The cooking area consisted of a single counter with rusted cook plate and broken dishes. Next to the counter, a lantern with a busted globe sat on top of an ice chest. No electricity. Not really surprising. A lot of the remote bayou houses lived without running water or electricity.

A tiny table was collapsed on the floor in front of the counter, its wooden legs rotted in two. A faded couch sat on the wall opposite the counter, its stuffing pulled out of the cushions and tucked into the corners in round bowls that looked out of place with the rest of the random chaos. Shaye hoped that whatever lived there had since moved on to nicer quarters.

The entire room couldn't have been more than two hundred square feet. One door stood on the interior wall, probably leading to the bedrooms. Given the remote location, a bathroom was probably a stretch. She lifted her gun up in ready position and approached the door.

She was just about to step through when her cell phone rang. Involuntarily, she jumped back and leveled her pistol at the doorway to fire. Then her mind caught up with her body and she pulled the phone out of her pocket and her pulse ticked up a notch when she saw it was Jackson. She hoped her service would hold long enough for him to talk.

"This is Shaye," she said, trying to stand very still so that she maintained reception.

"We found Ron Duhon."

Relief rushed through Shaye and she felt her body relax. "That's great!"

"I wish that were the case. He's dead. And he's been dead for at least a day."

Confusion coursed through her. "That's not possible. He killed the paramedic last night and attacked that patient…"

"It couldn't have been him. Shaye, the stalker is still out there, and Emma's not answering her phone."

Shaye struggled not to panic. She had to think. "Emma went back to her house to get some things. The police were still there."

"The last of the forensics team left ten minutes ago to come here and process the motel where we found Ron."

"You've got to get to her house. Make sure she's safe— Holy shit!"

Something banged at the back of the house and Shaye nearly dropped the phone.

"What's wrong?" Jackson asked. "Where are you?"

"I'm in the shack David lived in," she whispered. "Something else is here with me. Hold on."

"Wait—"

She slipped the phone in her pocket and brought her pistol back up to the ready position as she inched toward the doorway. The room she stepped into was smaller than the front room and contained three sets of twin mattresses, shoved next to each other in a corner. Like the couch, the stuffing had been pulled out and used to house God knows what. Her heart pounded in her chest, beating so loudly it sounded like a drum inside her head, breaking the absolute silence. A door stood on the left wall of the room, and she crept toward it, gun leveled and ready to fire.

She was completely unprepared for what was inside.

The woman whose arm was chained to the bed was nothing more than skin and bones with tattered rags draped over her wrinkled skin. Scars from cuts covered every square inch of her body that Shaye could see, the red and purple slits practically glowing against the stark white flesh.

326

Her head was slumped to the side, eyes closed and her tongue partially protruding from her dried white lips. But the worst part was the eyes, or what was left of them. They'd been carved out while she was still alive, a trail of dried blood falling from the sockets to her chest. Even though her face was haggard and bruised, Shaye recognized the jawline and cheekbones.

It was Helen Bourg.

A chunk of the ceiling lay on the floor at the end of the bed, dust still rising from tin sheets. That was the source of the noise Shaye had heard, but she had no explanation for the woman.

Decomposition hadn't yet begun, so she couldn't have been dead long, but the real question was how long she'd been shackled to her own bed and more importantly, who had done it? Had Jonathon returned home to "take care" of the person who'd shaped him into what he was?

A nightstand next to the bed had tipped over and the drawer had slid out. Shaye could see aged yellow paper and photos inside. She hesitated before inching toward the nightstand, then bent over and picked up two of the photos. The first was one of Helen Bourg holding her babies.

Her three babies!

Shaye's pulse quickened. The photo was cracked and yellowed, but there was no mistaking the three babies with blue blankets. Sissy had never mentioned a third child. Shaye blew out a breath. *Think.* This was a poor woman and probably a home birth. One of the babies probably didn't survive.

She reached down to pick up another photo and gasped. The three boys standing in front of the shack were at least ten years old. One was a couple inches shorter than the other two, but there was no doubt they were siblings. All three wore cutoff blue jeans and nothing else. Although their arms and legs were bruised and they were clearly malnourished, none of them appeared disabled. So why wasn't anyone in Port Sulphur, including the school district, aware of the third child?

A live sibling was a game changer. It would explain why Emma saw her husband even after she knew she'd killed him. It would explain why the stalker had intimate knowledge of her life. Jonathon must have been in touch with him.

She turned to leave and a bony hand reached out and grabbed her wrist. She screamed and jumped back from the bed as the woman she'd thought was a corpse came alive. Helen jerked up into a sitting position, her face contorted in rage, her empty sockets seeming to glare at Shaye.

"Get out of my house, whore! I smell the stench of lotion on you." Froth came out of Helen's mouth and bubbled up on her lips. She lunged at Shaye, swinging her free arm wildly to get hold of her again, but the chain on her other arm prevented her from reaching. Her bony fingers looked more like a cadaver than a live human being. Her fingernails were yellow and curled in circles under her fingers.

Disgust, fear, and panic coursed through Shaye as she

stepped backward, unable to take her eyes off the monstrosity in front of her. "Are you Helen Bourg? Who did this to you?"

"It said this was payback because of what I done to it. But I didn't do nothing. I couldn't turn it loose. It was evil. Just like you."

"Me?"

"You women, always conniving, always sneaking around, stealing someone's man, pretending you got rights you don't. You're all the same. And I wasn't going to have that evil living here. It had to change. But it was wily, that one. It didn't listen, so I had to chain it. I had to, don't you see? I had to until it learned its place. Until it learned how to be right."

Shaye stared at the woman, her stomach rolling, her mind racing. It sounded like nonsense, but it had to mean something. "Did your son do this?"

"It was never my son!" Helen screamed, spit flying from her mouth. "It was a monster and it had to be cleansed but now it's loose. It's out there and I can't protect the world from it any longer." The woman collapsed back on the bed, her eyeless sockets pointed at the ceiling.

Shaye clenched her hands, desperately trying to make sense of the woman's words. She lifted one hand and ran it across the top of her head. What the hell did she do now? Call the police, certainly, and an ambulance. It was clear the woman needed medical help, but Shaye needed to know how to find that third son. The one that must be the stalker.

She shifted her pistol to her left hand and pulled her phone out of her pocket. When she dropped her gaze down to look at the phone, she saw it. A business card stuck between two floor planks, behind one of the bed frame legs. She put the phone back in her pocket and inched forward, keeping a careful eye on Helen. Without vision, the woman's hearing had become more acute, and the last thing Shaye wanted was to feel the woman's skeletal fingers on her skin again. Keeping watch on Helen, she leaned over and picked up the card.

Patty Hebert
Serving all your real estate needs.

Suddenly, it all made sense. Awful, horrifying sense.

Chapter Twenty-Seven

Shaye ran out of the shack, pulling her phone from her pocket as she ran. No service. Shit! She leaped into her SUV and reversed as quickly as possible down the narrow path. At the end, she threw the SUV into drive and it slid in the dust before lurching forward. She tossed the phone in her cup holder, and gripping the steering wheel with both hands, she pressed the accelerator down and concentrated on staying in the center of the narrow road.

When she reached the highway, she hit the pavement and twisted the wheel, forcing the SUV to jump sideways. Before she'd gotten the vehicle straightened out, she slammed her foot down on the accelerator and it lurched forward, swinging from side to side a couple of times before the wheels finally locked onto the road and the SUV leaped forward. She grabbed her phone and checked. One bar.

She dialed Jackson's number, praying he'd listened to her earlier and was on his way to Emma's house. He answered on the first ring.

"It's Patty, the Realtor," Shaye said. "She's the stalker."

"What?" Jackson's tone left no doubt that he thought

she'd lost her mind.

"I know it sounds crazy, but you've got to trust me. Emma was going to drop her house key off to Patty. Patty will kill her. Game over!"

"Okay. Calm down. Detective Reynolds and I are already on our way."

"How long?"

"Fifteen…twenty minutes, tops."

The call dropped and Shaye cursed as she threw her phone onto the passenger's seat.

Then prayed that Jackson reached Emma in time.

Patty stood in the bedroom doorway, a pistol trained directly at Emma. "It pleases me that you're surprised. I worked long and hard at this disguise, and at no small expense to myself."

Emma stared at Patty in disbelief. It wasn't possible. Patty was tall, but her physique couldn't possibly be confused with that of a man, and her long hair and facial features only made it that much harder to believe. Patty couldn't be the man she saw in her bedroom that night. And besides, why in the world would Patty want to hurt her?

"I don't understand," Emma said.

Patty smirked. "Of course you don't. All this time, you've thought your dead husband was stalking you, or should I say, my dead brother."

"Your brother? David never told me he had a sister."

Patty's face flushed red. "I'm not his sister! I'm his brother. I've always been his brother."

Emma's mind whirled. Was it possible? Could Patty actually be a man?

"There were three of us...Nathan, Jonathon, and me. She called us her three blind mice because we couldn't see things like she did, but then when your mama is a crazy bitch, it's hard to agree with her. Nathan died when we were kids. Drowned. Mama was beside herself because Nathan was her favorite. She never beat Nathan. Never starved him. Never tied him up and cut him with a knife then laughed while he bled. Jonathon wasn't as lucky. He looked just a little bit too much like our no-show daddy. And then there was me."

Patty stepped closer to Emma. "I was the really unlucky one. You see, according to mama, I'd been born evil. You know why? Because I was born a woman. Mama hated women and she refused to acknowledge she'd given birth to one, so I become a boy. But she didn't trust me to keep my secret, so she never let anyone know I existed. Until Jonathon figured out how to undo my handcuffs when I was a teenager, my entire world was four walls and a moldy mattress on the floor. I watched closely and learned how to free myself, always careful to do it only when Mama passed out from her booze."

Emma tried to process the horror Patty described, but it was so far outside of anything she knew that she couldn't get a grasp on it.

"I didn't want to be a woman," Patty continued. "Women were bad, that much I knew to be true, because a bad woman stole our daddy away and left us destitute and living in a shack. I never wanted to be like the bad woman. I would never be a worthless whore. I would be a man. A man who protected my family rather than abandoning them. I shaved my head like my brothers, and we wore the same clothes. I knew I wasn't a woman and mama started to believe, but my body betrayed me. I grew breasts and my hips widened until I could no longer fit in my brothers' clothes."

Emma's heart sank. Patty was crazy. She'd known that whoever was stalking her wasn't completely right, but Patty was so far beyond rational thought, there would be no reasoning with her. And Emma had killed her only savior. She glanced down, but Patty's legs were hidden under one of the long skirts she always wore. She claimed her muscles were cramping earlier, but then if Patty was the stalker, she'd killed Mrs. Pearson and she was lying about that as well. Still, with her MS, Patty didn't have half the physical ability that Emma did. If Emma could launch at her before Patty got off a round, she might be able to get past. If she could get to the stairs, Emma had no doubt she could get away. Patty would never be able to keep up with her.

Patty cocked her head to the side and smiled. "You're wondering if you can get past me. Thinking that if you can, you'll be able to get away from a cripple. The problem is, I'm not a cripple. Never was. The MS was all part of my disguise, just like the dresses and makeup were. I knew a nurse wouldn't be able to resist someone with a disability. And I knew my disability is what you'd see before anything else, because that's what you were trained to do. I'm not overweight or out of shape either."

Patty reached under her shirt with one hand and yanked. Emma heard something rip and Patty tossed a pad with breasts and stomach padding at her feet. "As soon as I left home, I had my breasts removed. Had my uterus taken out as well. No bleeding for me. No sacks of fat on my chest taunting me. It was one of those back-alley jobs, but it worked. I was finally rid of the pieces that tried to betray me. Tried to betray what I was."

"You're sick, Patty," Emma said desperately. "You need help."

"Don't call me that! My name is Alan. Until David married you and moved to Algiers Point, I lived happily as Alan Frye, and as soon as I'm done here, that's exactly what I'm going back to. Back to my real life. I'm burning all these whore clothes and woman things. If it weren't for you, I could have been myself and been close to David, but you ruined it. I couldn't look like myself or you might have guessed our secret."

Patty reached up and pulled at the back of her head, ripping off her wig and exposing her military haircut. From her pocket, she withdrew a toilette and wiped it across her face, over and over again, until the thick, bright makeup she always wore had been almost stripped away.

Emma stared in horror at the thing in front of her. Eyeliner was smudged under her eyes and onto her cheeks.

The bright red lipstick clung to her lips in blotches. She stood there, in a white blouse and blue flowered skirt, smiling at Emma, those blank black eyes locked on her. No wonder she'd thought it was David in her room that night. Without makeup, Patty's square jawline and cheekbones were more prominent. She was a little shorter than David, but without the padding, her body was probably similar in size. Emma dropped her gaze to the chest pad and every ounce of hope drained out of her. No one would come to rescue her, because no one knew she was in trouble. She was out of options. Patty had won.

Even worse, no one would ever know what happened to her.

"He thought he could change," Patty said. "He joined the military to get away from our childhood, thinking he could become someone else. And he came close. With you, he almost managed it, at least for a little while. The only part of his past that he couldn't shed was me. He'd always been my protector and he didn't know how to stop, even though he was afraid to be around me."

Patty smirked. "Afraid I'd drag him back to the darkness. But I didn't have to. Something happened to him on his last tour. He wouldn't tell me what, but I could see it in his eyes. My brother was back."

Exhaustion and despair racked Emma's body. "Why didn't you just kill me?"

"Because you had to pay for what you took from me. You had to feel what it was like to suffer. What it was like for your life to be on the line and to have no one who could help you."

She was going to die. Emma knew it with complete certainty. She was trapped in this room with an insane woman who'd been bent on killing her from the beginning. She couldn't run faster than a bullet, and a single well-placed one would be all it took to drain the life from her.

But the longer Emma stared at that smirk that Patty wore, the angrier she became. God only knew how many people Patty had hurt beyond the carnage over her brother. Emma didn't believe for a moment that Patty had been leading a blameless life since she escaped her mother's grasp. People like Patty didn't magically appear. They were crafted over time.

She killed Mrs. Pearson and the paramedic. She tried to kill Corrine in order to hurt Shaye, and Shaye was the one person who believed you when no one else would.

Emma's jaw involuntarily clenched. She was going to die, but she refused to do it quietly.

She only had time for one play, and it had to be a good one. Even without the padding, Patty was still a large woman with four inches and at least forty pounds on her. She had to move fast. She had to be strong. She had to be clever.

Emma looked beyond Patty and out the window of the bedroom across the hall, and an idea formed. She stared over Patty's shoulder for a few more seconds, then smiled. "You stupid bitch. You didn't know the cops were coming to meet me here. They just pulled up. So you can kill me, but you're not going to get away with it. They'll be inside this house and standing at the bottom of those stairs the second that bullet leaves your gun."

Emma pointed at the window behind Patty and prayed that she took the bait. Patty frowned and turned slightly to look across the hall. That tiny loss of focus was all Emma was going to get, and she was ready to use it. As soon as Patty's eyes shifted off of her, she launched. She'd always stayed in good shape, but her recent martial arts training had made her quick and accurate. She hit Patty in the side with her shoulder, throwing all of her body weight against the woman.

Patty lost her balance and fell into the dresser, dropping her gun in front of her. Emma tried to run past her, but Patty managed to grab her leg. Emma twisted her leg and yanked, managing to pull it from Patty's grasp, then bolted out the bedroom door and down the stairs. She heard Patty cursing and footsteps pounding behind her.

Emma had just jumped off the last step when the first gunshot whizzed by her. Ducking, she ran for the front door, praying that she could get to her car before Patty made it down the stairs. With no weapon of her own, she'd be an easy target outside, and Patty was far beyond caring about anything but killing her. As she yanked open the front door, a second shot boomed and she cried out as the bullet grazed her arm and embedded in the wall just inches from her head.

She wasn't going to make it.

But by God, she was going to make sure everyone on the block knew exactly who had killed her. She practically tore the screen door off the hinges as she ran through it screaming. A third shot caught her in her shoulder, and the force and pain caused her to stumble down the stairs and crash onto the sidewalk. She glanced back as Patty ran out the door and leveled her pistol at her.

Patty smiled and started whistling. Emma closed her eyes and dropped into unconsciousness as the last shot rang out.

CHAPTER TWENTY-EIGHT

"Are you all right?" A man's voice sounded in Emma's dream.

She knew it was a dream because she'd died. Or maybe they had medical personnel in heaven to help the people who came through injured. Maybe she could get a position there.

"Emma? Talk to me."

Her mind sharpened so quickly that it sent a shot of pain through the top of her head, and her eyes flew open. She jerked upright, looking around wildly, and felt a hand on her arm. She turned her head toward the man kneeling beside her and blinked, bringing him into focus.

"Jackson!" She threw her arms around him. "Oh my God."

Jackson gently wrapped his arms around her and whispered, "It's all right. You're going to be all right."

"She's dead." Another detective stepped up beside them. "That was a hell of a shot, Lamotte. I've already called for a bus. Are you all right, ma'am?"

Emma released Jackson and looked up at him. "Hell no, I'm not all right. I've been stalked by a crazy woman and shot...twice."

Her lips quivered as she managed a smile. "But I'm going to be."

CHAPTER TWENTY-NINE

Emma looked up from her scrambled eggs as Shaye stepped into her hospital room and broke out into a smile. "You're up and out early."

Shaye stepped up to the side of her bed and placed a bouquet of flowers on the table. "I could say the same for you, about the up part, anyway."

"Don't worry. The out part is coming soon. I'm an impossible patient. They'll cut me loose as soon as they can."

"How are you feeling?"

"Like I've been shot. God, I can't believe I am actually saying that. This whole thing has been so surreal. I still haven't quite processed it all." Emma shook her head. From the time the paramedics had put her into the ambulance until the doctor finally gave her something to make her sleep, her mind had raced with everything Patty had said and the things Shaye told her about Hamet and Port Sulphur. If it hadn't actually happened, Emma would have sworn it wasn't possible. It was all so strange. So horrifying. So evil.

And so sad.

"I'm still working on processing it myself," Shaye said. "It's a lot to absorb."

Emma nodded. "I've already made up my mind. I'm allowed to dwell on it until I leave the hospital and not any longer than that. We know the big factors, but all the small things...all the things that went into turning those kids into monsters...I don't think I want to know."

"I think that's smart. So what are your plans after you ditch this rolling bed?"

"I'm still leaving New Orleans. I probably won't drive as quickly on my way out of town, but I need to go somewhere else. Start over where there aren't any reminders."

"No one giving you sympathetic looks. No one whispering and thinking you don't know it's about you."

Emma's heart tugged and she reached for Shaye's hand and squeezed. With what little she knew, Emma was certain she hadn't been through a quarter of what Shaye had. More importantly, Emma had answers and the security of knowing that the people who'd hurt her could never do so again. Shaye didn't have any of that.

Emma locked her gaze on Shaye's. "I have never been as impressed with someone as I am with you. You are an incredible person, Shaye. I owe you my life, and I'm going to remember that every single day I have left on this earth."

A flush ran up Shaye's neck and she looked down at the blanket. "Thank you," she said softly.

"You're going to do amazing things."

Shaye looked back up at her and smiled. "I hope so."

Emma sniffed and decided a change of topic was in order. "So, all of this means I'm going to need a new real estate agent."

Shaye's eyes widened and she laughed. "I can probably help you with that. Corrine has a friend—she'll pester you about fresh flowers and room deodorizers, but she'll get you top dollar. The best part is Corrine's known her and her family since preschool. They probably had gym together, so there's a good chance she's even seen her naked."

"Sold!"

Shaye beat Jackson to the café. Black coffee and one sweetener were already in place in front of his chair before he arrived. He looked at the cup and smiled as he sat down. "We're going to have to stop meeting like this."

She laughed and then marveled at how much she loved the sound. It had been a long time since she'd felt the way she did right now. She had no idea how long these moments of pure unadulterated glee would last, but she was going to enjoy the hell out of it as long as she could. Stark reality would creep back in soon enough.

"Have you seen Emma?" Jackson asked.

"I came here from the hospital. She's good. Great, actually, especially considering everything she's been through. The doctor removed the bullet in her shoulder. It had lodged in a muscle. It's going to hurt like hell for a good long time, and she'll have to be careful about infection, but if anyone's qualified to take care of it, Emma is."

"I guess she doesn't have to leave town now."

"She doesn't have to but she's going to anyway. Fresh start."

"Can't say that I blame her."

"Me either."

"How is your mother taking the news that her attack was related to your case?" he asked.

Shaye sighed, not even wanting to get into a discussion about the fallout she'd had with Corrine over the case. Her mother was convinced that if Shaye continued as a private investigator, she would be killed, or the world would spin off its axis, or the network would cancel HGTV. Something awful.

"Let's just say it's given her a whole new round of energy to try and convince me to change professions," Shaye said.

"Is it working?"

"I told her I'd quit my dangerous job when she did."

"Ha! Bet that one went over well."

"Yeah. Did you hear anything on Helen Bourg?" Shaye asked, changing the subject.

Jackson nodded. "I talked with the sheriff's department this morning. Your phone call yesterday set them all on their heels. They'd never seen anything like it and damned sure don't want to again. He said even in the shape she was in, they had to sedate her to get her out of the house. She screamed at the cops and tried to scratch and bite them."

"She's definitely disturbed, but even in her ranting, I think she told the truth."

"A team took all the paperwork they could find out of the place thinking they might be able to piece together how long Patty had kept her there that way."

Shaye shook her head. "You know, I've been thinking about what Patty told Emma, about Nathan being the favorite. Do you think she killed him? To punish her mother, or maybe because he wasn't abused the way she and Jonathon were?"

"It's definitely possible. Detective Reynolds has been trying to trace her movements since she left Port Sulphur, working backward using employment records and the name she gave Emma. So far, he's found three cities that she lived in. All three have unsolved murders where the victim had their eyes removed."

Shaye shook her head. "Is it wrong that I'm glad you killed her?"

"Hell no! There's no way she would have stopped with Emma. No telling how many bodies she could have racked up if she'd gotten away with it."

Shaye stared down at her latte for a bit, stirring the froth around. "On some level I get it...what makes a person turn. I think the absence of hope removes all empathy. Then all you want is for the rest of the world to suffer like you do."

She looked back up at Jackson, expecting to see

judgment, even frustration, but instead, he was frowning and appeared deep in thought. For a minute, she thought he wasn't going to comment, but finally he cleared his throat.

"I can't begin to imagine the kind of life Helen and Patty had, or Jonathon for that matter," he said. "Even knowing what I do, even with the medical facts that speak for them, I can't force my mind to make a leap that far into darkness. I can process it on a surface level—I wouldn't make a very good cop if I couldn't—but as far as deep understanding goes, I may as well be looking at a van Gogh."

"Sometimes beautiful. Sometimes horrifying."

He nodded. "Sometimes the picture is clear and makes sense. Other times, it's confusing and makes my brain hurt to even attempt to contemplate it." He locked his gaze on hers. "There's no one answer for people like Helen, Patty, and Jonathon. Every person has a different breaking point. Every person experiences a different set of inputs. Every person has a different support system."

"Or no support system," Shaye said quietly. She couldn't help but wonder what would have happened to her if Corrine hadn't taken her in. Jackson seemed to think she was tough and would have managed, but he didn't really know her. After nine years in Eleonore's office, Shaye still wasn't sure she knew herself. Not completely. And she knew why.

Because the pieces of her past were missing.

She couldn't address the unknown, but it was always

there. Lurking beneath the surface, compelling her to act and think in ways that she had no logical reason to support. Forcing her to attempt to deal with the symptoms rather than addressing the problem.

"You said you would help me," she said. "If I ever wanted to know…"

"And I will. Every step of the way."

Learn more about Shaye's past in SINISTER, coming Fall 2015.

About the Author

Jana DeLeon grew up among the bayous and gators of southwest Louisiana. She's never stumbled across a mystery like one of her heroines but is still hopeful. She lives in Dallas, Texas with a menagerie of animals and not a single ghost.

Visit Jana at:
Website: http://janadeleon.com
Facebook:
http://www.facebook.com/JanaDeLeonAuthor/
Twitter: @JanaDeLeon

For new release notification, to participate in a monthly $100 egift card drawing, and more, sign up for Jana's newsletter. http://janadeleon.com/newsletter-sign-up/

Stain $\widehat{D}$
20. Feb. 2020

Made in the USA
San Bernardino, CA
28 July 2015